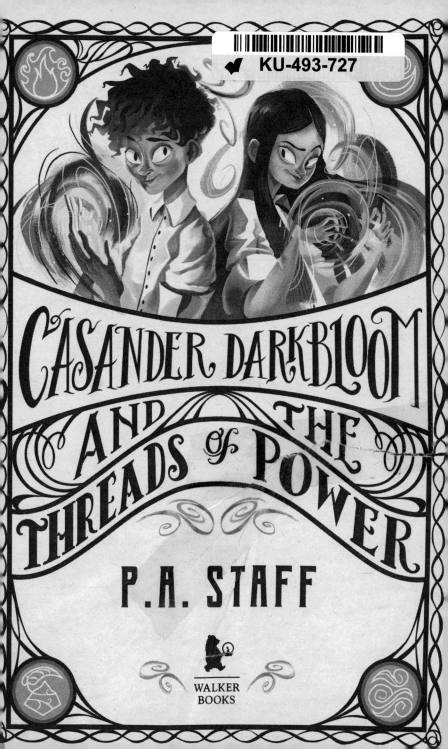

CASANDER DARKBLOOM AND THE THREADS OF POWER

P.A. STAFF

WALKER BOOKS

CONTENTS

CHAPTER 1
An Act Against Nature

PARIS, FRANCE

In the beginning, when the universe was merely stardust and night, the world was woven from powerful threads of twilight and white.

Life and death. Good and evil. Dawn and dusk. That was the way things were at the origin of time, before the clocks started spinning, the years flew by, and the strength of these threads weakened as people evolved and spread across the world.

In some, the threads changed into different shades of colour – but in many people, they dulled, faded and lost their powers altogether.

It was this fact that Claudius Bane liked to remind himself of often, especially on nights like this. Nights that were unusual. Nights when the uneasy sense of something terrible was brewing in the air and he needed his courage

"Who are you?" a small voice whispered from the other side.

A child.

This certainly wasn't who Claudius had been expecting to meet.

He swallowed hard. "My name is Dr Claudius Bane," he said, before clutching his bag protectively closer and taking a step back into the shadows. "Someone sent for me from Wayward School. I'm here to deliver a book, but I believe I may have the wrong address."

The door swung open.

"No," the boy standing inside replied determinedly. His ferocious amber eyes narrowed. "I summoned you here and you're late."

Words failed Claudius as he opened and closed his mouth like a gormless goldfish. The young boy staring back at him was merely ten or eleven years old. He was round-faced, but tall and lanky like a string bean, with soot-black hair. His eyes sparked like smokeless flames, causing Claudius to look away first.

Impossible.

He had expected to meet someone else – *anyone else* – but not this child. How had someone so young been smart and powerful enough to send a letter to the Balance Lands? What was this prodigy doing in the normal world? And, most worryingly of all, how did he know about *The Book of Skulls and Skin*?

Another uneasy feeling hummed in the air around Claudius now, thicker than before. *Fear*. He had seriously misjudged this encounter. The threads of power throbbed so violently within the boy before him that Claudius could feel them. Taste them. Smell them.

They felt like cold, lifeless fingers drawing lines up and down his spine. Like grave dirt on his tongue and the stale scent of something no longer living.

Deathmaker.

That was the Order of Others this boy belonged to.

"Come in," said the boy sternly, stepping aside so Claudius could pass.

Still shaken, Claudius silently obliged.

The apartment was furnished in a simple fashion. There was a plain brown table surrounded by plain brown chairs. Flaky teal wallpaper overlooked two rickety beds tucked away in a corner, one of which cradled a frail-looking woman with her head turned to the wall. Raspy breaths rattled through her ribcage as Claudius and the boy approached. Her skin was as white as chalk, her hair as fine as silk, and she wore a holey nightgown which had been eaten away by moths. For a second, a flicker of familiarity tickled Claudius's skin, but he had never met anyone so weak and sickly in his life.

"Don't worry, Mama," the boy said, snatching *The Book of Skulls and Skin* from Claudius's bag before Claudius could stop him. He knelt beside his mother and placed

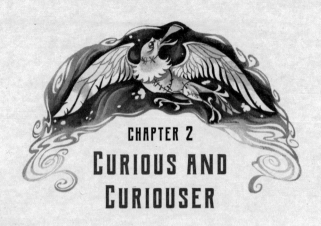

CHAPTER 2
CURIOUS AND CURIOUSER

LONDON, ENGLAND

SEVENTEEN YEARS LATER

CURIOUS MRS CRANE'S SHOP OF EVEN CURIOUSER Curiosities was the most special shop in all of London, though few people knew the real reason why. Behind its multicoloured awning and twinkling wind chimes, it was home to the most weird and wonderful objects which couldn't be found anywhere else. There were mirrors that, if you stared at them for long enough, gave you a glimpse into another world. Magical books whose ink whispered words from the pages and which jumped from shelf to shelf when you weren't looking. Snow globes with scenes that changed with the seasons and clocks that spun backwards. But what made it truly unique wasn't something that could be found inside the shop – it was outside of it.

And then the mysterious boy outside became very hard to ignore.

It all began on a wet, miserable Tuesday.

Casander didn't know much about himself, but he knew that he had always hated Tuesdays. Tuesdays were the nothing days. Not like dreaded Mondays, with the slog of a long week ahead, or Wednesdays, with their happy dance feeling when half of the week was already done. In fact, the only good thing about Tuesdays was that Crane's Curiosities was usually quiet, meaning there were fewer snooty stares from customers and Cas didn't get a headache every time the bell above the door tinkled when somebody entered or left.

On this particular Tuesday, it was raining cats and dogs.

Perhaps if Cas had been able to remember something – *anything* – then this would've been the first sign that something was going to be different about this day.

Not that it was literally raining cats and dogs, of course – that *would* have been a worrying sign to ignore – but that Crane's Curiosities was filled to the brim with people. Usually on rainy days like this, the howling weather deterred people from venturing to the shop. They preferred to stay cosied up at home or wait out the storm in the nearby Natural History Museum. But instead, something was propelling people into the shop in droves.

Trinkets and titbits were flying off the crooked shelves

18

in a frenzy. People seemed to be buying just about anything and everything to avoid going back out into the drizzle. As the shop's owner, Will should've been delighted. But every time a customer came or went, the open door revealed Cas shivering outside.

By late afternoon, the guilt became too much.

"Hold the till," Will finally sighed, turning to the girl who helped him and heading towards the door.

Even before he had pushed it open, Will was already having doubts. He'd had a funny feeling about the mysterious boy from the first time he saw him, though he couldn't remember exactly how long ago that was. Will had only caught glimpses of him at first; a flash of a dark silhouette or unusual-coloured eyes peering through the windows. The boy had been popping up randomly here and there throughout the summer, but Will had caught him snoozing outside almost every day recently. It was practically like he had become part of the shop. Luckily, the boy always showed up when Will's assistant was around, so the raven-haired girl could make sure he wasn't causing trouble.

But Will couldn't very well let the poor boy sit out there like a scolded puppy now.

"Look, kid," said Will, holding open the door. "I don't know who you are or where you're from, but you've been lurking around long enough that you've basically become my responsibility. You'll freeze to death in this rain, so come inside quickly before I change my mind."

nowhere. One

eeing, and

hat general

that seized

time.

his had

pped by

shot up

og, as if

ly frying

up. The

surprised

efore.

heir just as

appeared,

ull only be

get out

ffer help,

of the

stomach

eaved his

d twisted

he scales

him.

Spotting a quiet corner by a bunch of creepy taxidermized animals, Cas crouched behind a shelf. He pressed his forehead against the misty shop window. Leftover sparks of energy still made his arm twitch – but even though he didn't understand it, for some reason he wasn't afraid of it either. The feeling was like an old friend saying hello again. Whatever it was – whatever had happened to him – had clearly been a part of him for a long time.

Why did it have to happen in front of those people, though? thought Cas.

He could deal with being out of the ordinary – he was an impossibly forgetful nobody boy who slept outside a curiosity shop, after all. But if the shopkeeper and the girl didn't think he was a freak before, they certainly must now.

He sighed. "At least you don't have to worry about being a weirdo," he muttered to a stuffed raven on the shelf. "Your last dilemma was probably whether to have worms or bread scraps for breakfast."

It might have been a trick of the light, but Cas could've sworn he saw the bird *blink* in reply.

Shaking his head, Cas reached out to stroke the raven's cool feathers, trying to ignore the uncomfortable feeling still swirling in his belly. He needed a distraction. As it happened, two loud women were gossiping away like geese on the other side of the shelf.

"This place is an absolute hovel, Lupina!"

"ARGH!" Cas threw his arms up defensively and stumbled backwards into a bookcase.

"KRAA!" squawked the raven. With a ginormous flap of its wings, it took off into the air, smashing a blue vase and sending a grandfather clock swan-diving to the floor.

Immediately, the shop erupted into chaos.

The two gossiping ladies started screeching and frantically waving their arms, batting the bird away from their bouffants. Several others ran shrieking from the shop, whilst a little old man sprinted in circles screaming, "CALL THE POLICE! CALL THE POLICE!"

"KRAA! KRAA!"

Hurriedly, Will and his assistant scrambled behind the counter, searching for something with which to catch the creature. Meanwhile, the bird was now crashing into porcelain ornaments left, right and centre. Covering his head, Cas crawled out from his hiding spot, wincing amongst the torrential downpour of shattering ceramic. He cast a glance over his shoulder to check that the shopkeeper and the girl were still distracted, before spotting his chance to escape and darting towards the open door.

But just as he reached it, Cas skidded to an abrupt halt.

Two men, their faces hidden under the heavy hoods of their purple-and-white cloaks, blocked his way.

"Gotcha," one of them snarled, reaching out a strong fist and grabbing Cas's shoulder.

24

Cas didn't have time to react. Before he could shout or struggle, the first man closed his arms around Cas and lifted him off the floor. Cas bucked, kicked and squirmed as hard as he could. "Let go!"

"Hold still," the second man growled, trying to shove a black sack over Cas's head. Terrified, Cas desperately lashed out, but he couldn't break free until…

"RUN!"

In one swift motion, Will's assistant grabbed a twisted staff from one of the stands and swung it at the first man's knees. He released Cas with a crippling yelp and collapsed, whining and clutching his leg. The second man dropped the sack and sprang forward, but tripped over the first.

"Come on!" the girl urged, grabbing Cas's hand and tossing the staff aside.

Together, they barrelled out of the shop into the rain.

The grey pavement was slick with puddles as they ran. They splashed around bemused pedestrians and nipped between buses, until another set of footsteps joined theirs. Cas chanced a look behind. The hooded men were gaining on them. *Fast.* Cas had no idea what was happening, and even less of an idea where they were going. Thankfully, the dark-haired girl seemed to know the way. They took a sharp left at a red telephone box. A right turn at the cinema and another when they passed the toy shop. People gawked at them as they sped by, bumping into rowdy shoppers' bags and scattering pigeons in their wake. But the girl

bridge overlooking the
hands.

Without hesitation, she climbed up onto the railing.

... she said, breathless.

... him down, reaching out her hand. ...

... balked. *"Are you mad?!"*

"Not as mad as those men will be if they ...
me ...

"... I want you to *drown*."

He dared one final glance over his shoulder. The
... men were at the end of the bridge now, running
... toward ... with unbelievable speed.

He ... down at their reflection in the murky
river.

He ... looked at the girl's waiting hand, and the ...
... fighters closing in.

... took her hand.

... had barely touched the top of the ... when the
girl leapt off, taking him with her. Wind rushed past them
... a symphony of chaos. Passers-by on the bridge gasped
... called out in shock.

But Casander barely heard anything before they hit the
water, the grimy water swallowing them whole.

❧ ❧

CHAPTER 3
WELCOME TO WAYWARD

CASANDER DIDN'T KNOW IF HE COULD SWIM.

He thought he could, but then again it was hard to trust your own memory when you could probably claim the prize for World's Most Forgetful Boy.

Still, everyone could doggy paddle … right?

The dark waves of the Thames closed in around him. Cas flailed his arms and kicked his legs, but every stroke felt like ice against his skin. Water rushed into his ears, drowning his senses and dragging him down. It felt like being sucked into another world. A world where the time between seconds lived; where dreams and nightmares came to play when the sun was up; and where he imagined his memories scuttled off to when they slipped away from him at the end of every day.

But Cas knew he couldn't give up.

A tiny, kindling spark inside him wanted to fight.

Summoning every ounce of strength, he beat b...

the current and battled the waves. The dazzling...

surface shone above him, growing clearer as he...

Up, up and up, until...

GASP.

He broke through the surface, gulping...

Nothing had ever tasted so good.

A second later, the Crane's Curiosities...

up beside him. Chilled to their cores, they swam...

shore and clambered onto the bank, soaked...

glittering like a pair of soggy seal pups...

It was only then that Cassander realized they...

couldn't any more.

The rain-soaked roads and sullen skies...

replaced with sunny, green grass...

swaying willow trees. Chirping birds...

replacing the angry bells of...

most importantly of all, the sun...

For now.

None of it made any sense. Where had...

Where had the city gone?

Cas opened his mouth, but the words...

out to it. "Don't freak out," she said, putting her hands

out as if to steady him.

Cas's jaw dropped open. "I just..."

"Look, there's no time to explain..."

last drops of water out of h...

polite. The girl rolled her eyes and marched off ahead. Her strides were brisk and purposeful, like he was a nuisance fly she was trying to shake off.

Clearly, she wasn't the chatty type.

The girl was the same age as Cas, and too short and delicate to be frightening really – but something about her still thrilled and terrified him to the bone. She had poker-straight black hair, which was bright red at the ends, and narrow, hooded eyes, not dark enough to be brown yet too earthy to be amber. Her gaze was fierce enough though. It burned through Cas like a blazing north star. It was the gaze of someone who could be either your best friend or worst nightmare.

Maybe it was foolish, but Cas refused to silently trail along in her wake.

"Who were those people?" he asked, struggling to catch up.

"Heretics," Warrior called over her shoulder.

That information was about as useful as a chocolate teapot. "Why are they chasing us?"

"Not us, *you*." She shot him a look of utter disbelief. "Isn't it obvious?"

"Not to me," said Cas. "I don't know what I've done. I barely even know who I am!"

Warrior fixed him with a piercing stop-joking-around look, but Cas was too busy to explain. He was racking his brain, desperate for a speck of sense to fall out.

Crikey, he thought. *What* have *I done?*

The trouble with having no memory was that the possibilities were endless.

Had he robbed a bank? Tripped up a dithering old grandma? Run down the high street naked in only his most embarrassing rubber ducky socks? For all Cas knew, he could have been anyone from an international jewel thief to someone who had simply walked out of a newsagent's without paying for a bag of sweets. The hooded men hadn't looked like police, but they had to be something similar.

Heretics didn't sound friendly.

The one thing they surely couldn't be after him for was what had happened in the curiosity shop. They just *couldn't*. People weren't hunted for accidentally spooking a loose bird that must've got in through a window. Because that was all that had happened – what *must* have happened. There was no other explanation for it.

As he slipped and slid up the bank, Cas felt it again. That unusual tingling sensation. He tried to keep walking, but it was useless. Within moments, the same thrashing, jerking motion that had overcome him before seized control of his right leg and he was forced to stop moving until it did.

Warrior's eyes widened as she stopped too. "That happens to you a lot, doesn't it?"

Cas shrugged. "Honestly, I don't know."

"Well, I've seen it happen a bunch. Whenever you've

and cheerful, which made the gnawing confusion feel less heavy. And it was odd, which was exactly what the tingling felt like.

Cas grinned at Warrior, glad that they were finally talking. But when he looked back, he couldn't help noticing the ends of her hair were definitely bright red again.

Once they reached the top of the hill, Cas looked around for any sign of where he was. As if by magic, there was one literally in front of them. An old, rickety signpost was planted in the ground, with two crooked arrows pointing the same way towards a winding, dusty path: *Wayward Town, 782 paces and 1 hop* and *Wayward School, 1,203 steps, 3 skips and a jump.*

Warrior started walking along the track, but Cas thrust out an arm to grab her.

"Wait, where are we going?" he said. "I need answers. About who those men were. About where we are and what's going on."

Warrior glanced skyward again. *One day, the wind will change and her face will get stuck like that,* thought Cas. "I said I would tell you everything, remember? We just need to lose the Heretics first."

"Heretics, heretics," repeated Cas. "You keep calling them that, but I don't know what it means."

"Surely even you can figure out that they aren't exactly going around throwing tea parties and handing out kittens."

"No, wait," she said feverishly, her eyes scanning their surroundings as if she could sense something. She wasn't the only one. People around them were looking from ward to ward as well. *"Come on, come on."*

"What are you doing?" shouted Cas, panic spiking his voice now. The hooded figures were closing in. They were almost at the boundary.

He was on the brink of running away to save himself when a great shudder reverberated through the ground beneath their feet. Everyone at the boundary of Wayward stumbled. Everyone, that was, apart from Warrior – who wore a wicked, knowing smile. "Just wait a second – you'll see!"

Sure enough, a moment later, Cas did.

As the first tremor rocked the earth, the two purple-and-white-hooded men strained to stay standing. Their legs shook as they rode out the vibration, but as soon as it passed, they surged forward again, shoving brightly cloaked men, women and children aside. Their hungry eyes locked on Cas and Warrior in the same second another shudder hit.

Cas's stomach lurched as the world went sideways. He and everyone around him was knocked off their feet. *Great, an earthquake. Just what we need on top of everything.* Except the citizens milling about further into Wayward Town were still merrily going about their business, as if they hadn't felt a thing. As soon as he could, Cas scrambled upright, helplessly trying to figure out what had happened.

Only, when he glanced back across the boundary, he saw ... *nothing*.

Every person who had been outside the wards when the second, bigger impact hit had vanished. Instead, empty, rolling sand dunes stretched as far as the eye could see. Thundery clouds loomed outside the boundary, but when Cas glanced upwards, the sky directly above him was still clear and sunny.

It didn't make sense.

The town couldn't have *moved* ... could it?

"We need to keep going," said Warrior. "The Heretics will easily find us again soon."

Cas barely had time to brush down his knees, before Warrior was hurrying him along into the town once more.

"Are you going to start explaining things yet or not?" Cas demanded.

Warrior sighed. "Wayward is like a checkpoint," she called over her shoulder as he rushed to keep up. "A halfway place between this world and the Normie world. And everywhere else. That's how it got its name – *Wayward*. *Way* through the *wards*."

Cas had the overwhelming urge to pinch himself. If this wasn't a dream, maybe they really were in another world – nothing else could explain the impossibility of it all.

"Wayward has a tricky habit of moving about of its own accord. It jumps from place to place whenever it likes.

"Exactly." She cast him a half-threatening glare. "But don't go shouting about it from the rooftops – technically we're not supposed to travel through waygates alone until we're older. It's very difficult. It would've been almost impossible for you on your own if I hadn't taken you with me."

"*Kidnapped* me, you mean."

"*Saved your sorry butt,*" amended Warrior, raising an eyebrow. "You're welcome."

Ignoring her, Cas shuffled closer to the nearest mirror to get a better look. Its reflective surface rippled and shimmered like it was alive. Between one ripple and the next, he caught a fleeting glimpse of the Normie version of London. But when Cas reached out to touch the cityscape in the mirror's gilded frame, the image shattered and vanished without a trace.

Two entire worlds – both this one and the Normie one – were *literally* at their fingertips.

They could go anywhere. Do anything.

Cas's eyes lit up.

He imagined strutting along the whimsical, watery canals of Venice and scaling the dizzying heights of Machu Picchu in Peru. They could climb Mount Everest, or watch the sun rise over the Egyptian pyramids; go white-water rafting in New Zealand, or drink tea surrounded by perfectly pink cherry blossoms in Japan.

All his worries and fears slipped away. "Where are we going, then?"

Squeezing his eyes shut, Cas poked out his toe, edging across the boundary…

Nothing.

Only silence and a cool September breeze filled the air.

He opened his eyes and saw Warrior clutching her sides with laughter. "Your face!"

But Cas didn't care.

His stomach leapt back up into its rightful place. He had passed through the second set of wards without setting them off. Whatever he had done inside the shop, whatever reason the hooded men had for hunting him, it couldn't be that bad.

"Relax, we're safe now." Warrior patted his shoulder reassuringly. "Nobody can hurt us here."

Now that they were on the other side of the wards, Cas breathed and fully took in his surroundings. In front of him stood two heavy, wrought-iron gates shaped like the curling letters W and S. He and Warrior slipped between them and headed across a short, wooden bridge over a moat.

From there, Cas could see it all.

Wayward School was a magnificent old building, grander and more beautiful than anything he could ever have dreamed. The school looked like a cross between a stately home and a fortress. Ivy wound over the cream stone walls and wrapped around two ornate marble columns that bracketed the largest double doors he had ever seen.

To his left, a sky-high tower stood sentinel, whilst to his right the moat ran down into a deep boating lake. Enormous trees and vines spilled out of one wing of the building, creating a tunnel which led down to luscious green lawns and a dense forest, where a creaky greenhouse and little lodges sat dotted between the trees, puffing out plumes of homely charcoal smoke. The last thing he caught sight of was a small graveyard, sitting eerily undisturbed at the edge of the woods, before they were climbing up the marble steps leading to the front doors.

Up close, the school doubled in size. It was at least five storeys high and incredibly wide. An ornate wheelchair ramp sloped upwards. Above the doors, *Wayward School for Most Prestigious Others* gleamed in large, curling shiny script. As did the motto:

Vitas, Mortus, Terran, Ignuus, Aqus, Kaeli
- Omnus una cum trutina -

A platinum school crest made up of five separate seals (two entangled birds; a leafy plant woven around a rock; a wave; a fireball; and a swirl of air) sat below.

"Life. Death. Earth. Fire. Water. Air," said Warrior, translating the ancient script. "One is with the balance."

"Woah," Cas exhaled in surprise.

Warrior beamed. "Excellent goldfish impression. But yeah, I suppose this old hovel isn't half bad."

Half bad? Cas had never seen anything so spectacular in his life.

Her wrinkled face bore a striking resemblance to a cat's puckered bum hole.

"I'll let Headmaster Higgles know you're back, shall I, you ungrateful madam?" she snapped. "Goodness knows where you've been this summer. We were doubting whether you'd return for your second year at all."

"And miss our delightful chats like this? Never."

Dodging the daggers Miss Grimbly glared her way, Warrior flounced off down the hall, occasionally spinning merrily on her heel as if to agitate the old woman further.

They both seemed to have forgotten that Cas existed.

"Just wait until I fetch the headmaster," Miss Grimbly threatened.

"No need," said Warrior, her voice as sweet as syrup. "I spent the summer away on Dr Bane's orders. He needed my help with something."

"Well, I'll inform Bane of your arrival then."

"Again, don't hurry to toot the trumpets – I'm on my way there now. Besides, I wouldn't want to deprive Headmaster Higgles of his *wonderful* secretary's company."

Miss Grimbly made a noise that was somewhere between a huff and a growl. Then she turned back to Cas still lingering like a lemon in the entrance, and said, "Are you coming in or not, boy? You're letting all the blasted heat out."

Cas wasn't sure there really was any heat in the vast, airy building, but he didn't want to infuriate the secretary

everyone, even Headmaster Higgles who she works for. In fact, I think she only took the job because he doesn't mind Gripely keeping her children in the office."

"Her children?"

"Polly and Pieter. Two parakeets about as cranky and ancient as she is. She lets them nibble on her sandwiches and everything."

Cas grimaced. "Is that who you're taking me to?" He was desperate to finally get some answers. His head was spinning from all the new sights, sounds and information.

"Who? The parakeets?"

"No, Headmaster Huggles."

"*Higgles,*" Warrior corrected him, before shaking her head. "Hopeless Higgles probably doesn't even know that I left at the beginning of the summer, and it'll likely be next week before he clocks that you're here. No, Dr Bane is the one who sent me to the Normie world – to find you – so he can explain everything best. Right here."

They reached a single stone archway set at the end of the first-floor corridor. Unlike many of the doorways, this one didn't look like it belonged to a classroom. The dim lantern light broke through the gloom to illuminate a solid wooden door laden with latches, bolts and a double bird knocker. Warrior banged her fist below a silver plaque engraved with the words: *Dr C. M. Bane, Wayward Professor, Doctorate in Deathmaking (First Attempt, Astounding Standard).*

Around them, the school was deathly silent. Cas wondered whether the school year had started yet. Or was that what all the hubbub in town was about?

Regardless, the ominous emptiness made his skin prickle.

Abruptly, the door in front of them groaned open—

"Dr Bane! Dr Bane, I've found him!"

The words burst out of Warrior so loudly and violently that Cas jumped out of his skin.

A tall, greying man stood silhouetted in the entrance. Dr Bane instantly reminded Cas of a quick, silver fox. He had a shaggy mane of shoulder-length, silver-speckled hair and a wiry, grey beard, both of which were shot through with streaks of auburn. His amber eyes were crinkled and kind, but also smart and sharp, and he wore a neat plum suit under a matching cloak – not too dissimilar to the ones the hooded men had worn, except his was plain purple with only a hint of silver thread. His twilight-coloured garb contrasted starkly with the many pewter rings bejewelling his fingers, which twinkled and drew attention to the tattoos on his hands. The ink scrawls were variations of the same five symbols strewn around the school.

"Warrior, my dear," said Dr Bane, holding up a hand as if to soothe her. "Take a deep breath. Let's start over and say that again … *calmly* this time."

Warrior didn't bother to heed him. "Dr Bane, I've found him," she said breathlessly, gesturing to Cas. "It's him – it's really him. The One we've been looking for."

Dr Bane cast her a dubious stare. "Warrior," he warned, drawing her name out in a cautionary tone. He gave Cas the once-over. "I know you've been kind enough to assist me all summer – and that you're desperate to stay at Wayward for the entirety of this year – but if this is another of your waifs and strays, a ruse or pretender to persuade me not to send you back to the Normie world…"

"No, sir," insisted Warrior. "It's him. Honestly, I swear. The Heretics were hunting him and everything."

"Well, have you seen them? His powers?"

She nodded, nudging Cas in the ribs. "He brought a dead raven back to life—"

"Actually, it was more of a big crow," Cas chipped in unhelpfully.

"And his Deathmaker ones?"

Deathmaker ones?

"Um, no … not yet… But, sir—"

Dr Bane let out a long, weary sigh. "Then you must be mistaken. He can't be the Foretold," he said. "I'm sorry she's wasted your time," Dr Bane apologised to Cas, before rounding on Warrior. "I don't know what you think you saw, or how you've convinced this poor boy to pretend, but I thought you understood how important our mission is, Warrior. Send your friend on his way and get some rest before school starts tomorrow. We'll discuss when I'll next be sending you back to the Normie world in the morning."

At those last words, Warrior's hair turned as chalk white as her cheeks. She took a frantic step forward to plead with Dr Bane, but he promptly and firmly shut the door.

Cas felt more lost and confused than ever.

Turning away, Warrior's shoulders sagged as she began to trudge off in defeat.

But Cas was done.

Done with people speaking *at* or *around* him, not *to* him. Done with having no idea about what had happened in the curiosity shop. Or where he was. Or why he was here.

"Enough," he said, reaching out and catching Warrior's elbow. His voice sounded much braver and tougher than he felt. "Just because Dr Bane won't tell me what's going on, it doesn't mean that you can't."

There was a moment's hesitation – but then his words seemed to spark something inside her. Gone was the silly schoolgirl who had been banished to her bedroom, and back was the bold, courageous one who had jumped into the River Thames and faced off against two hunters to save him.

"You're right," said Warrior, throwing her shoulders back and tilting her chin up. Her cheeks grew brighter again, before she added in a low whisper, "But not here, Cas."

Maybe if his stomach hadn't been doing acrobatic somersaults at the thought of finding out the truth,

Cas might have found it strange how Warrior knew his name, when he was certain he had never told her.

Nevertheless, he didn't protest when she grabbed his hand and led him back along the corridor. Their shadows trembled apprehensively as they scurried past the glowing lanterns, which, Cas now realized, were filled with real fire-producing fireflies. Without stopping, they sped up to the second floor, passing a vast array of unusual classrooms, many of which had odd symbols and sketches drawn on the blackboards and even one which had a small, solitary rain-cloud suspended in mid-air, drizzling away in the corner of the room. Warrior tugged Cas into a secret passageway, hidden behind a rather disturbing statue of someone crushed under a pile of books (the plaque on the room next to it read: THE LIBRARY). It led to a spiral staircase so thin and narrow that Cas had to suck in a breath to fit, and they climbed endlessly upwards, until they emerged in a room on the very top floor of the school.

The words THE ATTIC were roughly hand-carved into the doorway.

The Attic was a squat, stuffy room that closely resembled a forgotten loft. The floorboards creaked ominously under their shoes, while low beams criss-crossed overhead, causing Cas to duck to avoid banging his head or getting a mouthful of cobwebs. The room was sparsely decorated with four single beds and four trunks. The beds sat in pairs on either side of a cold, draughty bay window, and a fat, grey mouse scampered out from under one of the pillows when Cas sat down.

They were utterly out of earshot and alone.

"Sorry it's a bit small and shabby," Warrior mumbled.

"No need," said Cas, glancing around. Compared to waking up on the cold, wet pavement outside the shop, it was brilliant. "So, where do you want to begin?"

Warrior shrugged. "How about with the fact that I think you're the Chosen One?"

The Chosen One.

"Well, not the Chosen One. The Foretold."

She said the words so nonchalantly that it took everything inside Cas not to laugh. That was what Dr Bane had called the person who he, Warrior and the Heretics had been looking for.

But that was absurd.

"Nice try," Cas chuckled half-heartedly. "But really, what's going on?"

Warrior fixed him with a pointed stare. "How much do you know about the Balance Lands, Cas?"

"In case you couldn't tell by my incredibly blank face, nothing."

"And what about our kind, the Others?"

Before today, he hadn't known there was an *our kind*.

"Zilch. Not a dicky bird. Outside the curiosity shop is all I've ever known."

Warrior looked at him, bewildered. "Seriously?"

"Yes," said Cas, imploring her to understand. He mulled over his words for a moment, thinking how best to explain. "My funny leg isn't the only thing wrong with me. I have a terrible memory, too, probably the worst in the world. All I can remember is waking up this morning on the pavement outside, then getting drenched in the rain until the incident with the bird happened. And I can only assume that's what every other day has been like too. I wake up and I know who I am, and how the world works, but yesterday is a mystery. It's like I never existed before today. I don't have a home. Parents. A family. Or at least, not that I know of. I can't even remember what I last ate for supper." He glanced down at his knees, fidgeting. "I'm broken."

"You're not broken," said Warrior shortly, considering this. "There's nothing *wrong* with you, you're just *different*. Everyone is. Some of us with more unusual magic are simply more different than others." She shot him a whisper of a smile, her eyes shining. "Speaking of which, when did you first come into your powers? You know, like the one to bring things to life?"

Cas blinked at her. "I didn't … I mean, I don't."

She cocked an eyebrow, giving him a please-take-this-seriously look. "You do. I know what I saw. How else can you explain what happened in the shop?"

Cas opened and closed his mouth several times, searching for a clever excuse, but instead he found himself saying, "In that case, I didn't know that I had powers. Not before the raven."

"Big crow," said Warrior, grinning.

Cas couldn't help smiling too. "Yeah, that. Look, for all I know, I could've always had this ... *ability*. Or never had it."

"Interesting." Warrior began pacing the room. "Very strange."

Is it? thought Cas. Was bringing something back to life not normal in this world? Was that why the Heretics were chasing him?

Typical, he thought. *Even in a world of impossibilities, I still can't be ordinary.*

"Let's start from the beginning," said Warrior, flopping down on the bed opposite. A dust plume *poofed* into the air. "Like I said, right now we're in the Balance Lands. A mirror of the Normie world in every way except one. Here, people are born with powers. We call ourselves the Others. Each Other belongs to one of five Orders, depending on what powers they possess. Together, it's our job to maintain the balance of nature – both in this world and the Normie one.

"Every cataclysmic event or natural disaster that's been averted in the ordinary world can be linked back to us. Those bush fires that rage on for days, then suddenly go out; those tsunamis and earthquakes that destroy everything in their path until they're miraculously stopped – *us, us* and *us*. The Orders each play their role and work together. You have the Earthshapers, the Airscapers, the Wavebreakers and the Firetamers. Those four Orders are easy enough to understand, but there's also a fifth Order – the Lifemakers and Deathmakers. The rarest, most powerful and most dangerous Others."

"And that's where I belong?"

"Steady, grasshopper," warned Warrior. "Sort of. You see, when an Other belonging to the fifth Order is born, they're either born a Lifemaker or a Deathmaker. Never both.

"Or at least, that's how it was until *he* came along."

Cas felt the hairs on the back of his neck stand on end. "Who?"

"The Master of All. The most terrible and terrifying Other alive today."

Cas swallowed hard. Fear prickled through him from the tips of his fingers to the points of his toes.

"No one calls the Master by his real name any more. He's not really an Other, not like the rest of us now. The Master of All is an Other who was born a Deathmaker, but somehow managed to steal another's Lifemaker abilities for himself. Honestly, it's not surprising. Deathmakers are the Others who are most likely to turn bad. But what's scary is that the Master of All is the first person to do it. To be a Lifemaker *and* a Deathmaker. To have power over both life *and* death."

"And that's such a bad thing because…" Cas trailed off unknowingly.

Warrior threw her hands up, exasperated. "Didn't you hear me?" she said, tension rising in her tone. "The whole reason the Others and the Balance Lands exist is to *protect the balance of nature.* Life and death are two sides of the same coin, but they're different. Sure, Lifemakers and Deathmakers are in the same Order because in many ways their powers overlap. They both control how the body works, how things come together or apart. But being both defies the very idea of balance. Their ultimate goals aren't the same. Lifemakers heal, whilst Deathmakers hurt. Lifemakers care, whilst Deathmakers kill. The Master doesn't just want to stop there, either – he's been tyrannising and wreaking havoc in our world, determined to find a way to take the other four Orders' powers for himself too.

"Ever since the Master of All stole those Lifemaker abilities, the balance of nature has been disrupted. The threads that make up the existence of everything in the Balance Lands and the Normie world are already beginning to unravel. If he succeeds, who knows what could happen – it could bring about the end of both worlds."

"I still don't see what this has to do with me," Cas prodded insistently. The end of the worlds sounded dire and all, but Cas was still equally – if not more – perplexed than before.

Surprisingly, Warrior's rigid, tense expression turned ecstatic.

"Around the same time the Master turned bad," she explained, finally getting to the crux of the matter, "the Oracle – an all-knowing Other in our world – made a prophecy that he could only be stopped by the Foretold. A Chosen One born sometime in the next twelve years with power equal to, or greater than, his."

Cas shifted uncomfortably. "And you think that's me?"

Warrior snapped her fingers. "Bingo."

Unfortunately, Cas wasn't convinced.

"I can't be," he blurted out. "It doesn't make sense. The prophecy said that the Foretold, the person born to defeat the Master, would have power at least equal to his, right? Well, I don't. I still can't believe that what I made happen in the shop was real, but even if it was, surely I can only be a Lifemaker? I'm not a Deathmaker. I would never hurt anyone!"

"You don't understand," said Warrior, leaning forward, her face alight with excitement. "Bane might not believe me about the raven, but I know what I saw. Just being able to do that is proof enough. Normally, an equal number of Others is born into each Order. But when the Master stole those Lifemaker powers, a tear was created in the balance of nature. There haven't been any new Lifemakers or Deathmakers born in the seventeen years since. And nearly all of the current fifth Order have lost their powers, too."

"Do you mean—"

"You're the first new one we've found."

Cas took a minute to let the revelation sink in.

It felt like someone had just sent an electric shock through him. His heart raced. His breathing quickened. His palms turned slick and sweaty.

But he couldn't understand how she could be sure.

He was Cas. Just Cas.

The mystery boy who lived outside the curiosity shop. The boy with a funny leg and the worst memory. The boy who had made something extraordinary happen and had no explanation for it but this.

Except he couldn't be the Foretold.

He could barely tie his own shoelaces, let alone take on and defeat the great, dangerous and ambitious Master of All.

A second realization settled on him then.

"That's why you rescued me from those hunters, wasn't it? Because you thought I was the Foretold. You'd never spoken to me before."

Warrior gave him a coy sideways glance. "Well, I did think it was odd that you were on your own like that. You always seemed to show up when I was there. It was a bit weird. Besides, I'm not exactly in the habit of sticking my neck out for anyone." She tapped her throat. "In all fairness, it is a pretty good neck to lose."

Cas frowned. This time, it was his turn to shoot her a please-take-this-seriously look.

"All right, all right," said Warrior. "Look, I may have only rescued you because I think you're the Foretold – but it wasn't like I hadn't been keeping an eye on you before that. That's why Dr Bane sent me to the Normie world – to look for the Foretold. For some reason, Crane's Curiosities seems to attract stuff like that."

"The objects inside the shop are magical, aren't they?" said Cas. "I mean, they come from this world."

"Like calls to like."

"But why spend so much time in the Normie world if you live here?"

"Because," Warrior admitted, half reluctantly, half excitedly, "people in the Balance Lands have been searching for the Foretold for the last twelve years."

"Including those hunters – the Heretics?"

"Yes, the Heretics are the Master of All's followers. After the Oracle made the prediction, our leaders – the Grand Council – ordered every corner of the Balance Lands to be scoured for the Foretold. Of course, the Master of All got wind of this and set his minions to the same task. But Dr Bane thought the Grand Council might be missing something. Others born and living in the Normie world are exceptionally rare, but it happens. As the deadline for the prophecy drew near, and he heard that the Heretics seemed to have the same idea, he started sending me to the Normie world every now and then on a secret mission to look for you. I – I had to find you," she said, her voice cracking and growing dimmer with each word. "For the sake of the Balance Lands. For Bane, because I – I owe him. He took me in when my parents abandoned me. When nobody else would."

One by one, the puzzle pieces slotted together in Cas's head. Miss Grimbly's snide remark about Warrior's mother. Dr Bane's comment about the waifs and strays Warrior had reportedly brought to Wayward School. Her passionate, resolute, stubborn determination that Cas was the one she had been seeking.

"But now that I've found you," said Warrior, raising her eyes hopefully, "I can finally come home."

Cas didn't share her enthusiasm. Quite the opposite – he felt like the room was spinning.

"What if I'm not who you think I am? How do we know for certain?"

Warrior jumped to her feet and rummaged around in the trunk at the end of her bed. "We don't," she said begrudgingly. "At least, not yet. There's only one way to know for sure. That's why" – she pulled a tatty old blanket and oversized pyjamas out of the trunk, before tossing them at Cas – "we're going to gatecrash the Oracle's Order Trials tomorrow."

Cas winced. "Why do I have no idea what that is, but still hate the sound of it?"

Warrior placed her hands on her hips. "How dare you. My plans are always genius, I'll have you know."

Cas regarded her doubtfully.

"Whenever a powerful Other is born, the Oracle senses it, and at eleven years old that person is invited to try out for Wayward School. It's called Wayward School for Most Prestigious Others for a reason, though. Everyone would sell their granny to get in, however only the most talented students do. Not everybody who arrives here has fully come into their powers yet, so that's where the Order Trials come in. At the start of each new school year, the Oracle tests the first years, the Wayones. First, she uses her uncanny abilities to sense the strength of your power, then she tells you your Order."

"And we're going to make her test me?"

"Ding ding." Warrior shot Cas a gleaming, toothy smile. "Once we've snuck in, the Oracle will confirm that you have both life and death magic. Technically, you're not allowed into the Order Trials unless you're being tested or a teacher... I'm a second year, a Waytwo, so that might be a little tricky ... but we'll find a way. Then, Dr Bane will have no choice but to admit you're the Foretold and let you come to school."

"What if the Oracle doesn't confirm it?" challenged Cas. "What if she says I only have life magic? Or no powers at all?"

Warrior matched Cas's stare with her own. Faint ghosts of fear and worry flickered there. "Then I hope you like travelling through waygates, because you'll be sent back to the Normie world. And as I won't have found the Foretold, I'll probably be forced to go with you."

That night, Cas couldn't sleep.

Not because he was worrying about the Order Trials and if he was a Lifemaker and Deathmaker in one. Nor because he was concerned about whether he was the Foretold, and what that would mean for his future – and the future of the Balance Lands.

No, he couldn't sleep for two very different reasons.

Firstly, what if Warrior was wrong? What if he wasn't the Foretold? It would be his fault if she got sent back to the Normie world. He could return to Crane's Curiosities the same person as before. He would likely forget that any of this had ever happened by the following morning – but he could see that Warrior wanted to stay at Wayward. If she was sent back to look for the Foretold again, when she clearly belonged here…

The other reason Cas couldn't sleep was his forgetfulness. He didn't want to wake up tomorrow and not remember that this had all happened.

For a brief moment, Cas allowed himself to imagine that he was the Foretold. The Chosen One, with a purpose and a destiny. The One who, for once in his life, was wanted and special. A small spark of hope ignited inside him – and despite how hard he tried to calm the flame, all he wanted to do was hold on to this feeling. To let it grow.

Eventually though, Cas couldn't fight it any more. His eyelids grew heavy, his limbs became limp, and slowly he drifted off into a soundless, dreamless sleep.

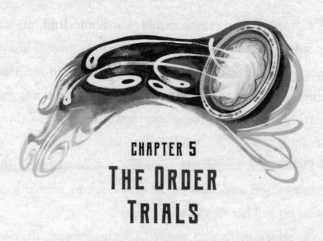

CHAPTER 5
THE ORDER TRIALS

THE NEXT MORNING BEGAN LIKE ANY OTHER.

As the sunny yolk of dawn cracked across the sky, Cas stirred from his slumber and rubbed the crusty sleepy-dust from his eyes. He stretched out his long legs from where they had been cramped on the bed overnight and looked around, ready for the onslaught of buzzing, nervous butterflies in his stomach when he couldn't remember where he was...

Except the butterflies never came.

As the clock bells chimed eight outside, Cas shot upright and tumbled out of bed.

He remembered.

He remembered *everything*.

All the events of the day before flew through his mind in a flurry: bringing the raven back to life, coming to the Balance Lands, learning about the Master of All and being the Foretold...

Potentially being the Foretold, Cas reminded himself.

Still, he leapt up from the floor and ran over to shake Warrior awake. She groaned groggily and buried her head deeper under her pillow, but Cas pulled her to her feet and began spinning her around the room, the pair of them blundering about like two baboons on hot coals.

"Who sent an electric shock up your bottom this morning?" groaned Warrior, sleepily cracking an eye open as Cas hoiked her this way and that.

"I remember!" Cas gasped, beaming and shaking her shoulders. "For the first time in my life, I actually remember!"

Warrior's mouth dropped open. Cas's smile widened. He had the distinct impression that she was rarely lost for words.

The silence was broken by Cas's stomach emitting an earth-shattering growl.

"Get dressed," said Warrior, digging out an old Wayward School uniform from one of the trunks. "I'll go and grab something to feed that grumbling monster in your belly. We've got a big day ahead."

As soon as Warrior departed down the spiral staircase, Cas pulled on the spare uniform she had laid out for him. The plain white shirt was too small and the black trousers were too itchy (not to mention the pockets were full of either mice droppings or mouldy chocolate chips – Cas didn't dare taste them to find out which), but he knew looking the part of a Wayone was crucial to Warrior's plan. Afterwards, he settled down in the big bay window and cast his gaze across the horizon, waiting for her to return.

Overnight, Wayward had changed location again. This morning, the sun crawled into the sky above a thick, vibrant bluish-green rainforest. Multicoloured tropical birds exploded out of the dense, leafy canopy that cast dappled shadows over the winding path leading off into the distance, like a mystical golden road. Cas still couldn't wrap his head around it. He could've sworn there had been a sprawling metropolis in the rainforest's place when he had woken up in the middle of the night.

Shaking his head, he switched his attention to the horde of students arriving for the first day of term. Wayones, twos, threes … and goodness knows how many other years flooded through the great big *WS* gates and across the courtyard below. Each student was dressed in the same uniform as Cas but with differently coloured cloaks or pristine blazers, each emblazoned with a unique symbol and trim.

Using his excellent powers of deduction (if he did say so himself), Cas guessed that the different colours must represent their Orders. The Earthshapers were clearly the ones wearing thick, green linen cloaks or green-and-brown-trimmed blazers, emblazoned with the sigil of a leafy plant woven around a rock. The Airscapers had to be those in wispy dove-grey cloaks or grey-and-white-trimmed blazers, with a swirl of wind emblem. The Wavebreakers wore shimmering blue cloaks or blue-and-navy-trimmed jackets, and a wave as their seal. And the Firetamers wore leather-cuffed scarlet cloaks or red-and-yellow-piped blazers, sporting a ball of flame.

A knot twisted in Cas's gut when he realized there weren't any students wearing any other colours – meaning there truly were no Life or Deathmakers among them. Just as he began searching the crowd for a second time, Warrior burst back into the room carrying a teetering breakfast tray piled high with jammy croissants, marmalade toast, cornflakes, dippy eggs and juice.

They filled their bellies until they were full to bursting, Cas smiling once more about his reason for leaping around the Attic like a springbok.

"I suppose it makes sense, you remembering," said Warrior, dunking a soldier of toast into her dripping egg. "Others' powers are strongest here in the Balance Lands, because this is where the threads of power come from."

"The threads of power?" asked Cas, taking a swig of orange juice.

"The threads are like a magical force," she said. "They exist within us, as well as around us. They make up everything in the universe, including our world and even the Normie one too. At the beginning of time, there were only purple and white threads of power. Life and death. Beginning and end. Dawn and dusk. They wove together to create everything. As time went on, some of the threads changed into different shades of colour, giving rise to the other powers – earth, air, water and fire – or dulled and lost their powers altogether, like with the Normies. Seeing as we still have powers and they don't, it's our job to help protect the Normie world, so the threads made the Balance Lands as our safe place. Our home. Others must always return here eventually because this is where our power is strongest. If an Other stays in the Normie world for too long, where there's no power, their abilities dwindle and their body withers and di—"

"So you think that's why I kept losing my memory in the Normie world?" Cas jumped in. "Because I belong here?"

"Like I said, it makes sense," said Warrior. "If your memories stick around now, that has to be the reason— Oh crumbs!"

Midway through her sentence, the clock bells outside had chimed nine.

"We're late!" exclaimed Warrior, tossing their breakfast plates aside with a loud *clatter*. Cereal milk and toast crusts splattered the walls, but Warrior didn't care. She grabbed Cas's hand and, to his surprise, dragged him towards one of the walls instead of down the spiral stairs. Frantically, she tapped around until she found a loose panel hiding a trap door.

It drew back, revealing a long, steep chute.

"Honestly – really – I'd rather take the steps," Cas mumbled, his stomach dropping into his shoes.

"No time," said Warrior. With a sharp shove, she sent him flying down the slide.

"ARGH!" cried Cas as he slid, uncontrollably, down and down, the metal slide twisting this way … and that … round one corner … looping so he was upside down … then round and down again…

It was dark inside the chute, but suddenly a flash of bright light was rushing towards him.

Faster…

And faster…

And faster…

SPLAT!

Cas's feet collided with a grated door and he shot off the end of the slide, somersaulted head over heels and landed in a crumpled heap on an old rug.

As the plume of dust from the rug cleared, Cas stood up, only to be knocked off his feet again seconds later by Warrior, who came toppling out and wiped the rug completely from underneath him.

"Ouch!" moaned Warrior. "I'm usually much more graceful."

Brushing the muck off his clothes, Cas realized they were in the library. Curving rows upon rows of bookshelves surrounded them, extending up to an impossibly high ceiling. Ladders at least fifteen metres tall reached up to the top shelves, and in the centre of the round room there was a large fireplace complete with an eclectic mix of brightly patterned, squishy armchairs.

"Come on," said Warrior, roughly tugging Cas along.

They streaked through the library, heading for the exit.

"Warrior Bane, is that you?" a voice called out after them. A bespectacled, untidy-haired woman stuck her head out from behind one of the bookcases, holding a tome suspended in mid-air.

"Not now, Mrs Crane," Warrior called over her shoulder.

"I hope you aren't causing too much trouble, dear!"

"No such thing as too much trouble!"

In a calamity of dishevelled hair and messy uniforms, Cas and Warrior careered out of the library and into the crowd of students. Warrior ducked and weaved through the sea of boys and girls taking the stairs down to the entrance hall. The manic mix of colours in the throng made Cas feel a bit queasy. It felt like they were passing shoulder to shoulder through a moving, living rainbow. Or swimming in a pool of multicoloured vomit from someone who had eaten too many pick 'n' mix sweets.

"Don't we need cloaks?" asked Cas, staring at the vivid students swarming around them. "You know, to blend in?"

"Not you," said Warrior, heading towards the end of the hallway. The crowd thinned here to a raucous gaggle of uncloaked, plain-shirted students and their parents. "Wayones haven't had their Orders declared yet, remember? If we want to sneak into the Order Trials, we need you to look bright and shiny and new."

"I *am* shiny and new," said Cas.

"Well, you know what I mean."

A sudden thought dawned on him. "Where's your cloak? What Order are you in?"

"Hush," said Warrior, brushing him off with the air of someone who was too busy to think.

Cas was sure she was avoiding his question, but he didn't have time to ask her again. They silently slipped into the bustle of uncloaked pupils and joined a queue waiting in front of the entrance to a grand room. A platinum plaque read THE ATRIUM in chipped letters. Sobbing, giddy parents with accents from all over the world hugged their children or kissed their cheeks, before pushing them into line and wishing them good luck for the Order Trials. At the front of the queue stood a stern-looking teacher holding a book of names. One by one, the hopeful first years introduced themselves. The teacher checked their name against her list before ushering them inside.

"This is where it gets tricky," whispered Warrior. She let out a deep groan when she spotted who the teacher was. "Oh no, not Madame Aster. *Anyone* but Aster."

"Why?" queried Cas. "What's wrong with her?"

"What's right with her is more like it," grumbled Warrior. Sure enough, the woman checking off the names looked very graceful but severe, with slick, waxy black hair pulled into a tight ponytail and high, sharp cheekbones – but how bad could she be?

"You'll see," said Warrior, answering Cas's unspoken question.

Soon enough, he did.

When their turn came, Warrior shoved Cas ahead of her as they stepped up to the front of the line.

"Name?" the teacher droned flatly, her coal-like eyes not bothering to look up from the book.

"C—" Cas began.

"Dewey Cricket," Warrior cut in, picking a name at random from the list and digging him sharply in the side with her elbow. *Oh, right,* Cas remembered. *I'm not on the Oracle's list.*

"Hey! I'm Dewey Cricket!" a strawberry-blond boy piped up from behind them.

Madame Aster glanced up, glowering. Her large, dark eyes suddenly narrowed, making Cas feel like they pierced right into his soul.

"No, she's right," lied Cas, chuckling nervously. "I'm Dewey Cricket. You probably know my cousin, Doughy Cockroach. He used to go here too."

For a moment, Cas thought they were rumbled. He swallowed hard and prepared himself for a scolding.

On the contrary, the stern teacher sighed and rolled her eyes.

"Both of you, inside now," she commanded in a slight, lilted French accent. "*Zut alors,* I don't have time for this. The Order Trials will be starting soon." Cas and Dewey both immediately scampered in – but when Warrior tried to squeeze by too, Madame Aster shot out her hand and grabbed a fistful of Warrior's shirt. "Of course you would be involved, Mademoiselle Bane. Where exactly do you think you're going?"

"Inside. With my friend."

Madame Aster laughed cruelly. "*Mais non,*" she snapped. "You do not have any friends. I believe you should be in Waygates and Portal Physics now, so hurry along. *Vite, vite!*"

Warrior shot a look of pure venom at Madame Aster, the ends of her hair turning a furious red.

But Aster didn't budge.

"Fine," said Warrior, kicking the ground in protest. She turned and reluctantly trudged off down the hall, desperately mouthing "sorry" to Cas over her shoulder.

Madame Aster gave a wicked smirk at Warrior's retreating figure.

"Did you not hear me?" she barked when she caught Cas lingering. "Inside! *Vite!*"

Totally lost with their plan up in smoke, Cas had no choice but to follow the real Dewey inside.

The Atrium was built like an amphitheatre. Its ridiculously high glass ceiling allowed bright light to pour into the room, reflecting the calm, sunny weather outside. Shimmering flags displaying each of the five Orders' symbols were draped from the walls, and seats for the students extended skyward in every direction. Above them, a viewing gallery stretched around the perimeter, where teachers – including Dr Bane – and a few older students who had somehow snuck in to watch sat chattering away.

Cas grabbed a seat between Dewey and another boy who introduced himself as Bracken Moonstrike. Once the last straggling prospective Wayone had entered, the Atrium's magnificent, intricately carved doors closed with a tremendous *thud*.

Madame Aster swept past them in her blue cloak and joined the other teachers up on the balcony.

For several minutes, everyone sat in silence.

People whispered behind their hands and nudged one another, pointing to a veiled figure sitting on a chair on a dais in the middle of the room. Cas weaved from side to side, trying to catch a glimpse himself, but he couldn't see anything properly until the figure suddenly threw back her veil, looked out at the audience with blind, milky eyes and stretched out a bony hand towards them.

The Oracle.

"Power," she breathed in a voice that was little more than a whisper, but which echoed and bounced around the room until it vibrated through their bones. "That is what resides in every one of you. In some, it is a smidge.

A drop. A trickle. But in others, the threads that bind your body together throb strongly – threads which tether you to this world and, in some cases, the next."

The Oracle moved her hovering hand slowly across the crowd, as if searching for something.

"Quinnberley Crestbourne!" she boomed, startling them all.

Every single head spun around wildly, looking for the owner of the name. Shakily, a brown-skinned girl with dark, frizzy hair and cornflower-blue doe eyes stood up.

"Come." The Oracle beckoned her. "It is time to judge the might of your power – to see if you are worthy of admittance to our esteemed Wayward School."

After a moment's hesitation, Quinnberley Crestbourne tentatively made her way down from the seats and up onto the dais. Her knees knocked together as she drew closer. The Oracle swept forward to meet her and reached out for Quinnberley's trembling hand. Around the Oracle, there were five objects: a mound of dirt; an empty, airy jar; a bowl of water; a single candle; and a strange dish with a luminous, glowing surface, from which Cas swore he could hear hushed voices coming.

Squeezing her eyes shut, Quinnberley took the Oracle's hand.

Instantly, an invisible wave of power pulsated out from them over the crowd. The water on the Oracle's left shook so uncontrollably that it burst out of the bowl. It rose into the air and enveloped the pair of them in humungous, graceful watery arcs, trapping them in a water-spun globe, before sloshing back into place. Out of nowhere, Cas could feel impossible sea spray spattering his cheeks. He tasted brine on his tongue and sensed a dampness in the air that suggested rain.

"Our first new student – a Wavebreaker!" the Oracle roared. A round of applause broke out, including from Madame Aster, who looked ambitiously thrilled that such a powerful Other was joining her Order's ranks. The Oracle released the shaken girl's hand and called towards the balcony. "Headmaster!"

Dr Bane stood and cleared his throat. "Headmaster Higgles is, erm – *busy* – at the moment. As deputy headmaster, I'm acting as envoy."

The Oracle didn't seem to care. "This one," she said, pointing at Quinnberley. "I see great talent and potential in her, more so than in any other in this room. Her gifts will be squandered into submission with basic Wayone classes. She needs proper teaching, proper taming – second year would be more suitable."

Second year?

Cas's cheeks heated. He felt like a fool for even showing up. He had never expected the Oracle to declare him to be the most powerful Other there – not when he'd had no knowledge of his powers before yesterday – but how could he possibly be the Foretold when the Quinnberley

77

Crestbournes of the Balance Lands were skipping school years because their talents were too precious to waste?

"Understood," said Dr Bane, nodding curtly and retaking his seat.

As he did so, Dr Bane glanced down and momentarily caught Cas's eye. Cas quickly looked away and sank lower in his own seat. He half expected Bane to shout out *"Imposter!"*, stop the ceremony and kick him out. Yet when Cas chanced a look up again, Dr Bane was simply watching him with a very curious, mildly amused expression. Bane winked, before turning back to the Trials below.

One at a time, the remaining students were called up to the Oracle's podium and tested. Quickly, Cas noticed a pattern. They were apparently being called up in dwindling order of power.

Akash Gill, the second new student to be accepted, was declared an Airscaper after he sent a miniature whirlwind twirling around the stage. He was followed by Ben Brooks, who joined Quinnberley in the Wavebreakers, though he didn't skip a year or make the water respond as violently. A golden-haired girl called Laula Spinks was the most talented of the Firetamers, making the candle flame sashay like a pair of tango dancers and grow to twice its size. Meanwhile, a run of three Earthshapers – Dewey Cricket, Bracken Moonstrike and Ellie Green – were enrolled after they made the mound of dirt transform into a muddy, growling bear, a grasshopper and a flowerpot respectively.

Charlotte Smelling, an Airscaper, was the first hopeful to be rejected when she couldn't even make the empty jar topple onto its side. She ran out of the room bawling, even though Dewey whispered to Cas that she would easily get into any other school with Wayward's recommendation.

With some of the students, the Oracle asked them a couple of hushed questions first. But the one constant which remained was that, with each passing person, the invisible waves of power pulsating over the crowd lessened, and Cas felt his chance of being the Foretold slipping further away. He waited with bated breath for the Oracle to sense him. But as the waves of power from the Wayones dulled to a barely there tickle over the skin, Cas began to panic.

The Oracle had just finished testing Elliott Icklepickle, another Firetamer, who was rejected, when Madame Aster rose, clapped her hands and ordered all the successful Wayones to line up outside again, ready to be taken to their first classes.

But as the successful students stood and began to leave, Cas stayed where he sat.

He wasn't sure if he felt more disappointed or amazed that he hadn't been called at all.

That's what you get for getting your hopes up, he thought, dread pooling like an icy puddle in his stomach.

Until, unexpectedly, the Oracle sprang forward.

"Wait!" she cried, her voice ringing out so loudly that

everybody froze. "There is another. Someone in this room who hasn't been tested yet. I can sense him not by his power, but by the hole he cleaves among you. He has no aura. No existence. He is a nothing boy." Her milky eyes found Cas in the crowd. "Come forward, child!"

The Wayones whipped their gazes to Cas – the only person still sitting – amidst whisperings and mutterings under their breaths.

Cas didn't move.

The Oracle was clearly talking about him ... but *no aura, no existence, a nothing boy ...* none of those things were good.

Standing beside him, Dewey Cricket nudged Cas. "Go on. It's not scary, I promise."

Despite his gut reaction to run, Cas reminded himself why he had come here. He stood on shaking legs. Over a hundred pairs of beady eyes tracked him as he passed by the other first years. He tried to ignore the gawking faces and speculations as he headed towards the Oracle's platform. Above him, every teacher and older student was craning their neck over the balcony. Cas had just spotted two very nasty-looking students, a pale pair of twins, leering at him like he was something disgusting on the bottom of their shoes, when he felt it again.

The tingling sensation in his leg.

He reached out a hand to brace himself on a nearby seat, but his leg began to jerk and twitch anyway. Soon it would be in full motion. He had two choices: try to walk or stay still until it passed.

Cas refused to be ashamed or afraid.

He chose to walk.

The mutterings and gasps swelled to a clamour as he pressed on unsteadily, staggering like a baby deer on ice towards the platform. His funny leg was moving this way and that, out of his control now, but he could just about keep heading forward if he concentrated hard on the direction he wanted to go in.

Triumphantly, Cas exhaled as he reached the bottom of the dais, but when he raised his foot to the first step, his knee buckled under him and he fell flat on his face to the floor.

The shocked gasps grew louder – but above them all, there was sniggering, no doubt from the nasty twins.

Shame. Anger. Fear. Confusion. All these emotions grew and roiled in Cas's stomach. He wanted nothing more than to curl up into a ball and wait for the ground to swallow him whole. But he wouldn't give in. Using the strength of those feelings, he pushed himself up and finished his climb onto the platform.

As his funny leg disappeared, Cas came face to face with the Oracle.

Her mysterious veiled appearance was even more intimidating up close; her costume seemed to flap in a non-existent breeze, and she had an unsettling sense of foreboding about her – like you wanted to ask her every question in the world but dreaded every answer.

"My child," the Oracle said. "Come closer."

Cas gulped, shuffling nearer.

The Oracle reached out her hand but didn't touch him yet. "My child," she mused, "you are strange, very strange – unlike anything I have ever sensed before. You are like fog. There, but barely there … like mist I cannot catch with my fingers." She curled a bony digit and beckoned him closer still. "Tell me, child – what is your name?"

"C-Cas," he stuttered. "I mean, Casander."

"And your last name?"

"No last name."

"Are you from this world, Casander No-Name?"

"Well, no, I'm from the Normie world," said Cas. "But I don't really know. I can't remember. I think I might belong in this one."

"And do you have a family?"

"No, miss."

"Have you been cleaned?"

Cleaned? What a weird question to ask.

"I suppose. I had a wash this morning."

The whole room broke into giggles.

"Not *cleaned*," the Oracle corrected him shortly. "*Gleaned*. Have you been Gleaned?"

This was even more confusing.

"Gleaned? What's Gleaned?"

82

The Oracle narrowed her cloudy white eyes. "Gleaning is the process of forcing an Other's powers out of them before they are ready," she explained in a low voice. "But as you have no knowledge of this, I assume that you haven't been."

"Oh no, definitely not," said Cas. "At least, I don't think so."

The Oracle huffed in approval, making it clear that whatever Gleaning was, it was frowned upon.

"Give me your hand," she commanded, opening her calloused palm to him.

Cas sucked in a deep breath and took it.

A tidal wave of power unlike any other rocketed through the room. Everyone, from staff to students, was thrown back in their retaken seats. The mound of dirt, the empty jar, the water bowl and the candle went flying, until only the strange, luminous dish remained. The hushed voices Cas could hear from within grew louder. Jets of violet and white light flew from the dish like bullets, taking on humanoid shapes and ricocheting around the room. The spirit-like things rattled the high glass window until cracks appeared, the glass threatening to cave in on them, and the sunny weather outside turned to black clouds and thunder.

"It can't be…" The Oracle gasped, before releasing him and uttering, "It is."

As soon as the Oracle relinquished Cas's hand, the

commotion stopped. The spirits vanished, the invisible wave ceased, and the stormy sky returned to perfect azure. Cas staggered backwards, clutching his hand like a deadly weapon.

But the Oracle took a great stride towards him, leaning in until they were practically nose to nose.

"My child," she cooed, and for the second time in two days, Cas felt like he had just become very hard to ignore. "*My child*. It is you. My prophecy came true."

CHAPTER 6
THE DARKBLOOM LEGACY

EVERYTHING HAPPENED IN A BLUR.

The hushed voices of the crowd grew into shouts of awe, wonder and amazement. The teachers leaning over the balcony either stood there gaping or, in Dr Bane's case, rushed down to rapidly usher Cas off the platform. Madame Aster tried to calm the roaring crowd, but it was useless. Dr Bane frog-marched Cas out of the Atrium to a crescendo of cries and pointed fingers.

"Who is it?"

"It's him! The one from the prophecy!"

"The Foretold!"

"His name's Dewey Cricket! I heard him say so outside!"

Another faint protest of *"Hey, no, I'm Dewey!"* was the last thing Cas heard before the Atrium's doors slammed behind them.

Outside wasn't much better.

Luckily, the parents from earlier had been escorted elsewhere, but there must've been another way down from the gallery because the entrance hall was teeming with jostling students, many of whom Cas recognized as those who had watched the proceedings. He spotted the pale twins, a boy and a girl, near the front of the throng. The smug smirks had been wiped off their faces.

Cas's heart soared with relief when he saw Warrior sprinting towards him.

"See, I told you!" she shouted at Dr Bane, beaming. The ends of her black hair glowed a victorious shade of yellow. "I saw the whole thing. You said I was wrong, but I told you! I told you!"

Dr Bane gripped Cas's shoulder so tightly that he thought his arm might fall off. "Not now, Warrior," said Dr Bane firmly. Out of the corner of his eye, he clocked the bespectacled librarian from earlier and called out to her. "Mrs Crane, alert the Grand Council. Tell them we've found the One they've been looking for!"

Mrs Crane instantly dropped the armful of hardbacks she was carrying and nodded, scurrying up the stairs, her glasses askew. "You can bring him to the library."

"Thank you, Dromeda," Dr Bane echoed back.

Dr Bane marched Cas all the way up to the second floor, the Oracle, Warrior and about half the school trailing in their wake. When they reached the library, he hurried their ragtag group inside, before barricading the doors. They could hear students scuffling among themselves, trying to peek through the keyholes or peer under the crack at the bottom of the doors, but Dr Bane rapped his hand on the wood and threatened to give everyone enough extra homework to last until Christmas if they didn't go away.

Thankfully, they did.

Mrs Crane promptly reappeared, panting. "They're – *GASP* – on their way – *GASP* – now," she wheezed, leaning on a bookcase to catch her breath.

A glint of sunlight caught Cas's eye as something shone from between the row of bookshelves Mrs Crane had emerged from. Seconds later, four figures in gold, orange-trimmed cloaks emerged from a gilded mirror.

"The Grand Council," Warrior gaped, starry-eyed, next to him.

As the four almighty figures approached, Cas and Warrior stumbled back, sinking into a mismatched pair of armchairs with a *poof.*

"I thought nobody could enter Wayward without going through the wards…" Cas began.

"*Shhh,*" Warrior hissed respectfully. "Not ordinarily, but the Grand Council Chambers has its own direct waygate to the school."

Neither of them could take their eyes off the two men and two women who had appeared in the room. "High Councillor Du Villaine, Head of Airscapers." Dr Bane greeted an older, silver-haired woman who had a fearsome, choking stare. "High Councillor Aster, Head of Earthshapers." He shook the hand of a tall, elegant man with tufty sideburns. "High Councillor Brooks, Head of Wavebreakers." A curt nod at the other man, who had a plaited beard down to his waist. "And High Councillor Hephaestus, Head of Firetamers." He bowed low in front of a woman with startlingly scarlet locks. "Thank you for coming."

"What is the meaning of this, Bane?" yapped High Councillor Du Villaine. Her thin lips curled back so ferociously that she made Miss Grimbly look like a cuddly teddy bear. "I swear on my family's honourable name, if this is a trick or joke you think is funny— You interrupted us in the middle of a *very* important meeting. We were on the brink of deploying a secret squadron of Earthshapers and Firetamers to deal with a volcano that keeps threatening to erupt on the Indonesian border. You better hope that what you've got to say is worth it, otherwise—"

"What Tyrannia means to say," cut in High Councillor Aster calmly, steepling his fingers, "is what is the nature of your call today?"

"This boy," said Dr Bane, unintimidated by Du Villaine and gesturing towards Cas, "is the One we've been searching for."

"It is true," said the Oracle in the same quiet, weighty voice she had used in the Atrium. "I tested him myself this morning."

"And where exactly did you find him?" said High Councillor Du Villaine stiffly, shooting Cas a suspicious look.

"Actually, I—" Warrior started to say, but Dr Bane sliced her off with a wide-eyed look.

"In the Normie world," Dr Bane said, spinning a vague and plausible tale as smoothly as if it were silk. "Warrior and I were holidaying there briefly before term started again. We happened upon the boy by chance."

Clearly, Dr Bane didn't want the Grand Council knowing about Warrior's unsanctioned, unsupervised mission to find Cas by herself.

"He has no memory of who he is," chimed in Warrior, seemingly determined to get a word in edgeways. "He didn't even know he had any powers."

"And does he really?" asked High Councillor Hephaestus, eyes aglimmer. "Have Life and Deathmaker abilities, I mean?"

Cas's throat dried up, but the Oracle answered for him. "Yes."

Relief and elation spread across three of the Grand Council members' faces like a cool, welcome breeze. High Councillor Aster smiled; High Councillor Brooks's shoulders sagged, free from an invisible weight; and High Councillor Hephaestus even did a little dance on the spot.

But not High Councillor Du Villaine.

The look she gave him made the weight that seemed to have shifted from Brooks's to Cas's shoulders feel heavier.

"How convenient," Du Villaine cawed. "A simple Normie boy, plucked from obscurity, with no memory of who or what he is, just happens to be our saviour. And you were the one who found him, Bane."

"I did," said Dr Bane, undeterred.

High Councillor Aster glanced skyward. "This isn't a competition, Tyrannia."

"The Foretold has come," butted in High Councillor Hephaestus. "You heard the prophecy as well as we did. *Only one born from the same stock, with power equal to or greater than the Master's, can stop him. They will grace us within the next twelve twirls around the sun.* We haven't seen a Lifemaker or Deathmaker in seventeen years – be grateful that we have finally found one."

"Well, how come *you* didn't know about this?" High Councillor Du Villaine sneered, focusing her wrath on the Oracle now. "Do you expect me to believe that your strange abilities were strong enough to know that the boy was coming, but not to know *when* he came? That's like inviting someone over and then being surprised when they ring the doorbell!"

"The threads of power work in great and mysterious ways," retorted the Oracle cryptically. She turned her unseeing eyes to stare dead straight at High Councillor Du Villaine. "He is the Foretold. The truth is what it is, whether you like it or not."

Something about the Oracle's hard tone made High

Councillor Du Villaine bite her tongue, seemingly cowed into acceptance.

"You must enrol him at once, Bane," High Councillor Aster commanded. "It is essential that he completes his proper education. Only then will he be ready to join us and stand a chance against the Master of All."

"Certainly," agreed Dr Bane, inclining his head as if he wanted to do nothing more than honour their wishes.

"And we must instigate a plan of counter-deception at once!" said High Councillor Brooks. "We can circulate false rumours about the boy and his whereabouts. Undoubtedly, the Master and his Heretics will hear whispers that the Foretold has been found soon enough!"

You have no idea how right you are, Cas thought worriedly.

"Is that what you want too, child?" asked High Councillor Hephaestus, turning to him. "To stay here and help us?"

Cas's eyebrows shot up in surprise. "I – I get a say in this?"

High Councillor Hephaestus grinned warmly. "Of course. This is your life we're talking about."

High Councillor Du Villaine snorted and stepped forward to protest, but Hephaestus held up a hand to stop her.

Unsure, Cas glanced around the room.

There was Warrior, sitting and smiling proudly beside

him; Dr Bane, shooting him a gentle and knowing look; Mrs Crane, who bobbed her head encouragingly and gave him the thumbs up; and the four Grand Council members staring back at him, waiting for an answer.

These people needed him. It was as simple as that.

"I do," said Cas, a kindling flame of belonging, of being wanted, striking up inside his chest.

He had never been surer of anything in his life.

"You'll need a proper name," Warrior said, as she escorted Cas away from the library towards the headmaster's office.

After the Grand Council and the Oracle had departed, repeatedly declining Mrs Crane's offer to stay for tea and custard creams, Cas had been shown out of the library by Dr Bane, who wanted to take him to meet the headteacher. Unfortunately, multiple students were still milling around outside, desperate to get a glimpse of the Foretold. So, whilst Dr Bane dealt with them, he had entrusted Warrior with the task instead.

"Make sure he signs the school register," Dr Bane said grimly, before rolling up his sleeves and venturing off to face the horde.

"I have a proper name," said Cas now.

"No, I mean a last name," said Warrior. "A family name. If you're the Foretold, you can't expect people to keep calling you Casander No-Name for ever."

"But I like it. *No-Name* sounds cool, mysterious… I bet nobody else is called it."

"Duh, for good reason. It's stupid."

"Well, so is Bane."

Warrior threw Cas a sidelong glance and chuckled. "Nice try. But I didn't get to pick my name, did I? Dr Bane gave it to me when he took me in."

The headmaster's office was located at the end of a wide corridor on the far side of the Atrium. A marble archway led into a foyer, complete with gilded statues of the five emblems, a sculpture of the world flipped on its head and a mahogany desk, behind which sat Miss Grimbly.

"Good morning, Miss Grumply," said Warrior, putting on her best sickly sweet voice, the one she knew annoyed the secretary the most.

Miss Grimbly stopped feeding pieces of bread to the two crusty parakeets in the cage behind her and whirled around. She gripped the sandwich ends so hard that her knuckles turned white. "What do you want, heathen?" She scowled. "Didn't I tell you not to hang around with this one, boy? She's nothing but trouble, I tell you. Nothing."

Cas remained silent and looked at his feet.

"Could you please tell Headmaster Higgles that Trouble is here to see him?" said Warrior, batting her eyelashes frantically. "Or I could go and tell him myself…"

Like a cat on a hot stove, Miss Grimbly leapt from

her chair and threw her frail, brittle body in front of the headmaster's door.

"Don't you dare," she said sharply, raspy breaths rattling through her fragile chest. "You'll have to make an appointment."

"Headmaster Higgles is expecting me now."

"And how *exactly* would that be the case?"

"Dr Bane sent an Airscaper note ahead—"

The waging war between Miss Grimbly and Warrior was abruptly interrupted by Headmaster Higgles opening his door.

"Well, well," guffawed the huge figure who filled the doorway. "If it isn't Bane's ward and the Foretold himself."

Headmaster Higgles was a very tall man who largely resembled a garden rake. His tufty head of hair brushed against the top of the door frame as he towered above the rest of them. He had the distinctly wide-eyed, bemused expression of someone who has been hit over the head with a frying pan. His spindly arms and legs folded unnaturally this way and that like a giant spider as he passed through the entrance, almost dislodging the small napping pillow tucked under one arm and the half-eaten blueberry muffin sticking out of the opposite breast pocket.

Cas wondered which had been the urgent business Headmaster Higgles was attending to instead of watching the Oracle's ceremony: his mid-morning snooze or early lunch.

"Let's get a good look at you, boy," said Headmaster Higgles, blundering towards Cas in an oversized green cloak. "Yes, that's it – turn left, now right – spin around a bit – my goodness, you're nothing like I expected."

"Like you expected, sir?" prodded Cas.

Warrior shot him a look that said, *Trust me, you don't want to know.*

"No, I suppose I expected the Foretold to be, well – something more, something greater – a strong, strapping lad, quite like myself," said Higgles. "But I'm sure you'll look the part once we've fed and trained you up a bit, got a bit more than fluff going on in your head and some meat on your bones."

You're one to talk, thought Cas, spying a ham sandwich sticking out of Higgles's other pocket.

"We're here to sign the register, sir," Warrior informed him, as the headmaster started making Cas spin around again like a new toy.

"Oh yes, right." Headmaster Higgles's words were muffled by the giant bite of muffin he had just taken, thick dribbles of drool sliding down his pointed chin. Cas wondered if the headmaster grew continuously up instead of out. "Get it out for them, Grimbly. That's it, hurry up – then scurry along and see if Cook Fiddlepot has prepared my second brunch yet."

Miss Grimbly looked downright offended. "But, headmaster—"

"Chop, chop," said Headmaster Higgles, clapping his hands. "Second brunch."

With a disgruntled noise, Miss Grimbly pulled a heavy calf-hide book out from her desk, but hovered for a moment, reluctant to leave them alone with it, before striding past them towards the kitchens with a grimace.

"Just pop it away when you're done," instructed Headmaster Higgles, licking his lips and returning to his office to polish off his muffin.

"Ah, this is the life," said Warrior, plopping down on Miss Grimbly's chair and lazily kicking her feet onto the desk.

Cas peeled back the register's front cover tentatively. "So, what do I do?"

"Sign it. Everyone who attends Wayward School has to."

On the pages in front of Cas, there were columns upon columns of students' names listed under each of the Orders. It seemed to date back centuries.

"Flip to the back," said Warrior, deliberately smudging a muddy footprint into the centre of the desk. "That's where all the available last names are."

"Available last names?"

Sure enough, on the back pages of the book there were more columns, though these were sparsely populated.

"Names that are used by people who come to Wayward

without one," she explained. "People like us. Orphans. Others born in the Normie world. Those who don't want to use their real last name because they're estranged from their family."

Cas scanned the lists in front of him. There was certainly an interesting selection to choose from:

EARTHSHAPERS
Rockforth
Ivywove
Fernheath
Mudstroke
Forrester

AIRSCAPERS
Gale
Windfierce
Draftblast
Gustpuff
Blowbreath

WAVEBREAKERS
Covey
Shorenear
Dropper
Pitterpat
Splosher

FIRETAMERS

Sparkshooter

Flintflick

Embershade

Kindler

Forger

LIFEMAKERS AND DEATHMAKERS

Darkbloom

Lightfall

Crowblight

Newbone

Bleakdawn

Dustbringer

"How am I supposed to know which one to pick?"

Warrior shrugged unhelpfully. "Just choose carefully."

"Because this is like a *the name chooses the Other* type situation or…"

"No, because once you write your name in the register, there's no turning back. You're stuck with it."

Cas raked his gaze over the list of names again. Whichever one he chose, this was going to be his new identity. His *true* identity. Or at least, the only one that he could remember. Maybe if Warrior was right and he was originally from the Balance Lands, then one of his family members' names could be in this book already.

His blank-faced parents. His unknown brother or sister. A mysterious aunt, uncle or cousin, who'd never know he was about to sign his name at the back of the book, renouncing theirs and claiming a new one of his own.

But that's all I can do, mused Cas.

In a way, it didn't matter what life he might have had before, whether in the Normie world or the Balance Lands. This was the first one he could remember. It was the first time he could remember being himself, *claiming* himself, being able to decide who he was and actually stick with it.

One particular name called to him above the others, until he could see nothing else.

"This one," Cas said, tapping his finger against the first surname on the Lifemakers and Deathmakers' list: *Darkbloom*. He flicked to the fifth Order's page at the front of the book, picked up a pen and dipped it in a pot of ink. He started to scrawl his new name – but faltered halfway through. "Hey, how come this name is scratched out?"

Jumping off Miss Grimbly's chair, Warrior peered over Cas's shoulder to see what he was pointing at. There was only one other *Darkbloom* in the book, but the name had been repeatedly struck through. Cas squinted hard to see if he could make out the letters.

Aeurdan Darkbloom

Warrior's face drained of colour and her hair turned ashen grey.

She swallowed hard. "Do you remember me telling you how we don't call the Master of All by his real name any more?"

Cas nodded, a chill sweeping through his bones. He could sense what she was about to say before she did.

"That was his name," said Warrior coldly, "before he renounced it. He turned up here, a mysterious boy from the Normie world with no family or parents, like you. I must've completely forgotten; it's been years since I've heard it."

At the look of dread on Warrior's face, Cas quickly dipped his pen back in the pot. "I'll choose something else."

But Warrior clamped her hand on his to stop him.

"No," she said quietly, eyes transfixed on the book with a mix of wonder and fear. "You chose that name. For whatever reason, the threads made it speak to you." She shuddered. "It's just … spooky … that's all."

A slow and terrible shiver ran down Cas's spine.

"Yeah," he agreed, finishing writing his name in the register. "Spooky."

CHAPTER 7
THE ABNORMIES

THE WHOLE OF WAYWARD SCHOOL WAS STILL desperate to get a glimpse of the Foretold, so Dr Bane decided that it would be best for Cas to start his lessons the following day, meaning Warrior was granted a free pass out of classes to give Cas a private – but discreet – tour of the grounds.

Delighted, Warrior led Cas down narrow passageways, forgotten, cobwebby corridors and at one point even over a low roof to avoid the other students. The fortified stately mansion that was Wayward School just seemed to grow bigger the more they explored it. Even Warrior got lost a few times and they ended up walking in circles or retracing their steps.

Yet despite being shown everything from the Wavebreakers' creaky boathouse (and the "seaweed monster" who allegedly lurked in the impossibly deep boating lake) to the Earthshapers' homely woodland cabins, Cas couldn't shake the chill that the register had given him for the rest of the day.

Perhaps choosing the same name as the Master of All was a coincidence.

But what if it wasn't?

Only when Cas and Warrior collapsed into the squashy comfort of the library's armchairs at the end of the day, too tired to explore another inch, did Cas cease dwelling on it. It was nice to seek refuge amongst the bookshelves – until people quickly figured out where they were.

Thankfully, Mrs Crane was prepared.

Armed with a firefly lantern and feather duster, she chased away any prying eyes that she caught squinting through the doors' cracks.

Cas had to stifle his laughter each time as Mrs Crane was a particularly unusual-looking lady. She had large, gleaming eyes that loomed behind a ginormous pair of jam-jar spectacles, and curly, sandy-blonde, salt-and-pepper-speckled hair that stuck out in every direction. However, her clothes were undoubtedly the oddest thing about her. She wore an awful lot of tweed. From her tweed pinafore to the little tweed pompoms on her shoes, each item was a different clashing colour. It looked like she had been eaten and spat out again by some great tweedy monster.

Mrs Crane let them stay in the library until everyone

had gone home for the day. They ate dinner together, sipped steaming hot tea and gorged themselves silly on custard creams, whilst she regaled them with wondrous tales about her time spent in the Normie world.

"My first job after graduating from Wayward was working for the Grand Council," she told them. "Not doing anything important and life-saving like the secret Order squadrons, just a small job transporting the occasional valuable artefact or document. Then I spent six months travelling, trying to find the wackiest souvenirs possible. I like collecting things, you see."

"What sort of things?" said Cas.

Mrs Crane smiled. "Well, there was the bicycle wheel from the time I hitchhiked from Prague to Edinburgh solely on the back of tandem bikes. And Harry the Hippopotamus" – she fished out a dusty blue porcelain animal figure from under her desk – "from the week I spent posing as an art expert at the Louvre. Paris is Dr Bane's favourite city and I came *this* close to stealing the 'Mona Lisa' for him, if only that pesky bumblebee and mouldy baguette hadn't ruined my heist."

Cas made a mental note to ask Mrs Crane about that later.

"Then I suppose you could count the restraining order I got from the Sydney Opera House as a souvenir too. I was *wrongly* banned for life after a choirmaster described my singing voice as 'a caterwauling bag of screaming foxes being banged against a brick wall'. Obviously, he must've been tone-deaf. Oh, and there was the time I bought out an entire Marrakech bazaar by exchanging trinkets I'd brought with me from the Balance Lands."

"Hang on," said Cas slowly, realization dawning on him midway through a mouthful of buttery biscuits. "Curious Mrs Crane's Shop of Even Curiouser Curiosities. It was your shop I was found outside!"

Mrs Crane gave a secretive wink. *"Shh."* She pressed a finger to her lips. "Don't tell the Grand Council about my side hobby. They don't mind Others visiting the Normie world occasionally, but you're not supposed to put down roots there."

"Is that why someone else looks after it for you?"

"Why yes, you must've met Will!" Mrs Crane clapped her hands in delight. "He's a lovely lad."

"Is he an Other too?"

The exceptionally ordinary shopkeeper seemed completely at odds with Cas's idea of someone with incredible, otherworldly powers.

"Hm-mm," said Mrs Crane vaguely, chugging her tea and quickly starting to tidy up the teacups.

Before Cas could ask anything else, Mrs Crane clucked her tongue and ushered them off to bed.

Sleepy and content, Cas and Warrior reluctantly lugged their biscuit-laden bodies away from the library's roaring fire. For once, Cas wasn't dreading sleep. He couldn't wait to lie down and wake up tomorrow with all the memories of today fresh in his head.

Warrior, though, had other ideas. "There's a couple of people I want you to meet first."

Following her up the spiral staircase to the Attic, Cas shivered at the brisk autumnal chill clinging to the air. He wished he had an Order cloak of his own to wrap around himself for warmth. Suddenly, something occurred to him for the second time that day.

"You still haven't told me which Order you're in, Warrior?"

Warrior opened her mouth to answer, but before she could, the Attic's door at the top of the stairs swung open and the most hideous-looking creature Cas had ever seen came bounding out.

"*YIKES!*" he shrieked, scooting across the landing.

"*Yip-yap. Yip-yap,*" the creature half barked, half squeaked.

Chasing its tail on the landing in front of them was an animal about the size and build of a small dog, but different in several very peculiar ways. It had big, hairy, pointed ears, a long, narrow muzzle, large paws, bulging violet eyes and furry, scaled legs.

"Meet Hobdogglin," said Warrior proudly, slapping her knees so the creature ran to her affectionately. She stroked the weird animal like it was her most beloved pet. "He's my creation. I'm an Illusionist."

"A what?" said Cas, puzzled. He stumbled past them into the Attic, unable to take his eyes off the creature.

"An Illusionist. It means—"

Warrior's words were drowned out by Hobdogglin growling at Cas, revealing two rows of razor-sharp, pinprick teeth. The creature let out another *yip-yap* and lunged. Cas cringed and threw up his arms, but the funny creature passed straight through him. It landed on the other side, re-formed, and then turned around to trot back and rub itself against Cas's legs. Cas cautiously knelt down and patted the creature; it felt very real and solid again.

"An Illusionist," repeated Warrior. "It means I can create realistic, touchable illusions – at least sometimes. It's an odd ability to have. It falls outside of the five Orders, that's why everyone thinks I'm a freak—"

"But not us," a voice piped up. Cas turned to see a girl in a wheelchair rolling towards them from the far side of the room. "People might call us Abnormies, but it's just because they don't understand our powers. We're not like most Others. Come here, Hobdogglin!"

At the sight of the girl, Hobdogglin neglected Cas and leapt into the girl's lap – but passed right through again. She giggled.

"You're way too nice about other people," said Warrior, groaning and rolling her eyes.

The girl ignored her, staring fixedly at Cas. "Aren't you going to introduce us?"

"Cas, this is Paws," said Warrior. "Paws, this is Cas. The Foretold."

The girl rolled her wheelchair closer, smiling. Cas shook her outstretched hand.

"I know," she said, her voice feather-soft and dreamy. "Everyone's buzzing about it. I'm Amalia, by the way. Amalia Grover-Rosales. But everybody calls me Paws."

Paws had kind, muddy-brown eyes and matching hair, with a plait running across the front, framing her dark, olive-skinned face. She wore a tatty green Earthshaper cloak embroidered with colourful patterns that she had clearly hand-stitched herself, and a scruffy scarf was slung around her neck. Except, Cas realized when it opened its mouth and yawned, it wasn't a scarf at all. It was a scabby ragdoll cat with mangy fur and half of its teeth missing.

"This is Mogget," said Paws, nudging her shoulder to wake the cat again, but it had fallen back into a sleep so deep it barely looked alive.

"Um, hi, Mogget," mumbled Cas, reaching out to stroke the cat. The animal felt stiff and cold as ice beneath his touch.

"Feels dead, doesn't she?" said a fourth voice, chuckling.

A boy with fiery red-orange hair leapt off one of the Attic's beds and came to join them. His face was splattered with freckles beneath his crooked glasses and a single orange curl hung in the middle of his forehead. The strand of hair skimmed a puckered burn scar running from his eyebrow to his knobbly chin. As he approached, Cas was hit by a whiff of burnt coals and smoke. The boy's bed was scattered with bits of wire and bundles of string from where he had clearly been tinkering with something, and when he stuck out his oil-covered hand, Cas wondered if the boy had been soldering.

"That's why we call her Mogget," he continued, "because she looks like a maggoty corpse most of the time."

"Don't be mean," scolded Paws, covering Mogget's ears so she couldn't hear.

"There's no use doing that," said Warrior. "She's definitely deaf."

"I'm sorry, I didn't mean to insult her…" said the boy sheepishly, his ears flushing as red as his hair. "Anyway, it's good to meet you, Cas. I'm—"

Cas reached out to shake the boy's hand, but the minute he did so, the boy's whole arm went up in flames. Instinctively, Cas snatched his hand back. The boy was *literally on fire* in front of him.

The boy rapidly clutched his own hand to his chest and the fire died.

"Oh, gosh, I'm so sorry, did I hurt you…?" he stammered nervously, his eyes wide with concern. "I – I didn't mean to, I'm sorry … drat, I already said that didn't I… I'm just so nervous…"

But Cas wasn't interested in the boy's apology.

"Woah," he breathed. "That's so cool. You're a Fire-tamer, aren't you?"

The boy nodded stiffly. That explained the scent.

"Can all Firetamers do that?"

The boy chuckled half-heartedly, rubbing the back of his neck. "No, erm, not exactly," he stammered. "I'm a bit different. My name's Felix Embershade, but people call me Fenix... You know, a cross between *Felix* and *Phoenix*, for obvious reasons."

"Of course," said Cas. Then, realizing that might've sounded a little rude, he hastily added, "I wish I had your power."

Sadly, his words didn't have the desired effect.

"Um, thanks, but you probably don't..." Fenix flickered his gaze from Cas's knees to the ground. "Yours is much cooler, being the Foretold... No, sorry, that was really insensitive to say, you have a lot of responsibility on your shoulders. I just mean, well, my power's not so awesome when you end up ... doing ... doing this to yourself." He tapped the burn scar taking up a good portion of his face. "I lost control quite badly once."

Cas didn't know what to say. *Sorry* didn't feel right for something that had clearly happened so long ago, but he didn't want to steer away from the subject like it unsettled him either.

"Well, I think it looks badass," said Cas.

It was simply another difference about Fenix. Everyone had them.

"So, let me get this right," Cas summarised, pointing at them each in turn. "Warrior, you can create illusions that aren't real, but which can physically touch things. Fenix, you're a Firetamer who can set himself alight. And, Paws, you're an Earthshaper who…"

Paws gave a coy smile. "Let's just say I have a special knack with animals," she said, tapping her nose.

Cas didn't know what she meant, but he was sure he would soon find out.

"And you all live up here together?"

Warrior nodded. "Originally, Wayward was a boarding school, but most students choose to stay with their families now. I suppose having an evil tyrant like the Master on the loose does that to people. I live up here because I don't have anywhere else to go. Dr Bane took me in, and since he lives at the school, I do too – but the quarters above his office are too small for the both of us. Seeing as I don't belong in an Order, I'm not allowed to use the old, abandoned Order dorms. Traditions and customs … yada, yada … some old, stuffy nonsense like that. So, even though Paws could stay with her parents in town, or Fenix could sleep in the Firetamers' dorm—"

"We choose to stay up here to keep each other company," Paws butted in.

Warrior smirked. "It's much more fun this way."

"Cool." Cas beamed. "I can't wait—"

"Can't wait to what?" an ice-cold voice sliced across the room.

They felt the intruder's frosty presence before they saw them.

"Good evening, Mademoiselle Bane, Monsieur Darkbloom," said Madame Aster, stepping out of the shadows, her dreadful, melodic voice ringing out like a funeral bell.

Warrior's hair grew a deep and dangerous shade of red. "What are you doing here?"

Outside the windows, the sky had turned the velvety purple of twilight and twinkling silver stars were beginning to peek through the clouds. But inside, it felt like a storm was brewing. An invisible charge crackled through the air, in the same way it always did whenever Warrior and her least favourite teacher were in the same room.

"Trust me, I take no pleasure in venturing to this … *place*," said Madame Aster, wrinkling her nose and dragging a long finger through the layer of dust clinging to the Attic's door frame. "But Dr Bane asked me to find and inform you that the old Deathmaker dormitories have been prepared for Monsieur Darkbloom. I would think he would want to get settled into his new lodgings early after such a long day, *non*?"

"*Non*," mimicked Warrior. "It's only seven o'clock. Besides, I was thinking Cas could sleep here with us in the Attic."

"Ha," cawed Madame Aster, flicking her dark hair gracefully over her shoulder, "you do not make the rules. This place is for people who do not belong to an Order … or those who take pity on them. Monsieur Darkbloom, on the other hand, does. In fact, he will have the whole mausoleum to himself."

The whole mausoleum?

"Downstairs. Two minutes, Darkbloom," Madame Aster commanded, striding out of the room.

Cas blanched.

"The mausoleum? Why do I have to sleep in the mausoleum?"

Paws and Fenix winced.

"I'm sure it'll be fine," said Paws gently.

"Yeah, there'll only be a couple of dead bodies in the room below."

"There will be *dead bodies* beneath me?" said Cas, his eyes almost bulging out of his head.

"What else do you think mausoleums are for?" said Warrior. "Don't worry. It's only a few rotting headmasters and headmistresses. The rest are buried in the graveyard outside."

"I'd like to see you sleep soundly in a place like that!"

"Look, it's not great, I know—"

"Not great?!"

"But we don't have much choice," Warrior spoke over him. "You heard Aster. It's what Dr Bane has ordered. Usually, I'd fight tooth and nail over something like this, but

I don't think we can risk upsetting the teachers any more. I was lucky not to get expelled for sneaking you into the Order Trials earlier, even if I *was* right. And there's always the chance that if we don't behave, they'll separate you from us completely – they'll say it's for your own protection as the Foretold. You'll just have to sleep in the mausoleum's dorms, at least for tonight. Maybe in the future you could move to the old Lifemaker dorms above the Nurse's Quarters, but there's a nasty whatsit infestation up there right now."

Cas clenched his jaw and crossed his arms. There was no way he was sleeping in a building full of dead bodies.

NO. WAY.

"Please." Warrior put on her best pleading puppy-dog eyes.

However much Cas didn't want to share a dorm with a bunch of corpses, his mind was changed. He owed her this much.

"Fine," Cas huffed in defeat, making a show of dragging his feet as he trudged towards the door. "But if I die when those dead bodies come back to life and eat me, I'm going to murder you, Warrior."

Darkness fell fast as Madame Aster escorted Cas and his only belongings – the oversized pair of pyjamas he had worn the night before – across the rolling lawns down to Wayward School's cemetery.

During the day, the small graveyard with its cluster of tombstones wasn't scary at all. But set against the canvas of night, the gravestones shone stark and menacing against the silvery gloom that illuminated the three mausoleums where the dorms were housed, waiting to welcome Cas to his doom. He cast a longing glance back towards the warmly lit school, where the tiny specks of Warrior and the Abnormies watched him from the Attic's faraway window. Yet despite his apprehension, Cas couldn't deny that a small part of him felt morbidly drawn to the cemetery. Its Deathmaker magic seemed to spill out of every crack, calling to his powers within.

The darkness only deepened when Cas shut the mausoleum's door and ventured up to the dorm. The thick, black nothing skulked in the corners, immune to his firefly lantern, and the whole place reeked of wet, muddy grave dirt and the stale smell of decay. Crawling into one of the beds, Cas tried to get settled. But portraits of dead headteachers lined the walls, their chilling gazes following him as he tossed this way and that.

Rain beat against the mausoleum's walls. The cold autumn breeze whistled through the gaps in the windowpanes and curled around Cas's body as he slipped into a light and fitful sleep.

Either moments or minutes later, he awoke to a loud and terrifying crash as a nightjar bird smashed through the window, shattering glass across the floor. It shook its bulbous head before flying off again, but Cas couldn't go back to sleep after that.

Creaks and groans continued to echo through the room. Cas tried to convince himself that he was imagining the sounds, but the noises only grew louder.

And louder.

Closer.

And closer.

BANG!

Something boomed against the dormitory's door.

Cas leapt to his feet. He spun around wildly, searching for a weapon to defend himself with.

"Who is it?" he called out, gathering the sheets together from his bed.

Stupid. An intruder wasn't exactly about to announce themselves.

BANG!

"I'm armed with a blanky and I'm not afraid to use it!" Cas yelled.

He tiptoed towards the door, reached out and curled his hand around the rusty doorknob. Readying the bed sheets in a ball in his hand, Cas took a deep breath, pulled open the door and...

"ARGH!" Cas screamed.

"ARGH!" the person on the other side of the door wailed.

Cas blinked in the blackness. "Warrior?"

She stood in front of him wearing a fluffy, mud-splattered dressing-gown and wellington boots.

"What are you doing here?" Cas gulped in air to catch his breath.

Warrior squinted blearily, her eyes shining like a cat's. She kicked off her wellingtons and pushed past him into the room.

"What are you doing is more like it," she said. "*I'm armed with a blanky and I'm not afraid to use it?!* By the threads, you scare easily. First the raven, then Hobdogglin, and now this."

Cas threw his blanket on the floor moodily. "In case you haven't noticed, I'm alone, in a strange new world, sleeping in a haunted crypt. I have every right to be afraid!"

"Alright, wussy-pants," said Warrior, shooting him a wink. "That's why I'm here, to protect you." She held up a biscuit tin and rattled it. "I brought cookies."

Cas felt his anger ebbing away as his stomach took control. "Well, erm, thanks, but you didn't need to frighten the life out of me."

Warrior waved him away. "Oh, you're fine. I've been outside ever since Aster left. I only came in because I'm cold."

She jumped onto one of the beds, screwing her face up when she saw the haunting portraits. "Gosh, I forgot about these. They're quite … *creepy* … aren't they?"

Cas nodded, his gaze flickering from the painted faces to Warrior's. "Hang on, you've stayed here before?"

"Once," she said, wriggling under the covers and closing her eyes. "When I was little, Dr Bane locked me in here overnight. I practically screamed the place down until they found me curled up in a ball the next morning."

"Locked you in here by accident?"

"No, um…" Warrior's voice grew unexpectedly quiet. "Not exactly." She drew the bed sheets so high over her head that they muffled her words. "He did it to try to bring out my powers."

Instantly, Cas's mind flashed back to the Oracle's question at the Order Trials.

Have you ever been Gleaned?

"Isn't that…"

"Gleaning, yeah," said Warrior, quickly and stiffly. "But it's not as bad as you think."

Cas didn't know what he thought.

"On the same day I was born, the Oracle made the prediction about the Foretold. Clearly, we know it was talking about you now, but at the time after hearing it, Dr Bane returned to Wayward School to find me dumped on his doorstep. All I had to my name was a letter from my mother and this." She poked her wrist out from under the covers. "A smudgy birthmark. Dr Bane thought that if you squinted hard enough it looked like an ancient symbol meaning *soldier* or *warrior*. He didn't think the two were

117

related at first. But after a few years, when the Grand Council still hadn't found the Foretold and was growing desperate, Dr Bane tried to pull the loose threads together. On the off chance that the prophecy and me showing up might be related, Bane locked me in here one night to see if the old Deathmaker dorms would coax any life or death magic out of me. It obviously didn't work. I was too young for my powers to have manifested yet and all I ended up producing was a wet pair of pants. But I got through it by pretending I had an imaginary friend who kept me company. My illusion abilities appeared shortly after that. And I'm glad. I've never wanted to be the Foretold."

Cas was lost for what to say.

When Warrior put it like that, Bane's actions almost seemed sensible. Logical. But the Oracle had made Gleaning sound like something unnatural, something wrong. Not to mention the idea of being trapped in the crypts, young, alone and helpless...

Silently, they both settled down in their beds.

But even with Warrior close by, sleep didn't come easily to Cas. He rolled one way and then the other, pulling the covers over himself and then kicking them off again, lolling one leg off the bed, then imagining a skeletal hand reaching out from under it to grab him, and swiftly retracting it.

In the early hours of the morning, his fidgeting finally got the better of Warrior.

"What are you doing?" she groaned, yanking the covers free from her head.

"I can't sleep," whispered Cas.

"Try counting whatsits."

"What are whatsits?"

"These gnarly little pests we get."

"I can't count. I'm thinking."

"About what?" she hissed.

"Anything other than the rotting bodies in the room below. Right now, I'm thinking about how weird it is that our noses run but our feet smell. Before that, I was thinking about how our bellies think all potatoes are mashed and wondering whether I would rather control one hundred mouse-sized lions or one lion-sized mouse."

Warrior snorted. "One hundred mouse-sized lions," she said, burying her face under her pillow, "so I could set them all on you."

CHAPTER 8
DU VILLAINE AND SNOUT

IRONICALLY, WHEN CAS AND WARRIOR FINALLY drifted off, they slept like the dead – which was why neither of them knew anything was wrong until they awoke, crusty-eyed and sleep-dazed, to the sight of Dr Bane's furious face looming over them.

"Didn't either of you hear the sirens?!"

It took a long minute for Bane's words to register. Warrior groaned and buried deeper into the cocoon of her covers, but Cas yawned, stretched … and then sat bolt upright.

"S-sirens?" he gulped. "What sirens? We didn't hear anything."

Dr Bane stood at the foot of their beds, tight-lipped and angry. He was flanked on either side by Mrs Crane and Madame Aster. Mrs Crane wore tweed pyjamas and her unruly hair was tidied away in a frilly sleep bonnet.

She was wringing her hands so anxiously that Cas thought she might rub all the skin off, whilst Madame Aster stood in her sleek blue Wavebreaker cloak, arms firmly folded, haughty and severe.

The only thing that could have made Dr Bane look angrier was if steam had been pouring out of his nostrils.

"The school's sirens!" said Dr Bane, flinging an arm towards the shattered window. "The ones that went off only minutes ago."

Following Bane's gesture, Cas glanced outside to see that dawn had barely broken. A faint red glow pierced the eerie gloom from the boundary, but overhead the moon and the sun were still crossing paths in the inky violet sky.

"Excuse me. What happened here?" asked Dr Bane, eyes widening at the sight of the broken glass.

"It was nothing. A bird." Cas brushed him off. He leapt out from his covers, fixated on Dr Bane's news, but loitered by his bed. Bane looked so enraged that Cas didn't dare approach.

No, thought Cas as he examined Dr Bane again. That wasn't right.

From the tense, wrinkled lines of his brow, to his pursed mouth and hands curled into balls at his side, Cas realized with an unsettling jolt that Dr Bane wasn't mad. He was worried. Terrified. Petrified with concern.

Without answering, Dr Bane strode forward and reached out to grab Cas. For a stupid, crazy moment, Cas thought Bane was about to grasp him by the collar and march him out of Wayward School's gates, yelling at him never to return. But instead, Dr Bane stretched out his arms as if to hug him, relieved, before he stopped himself at the last moment and instead patted Cas down as if he was making sure he was still real. As if he was making sure Cas was still alive.

Dr Bane let out an almighty sigh. "You're both all right," he wheezed, pressing a hand to his forehead as his usual calm returned. "That's the main thing."

"Wait a second," said Warrior, suddenly jumping out of bed too. "The school's wards went off? Do you mean—"

"Yes," Dr Bane cut her off, frowning again. "Someone tried to break in."

Cas's stomach plummeted.

A break-in?

Not even Dr Bane's eyes flickering towards him with the greatest care in the world could quell the thought that instantly came to mind.

The Master of All.

Or, more likely, one of his Heretics.

But how could it be?

Cas hadn't even known for certain that he was the Foretold until yesterday. Warrior had said that Wayward School was the safest place for them. She had made it seem like Cas would be untouchable here. It was one thing if the Master suspected where Cas was – his Heretics had followed them to Wayward Town, after all – but did he now know that Cas was the definitely the Foretold, too?

A dread unlike any other flooded Cas from head to toe. Maybe it was cowardly, but he wanted to run. He wanted to hide. Every good and hopeful feeling that had come with being the Foretold was replaced by ice-cold terror. The Master was coming.

The Master was coming for *him*.

Cas couldn't help but look at the crumpled sheets on his bed. The ones he had ridiculously tried to use as a weapon to defend himself last night. How dumb and reckless had he been to let Warrior in like that?

She could've been anyone.

Dr Bane moved to embrace Warrior, but then switched tack and flicked a speck of lint off her shoulder.

"It's probably just some kids from Aurelius Academy," said Warrior, shrugging the incident off. "They're our rival school. They try to mess with us every year. Last September, they trashed the boathouse and released a bogwumpy into the woods."

"She's right, Claudius," said Mrs Crane, her voice waveringly hopeful. "Wardsmen are searching the school as we speak. Whoever it was seems to have been spooked by the wards. If someone had got in, the guards would've found them by now."

Cas wasn't sure who Mrs Crane was trying to convince: Dr Bane or herself.

"Oui," agreed Madame Aster. "Nevertheless, Monseiur Darkbloom, Mademoiselle Bane, we were very concerned when you didn't show up in the Atrium with everyone else, like we've practised in our drills. Instead, Mademoiselle Bane, it seems you chose to leave the Attic in the middle of the night, unsupervised, to sleep somewhere you were not supposed to. And you didn't even have the common sense to inform Monseiur Darkbloom about our procedures when the wards sounded, compromising both of your safeties—"

"We didn't hear them!" insisted Warrior.

"Enough." Dr Bane held up his hand sternly. "Warrior, Madame Aster is right; you shouldn't have left the Attic without telling anyone. Of course we were going to worry when you weren't up there and we couldn't find either of you. But thank you, Morgane." Bane sounded distinctly sarcastic. "I am more than capable of knowing when to discipline my ward."

Madame Aster shrank back, sour-faced and submissive.

"You're right, Dromeda." Dr Bane nodded at Mrs Crane. "It was probably just Aurelius Academy trying to pull another prank, but even so…" He trailed off, glancing back to Cas. "I think it's best if Cas rejoins Warrior and her friends in the Attic."

Dr Bane took a step closer, gripping Cas's shoulders fiercely.

"We need to keep you safe, Cas." His tired eyes swam with years of longing and desperation. Cas felt something squeeze hard and fast behind his ribcage. "You're the only hope we've got."

Everyone was buzzing with the news about the break-in when Cas and Warrior entered the dining hall for breakfast.

Normally, Cook Fiddlepot only needed to cater for Warrior, her friends and the live-in teachers who had breakfast at the school, but today the hall was packed to the brim with students. For a second, Cas was grateful that he was yesterday's news – until suddenly the room grew silent as all eyes swivelled towards him. Then noise exploded again as half the school rushed towards him, jabbing their fingers and pulling him this way and that.

"Cas! Cas! Come here!"

"Sit with us, Cas!"

"No, you're welcome at *our* table, you can even have my eggs and bacon!"

Roughly, Cas was jostled from side to side as he ripped his hands and elbows free from people trying to grasp him. Some wanted to tug him down to sit beside them, whilst others simply wanted to touch him. Perhaps wearing the ratty purple Deathmaker cloak Dr Bane had lent him wasn't the best idea today.

"Make way, make way, Foretold coming through," Warrior sing-sang, shoving people away from Cas as they waded through the throng. "Get off, get off – I swear by the threads, Laula Spinks, if you don't get your grubby Firetamer hands off him, I'll bite you!"

"Where do you want to go, Cas?" Warrior whispered in his ear.

Cas pointed towards a secluded table nestled away at the back of the room, where Paws and Fenix were sitting with Dewey Cricket and his two Earthshaper friends, Bracken Moonstrike and Ellie Green.

Finally, after batting and slapping away countless hands, they broke free from the crowd and plopped down at the table beside them. Paws and Fenix had also been joined by an Airscaper girl, who introduced herself as Neerja Gill.

"They're animals," said Warrior, running her fingers through her ruffled hair. "Animals, the lot of them."

"Oh, they're only excited," said Paws sympathetically. "For twelve years, we Others have been searching for the Foretold. You can't expect people not to be happy."

"Happy I can deal with," grumbled Warrior, inspecting a tear in her plain blazer. "But they could at least have a bit of respect."

"*Respect?*" sniggered a voice from behind them. "Who on earth would ever respect *you*?"

Their whole table spun around to see the pale twins from yesterday standing behind them. The twins were flanked on either side by a big, burly boy and a long, narrow girl. The burly boy looked like the kind of person who ate nothing but spinach for breakfast, whilst the narrow girl's mouth was hooked in a permanent sneer, making her seem like the kind of person who could be found pressed up against walls or hiding in crevices, fishing for secrets which weren't hers to know. To Cas's utter amazement, Quinnberley Crestbourne – the talented Wavebreaker – was there too. Unlike the others, though, she cringed back as if she had been dragged there against her will.

"Du Villaines," said Warrior through gritted teeth.

What a surprise. The pale twins were related to the wrathful High Councillor from the library.

"Nice summer, Riff-Raff?" the female twin sniped. "We heard Dr Bane shipped you off to the Normie world because he couldn't stand the sight of you."

"I'm surprised you can stand the sight of yourself," retorted Warrior, "looking at your ugly face in the mirror every day."

The girl snickered again as the insult fell flat. *Ugly* couldn't have been further from the truth. The twins were identical in every way except the obvious. Both had silver hair, moonshine skin and poison-ivy green eyes.

"Maybe Bane was hoping you'd get stuck there," said the male twin. "Everyone knows what happens to Others who stay too long in the Normie world. They shrivel up and—"

"Stop it," said Cas, standing up and facing them eye to eye.

The boy and girl beside the twins let out an antagonising *oooh*, but the twins didn't seem to care. In fact, their faces softened into chillingly pleasant smiles.

"Casander No-Name, right?" said the female twin, her hungry gaze roaming over him. "From the Order Trials?"

"Actually, it's Casander Darkbloom," said Cas. He wanted the twins to know his new name, to push home the point of who he was. They had been there at the Oracle's ceremony, which meant they knew that he was the Foretold. And if there was any chance this might dissuade them from taunting Warrior and the others, Cas intended to use it.

The male twin only smiled wider. "We thought as much," he said politely. "That's why we came over."

"To invite you to come and sit with us."

"Because you must be lost."

"Or confused."

The male twin jerked his chin towards the table. "There's no way the great and special Foretold should be caught dead sitting with people like *this*."

"Thanks for the concern," said Cas coldly, "but I think you're more lost than me. I believe the Basic Manners for Nitwits and Numpties class is located down the hall."

In an instant, the male twin's smile slipped into a scowl. "Is that so?"

The sound of clattering cutlery around them ceased as the room grew quiet. Everyone was watching them.

"You're making a big mistake, Foretold," the male twin warned, puffing out his chest importantly. "My sister and I would make much better friends than this lot. Our family is very well known in the Balance Lands. We know what it's like to be in your shoes, to be famous. We practically run Wayward School, you'll see."

"Really?" said Cas. "Because you don't look like you could run a bath."

The onlookers sucked in a breath.

"Snouts!" ordered the female twin, stamping her foot. The twins' cronies inched forward. "I think it's time we taught the Foretold his first real lesson at Wayward."

Even though she was clearly part of their gang now, Quinnberley Crestbourne gave a trembling squeak.

"I'd like to see you try," Cas challenged, clenching his fists and stepping towards them. It would have been a bold move, except his step landed awkwardly as he felt the tingling sensation of his funny leg starting.

Cas tried to hide it, but it was hopeless.

"Hey, look, everyone!" howled the male twin, pointing and smirking. "The Foretold really is 'special' after all."

"How can you be the Foretold if you're broken?" snapped the female twin. "What use are you to us like *that*?"

Warrior rose and slammed her breakfast bowl against the table. "Leave him alone, Lucie."

The pale female twin faltered for a second, then quickly regained her cool, callous composure. "It's *Lucille*

129

Du Villaine to you," she snarled. "Only my friends get to call me Lucie. And I wouldn't be seen with you as my friend if you were the last slimy limpet on earth."

"Maybe we should just leave it, Sam," stammered Quinnberley, tugging on Lucie's brother's sleeve.

But Sam swatted her away. "Do you want to hang out with us or not, Crestbourne?" he threatened, before throwing his gaze back to Cas and his table. "You wouldn't want to be associated with the likes of Riff-Raff, Furball and Phoenix Boy, would you?"

Quinnberley shot Cas and his friends an apologetic stare. Cas felt sorry for her. He could only imagine that she'd been waylaid by the Du Villaines in a dark corner of the school after the Order Trials. They would have been desperate to acquire her gifts for their ranks. If Cas didn't have Warrior and the others, that could've easily been him.

But he *did* have Warrior. And Paws and Fenix.

And he was Casander Darkbloom. The Foretold.

Nobody spoke to his friends like that.

"How about you mind your own business?" said Cas determinedly, taking a wobbly step despite his twitching leg.

The Du Villaine twins and the Snout brother and sister burst out laughing.

"Come on, Luce," said Sam. "Let's not waste our time on these freaks any more. Maxwell, Aubria, let's go."

Lucille shot Cas a dirty look. "We'll be watching you,

130

Foretold. It's only a matter of time before you slip up, then everyone will see you for the fraud you are."

The crew of bullies turned on their heels and stalked off. As they did, Warrior slumped back down in relief, but Cas refused to take his eyes off them until Maxwell Snout had dunked a Wayone's head into his cereal bowl on their way out of the room.

"Poor Quinnberley," said Paws, once they sat down. "She's a lovely girl, I was speaking to her in class yesterday. She doesn't know what she's got herself into."

"Poor Quinnberley?" said Warrior exasperatedly. "How about *poor us*? We were the ones about to get walloped into next Wednesday by the Snouts."

"The Snouts?" asked Cas. "I thought—"

"The Du Villaines never do their own dirty work," said Warrior, gripping her spoon so hard that her knuckles transformed into white stars. "They get their cronies, the Snouts, to do it for them. Maxwell might be brilliant for beatings, but if brains were dynamite, he wouldn't have enough to blow his own nose. That's when they use Aubria to dig up dirt on anyone they want to intimidate."

"If it makes you feel better," piped up Neerja Gill, "they aren't any nicer to anyone in their own Order. I have all my Airscaper lessons with them and it's just –" she shuddered – "*horrible.*"

"Well, um, antagonising them isn't the answer," said Fenix.

"He's right," agreed Paws. "You know what you should say: *I am rubber, you are glue. Whatever you say bounces off me and sticks to you.*"

Warrior looked between the pair of them like they were muppets.

"Honestly, Fe," she said despairingly, "sometimes, you're like a lighthouse in the Sahara: bright but not a lot of use. The Du Villaines only speak one language and it isn't the one we're using right now."

"Maybe it's not their fault," said Fenix. "Everyone knows Mr and Mrs Du Villaine likely, erm, Gleaned the twins when they were younger. Putting someone through something as, um, traumatic as that can mess you up for life."

Warrior grew uncharacteristically silent and glanced down at her plate. Cas knew they were both thinking about what she had told him last night about her own Gleaning.

Hadn't she ever told anyone else before?

"Or maybe they're jealous of you," suggested Dewey Cricket, tossing Cas a bucktoothed, comforting grin. The gesture was so genuine that Cas smiled too.

"I doubt it, Dewey," muttered Cas.

"Actually, he's probably right," said Warrior, speaking up again and grabbing a piece of toast off the rack to butter it. "That's why High Councillor Du Villaine was so mean yesterday. She didn't want to accept that you, a nothing boy from nowhere, is the Foretold instead of one of her grandchildren."

"*Nothing boy from nowhere*. Splendid, I think I'll get that tattooed on my forehead."

"Groo know whab I mean," Warrior mumbled through her mouthful.

"Let's just hope I don't have many classes with them."

"Oh, that reminds me!" said Paws, grabbing something stuffed down the side of her wheelchair. "Miss Grimbly gave this to me for you, Cas. It's your class timetable."

"Bwet dat was wuvley," said Warrior, still chewing, before she gave a mighty swallow. "Seeing gorgeous Gruffly first thing this morning."

Paws pouted, offended. "Miss Grimbly's not so bad, if you'd just get to know her," she said, stroking the cat still snoozing on her shoulders. "Though Mogget isn't too fond of her parakeets. But then again, she doesn't like many other animals. Speaking of which! Did you get my bird last night?"

"Bird?" Cas and Warrior said at once.

"Yeah, my nightjar," said Paws. She registered the look of unbridled confusion on Cas's face. "I tried to send one to the mausoleum to check on you. I don't control mud and rocks and plants like other Earthshapers. I can control animals – speak to them, speak *through* them, read their thoughts, jump into their bodies and see the world through their eyes."

"Wow," Cas breathed, astonished.

The Abnormies' powers just kept getting cooler.

"What does it feel like, being apart from your body?"

With his funny leg, Cas wondered what it must be like to slide into a body which wasn't his own.

Paws shrugged. "It's not really like being apart from my body, more like I am them and they are me. I've always been drawn to animals. To understanding them. I couldn't leap inside an animal's mind if they didn't want me there, nor could I return my own body if I didn't feel at home in it. But, as you might've seen from the nightjar, I haven't been able to successfully jump into another creature's body yet, aside from Mogget. That's why she stays so close."

Cas studied his class timetable. Like Quinnberley Crestbourne, it looked like he had been bumped straight up into second year with students his own age.

"First year's a dud," said Warrior, peeking at the schedule over his shoulder. "You don't have Order-specific lessons and it's mostly to get everyone on the same level. I see you do have some Wayone classes, though, to get you up to speed. Look, there's Thread Theory 101, that's not too tricky – oh, and History of the Balance Lands, but they've changed you from the beginner's class to our Waytwo class after week two. Urgh, Order Studies with Madame Aster is the worst – but at least we're together for Special Studies after that."

"What's Special Studies?"

Everything else on his timetable seemed self-explanatory: Waygates and Portal Physics; Power and Politics of the Ages; Calligraphy and Cartography; Twisted Tongues and Languishing Languages; and Maths (apparently there wasn't a way to make such a dreadful subject sound exciting).

"Special Studies and Order Studies go hand in hand," elaborated Warrior. "Everyone is together for Order Studies, where you learn about the different Orders: their traditions, cultures and the Elementie creatures associated with them. Then every few weeks, we go and observe one Order's Special Studies class. Now, that's the one where everyone is separated into their Orders. Earthshapers learn how to control dirt and stuff, Wavebreakers learn to control water, and so on… But us – you and me – we get our own private lessons with Dr Bane. I don't fit into any of the Orders, so Bane has always taught me himself. But I bet he can't wait to get hold of you. He hasn't been able to teach his Deathmaker powers for seventeen years."

"Dr Bane still has his powers?" said Cas disbelievingly.

Warrior nodded. "The last fifth Order member alive with any of his magic still intact. You couldn't ask for a better teacher."

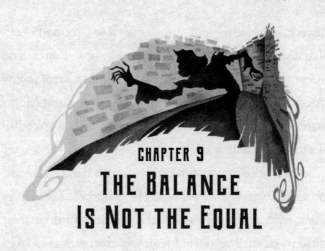

CHAPTER 9
THE BALANCE
IS NOT THE EQUAL

Cas's first class was Thread Theory 101, so he followed Dewey Cricket and company to where the Wayone class was located on the third floor. Unlike many of the classrooms they passed, which had extraordinary things like swirls of raging wind rattling the doors or crisp, autumnal leaves floating down from the ceiling, the Thread Theory 101 classroom was very dull. It simply had rows of desks and chairs, a smudged blackboard at the front, and Professor Vulcan, a Firetamer teacher who had evidently been roped into taking the class, droning on about the threads of power.

Without thinking, Dewey Cricket and Bracken Moonstrike nabbed a table and a pair of chairs together, but when Cas turned to their Earthshaper friend Ellie Green, and jerked his thumb towards another desk with a smile, she shot him a look like a rabbit in headlights and scampered off to sit next to Neerja's Airscaper brother, Akash, instead.

Cas plonked himself down at an empty desk at the back of the classroom, alone.

Apparently, his confrontation with the Du Villaines at breakfast had put a black mark against his name. People whispered and turned around to stare at him in their seats, but otherwise they avoided him like the plague. In the space of an hour, Cas had gone from being the most popular boy in the school to an outcast nobody dared poke with a ten-foot barge pole.

Professor Vulcan cleared his throat and the class began.

"The threads of power are a great and mystical force. A magic as old as existence itself. They make up everything around us, as well as within us. As many of you know, at the dawn of time, the universe was woven from two coloured threads: white and purple. Life and death. Beginning and end. Yet over the years, these threads changed into different colours, giving rise to the earth, air, water and fire powers we see in most Others today. However, in some people, they grew so dull that they lost their powers altogether, like in the case of the Normies and the Normie world we are sworn to protect…"

Cas tried to listen as Professor Vulcan dug out metres of multicoloured yarn, attempting to demonstrate how the different invisible threads wove together to create different bits of the world. But not even Vulcan explaining how Abnormies – people like Warrior, Paws, Fenix and, Cas supposed, himself – were unique, because they were woven together from lots of differently coloured threads, piqued his interest. All he could think about was the emotional whiplash he felt from the breakfast encounter.

The Du Villaines' words rang in his ears.

Broken. Freak. Fraud. Cas wasn't ashamed of his funny leg – on the contrary, he knew it was just a part of him. But what if they were right about him being useless as the Foretold? What if the Oracle's first assumption about him – *a nothing boy* – was true?

The Oracle could have still made a mistake.

"Threadologists have studied and speculated about the origins of the threads of power for millennia," Vulcan droned on. "As of yet, no solid conclusion has been reached about where they come from. Exactly how or why Others like Abnormies came to be remains one of the threads' greatest mysteries."

By the time the bell rang for break, Cas had been stewing in his stupor for so long that he practically reeked of it. As all the students filed out of the classroom, the whispers and wide berths only grew louder and larger – something which persisted for the next few days.

Initially, Cas did his best to bear the brunt of it, but by the time their attitudes had eventually faded to bored indifference by the end of his first week, he was exhausted.

There was only one place where he could escape his relentless thoughts: the library.

From the instant Mrs Crane saw him, it was like she knew.

"No Warrior, dear?" Mrs Crane had asked, when Cas sank into one of the armchairs promptly following Thread Theory 101.

He shook his head, hoping the seat would swallow him whole.

Ever since then, Mrs Crane had plied him with copious mugs of hot cocoa every visit – and whenever Warrior and the others showed up to find him, she swept over to distract them with various activities, sensing that Cas wanted to be alone.

"Is this seat taken?" a voice asked on the Friday, breaking a week's spell of silent treatment.

It was morning break. Cas jumped as there was a tap against his chair leg, almost spilling hot cocoa in his lap. A boy with white dreadlocks and a purple beanie hat lingered over him, rapping his walking stick. He looked somewhat similar to Cas – he had the same slender build and grey eyes, with dark skin – but he was older and wasn't wearing a cloak or blazer, making it impossible to tell which Order he was in.

Intrigued, Cas nodded. "It's free."

The boy sat down. "I'm Cecil Igwe," he said quietly, careful not to break the peace of the library. Cas was grateful; Warrior knew something was off and had shown up to find him again. She was currently shooting him concerned looks from where Mrs Crane was trying to get the Abnormies to help her rearrange the bookshelves.

"I'm Casander Darkbloom."

The crooked beam on the boy's face fell. "Threads, I didn't know it was you." Hurriedly, Cecil started to grapple around for where he had dropped his walking stick and school bag on the ground. "I'll move."

"No, please," said Cas quickly. *Too* quickly. "Stay."

He didn't know why he said it, why he was begging a stranger not to leave, but suddenly the last thing he wanted was to be alone. Perhaps it was because he could still spy Warrior watching him, and he wanted to reassure her that everything was fine. Or perhaps it was just because Cas wanted to feel like someone, anyone, who *wasn't* Warrior, Paws or Fenix still wanted to be seen with him.

Cecil hesitated, then let his things drop back to the floor with a *thunk*. "Are you sure? You're the Foretold. Surely you don't want to be seen sitting with me."

Cas chuckled. "No, it's me you don't want to be seen with. The Du Villaines have marked me for lonerdom."

"The Du Villaines?" asked Cecil, his face blank. "Sorry, I don't know them. I tend to keep to myself."

This was a refreshing surprise. "Probably best," said Cas.

"I doubt they'd like me anyway." Cecil sighed, pulling

a book with braille on the front cover out of his bag. "I'm an Abnormie."

Cas's face lit up.

"No way," he said hopefully. That explained the lack of coloured cloak. "Me too."

Cecil exhaled. "They think I might be the next Oracle," he told Cas in a rush, as if he had never had a chance to tell anyone this before. "I'm partially sighted; I can't see out of my left eye and I've been losing sight in my right one ever since I was born. But I get these funny visions sometimes. Like swirly pictures in my head. I'm here at Wayward School until the Grand Council takes me on for training."

"That's awesome."

Cecil didn't give Cas the same on-edge vibe as the current Oracle.

But Cecil's voice unexpectedly shifted. "Not really," he said dejectedly. "The Grand Council won't take me on until they're sure of my powers. The current Oracle has to sense that one of my predictions is true first, so I'm stuck at Wayward until that happens. I don't know how she'll be able to tell, but the Council say she'll feel it. Trouble is, she hasn't confirmed anything I've seen yet."

"Oh, I'm sorry."

"Don't be. That's why people steer clear of me. They're either terrified I'll predict something horrible about them or they think I'm useless."

A brilliant idea hit Cas then. Maybe there was a way they could help each other out. A way Cas could feel a little surer about being the Foretold *and* give Cecil what he needed.

"You can try and make a prediction about me, if you like," Cas offered.

Checking no one in the library was watching, Cas set down his mug and held out his hand in the same way he had done during the Order Trials. "I don't know, maybe being the Foretold will make it easier or something."

At the suggestion, Cecil's doom-ridden face brightened. "Seriously?"

"Of course!"

Gleefully, Cecil reached out and latched his fingers around Cas's arm. "OK. Just to warn you, though, I don't know what I'll sense. I get visions about lots of different things, good and bad, and they're not always one hundred per cent true. Like yesterday, I predicted my homework would get eaten by my dog – it was actually the hamster who ate it. And today, I thought I sensed Cook Fiddlepot would be serving shepherd's pie for lunch, but it's Fritter Friday."

Cas snorted. Cecil squeezed his eyes shut and poked out his tongue in concentration. His face grew hopeful for a second, then dimmed. "Drat. Sorry, I thought I saw something … right there … but I'm not getting anything now."

Cas's heart sank. "Nothing?"

Still concentrating, Cecil shook his head. "Not really... Well, there is maybe something ... you..."

Cas's heart began to soar once more. "Yes..."

"And a girl, with black, no, *red ... purple ... blue ...* colour-changing hair..."

"That's Warrior. She's the one who found me."

"And..."

Cecil grew quiet, his expression turning grim.

"And what?" Cas pressed, as the Oracle-in-training's visage grew taut in stony dismay. He released Cas's arm as if he had been burned, eyes flying open.

"Hollowness. Cold. And him, the Master of All, skulking around with the echo of a handful of words." Cecil sucked in a huge breath. "You're going to fail as the Foretold."

Cas's heart turned to lead.

"What?"

Cecil's face was the perfect picture of horror: unseeing eyes watering, lips aquiver and brow deeply furrowed. "That's all I see."

"That can't be..." Cas choked out. "That's what the words are? *You're going to fail as the Foretold?*"

"No," hissed Cecil quickly, gripping on to Cas's arm to silence him. "Keep your voice down. If anyone hears you say that, there'll be a riot. They'll think I'm dismissing the *real* Oracle's prophecy."

"Well, aren't you?"

Cas's eyes immediately flew to Warrior and the others. Thankfully nobody else was near by. Paws and Fenix were laughing jovially with Mrs Crane, but Warrior was still sneaking him furtive glances like a hawk.

"No," repeated Cecil in a hushed tone. The only saving grace about his prediction was that he had been sensible enough to mutter it too quietly for anyone to hear. "It's just... I've ... I've only ever felt something like this hollow, cold feeling once before, shortly prior to my Great-Nanna Pat's passing. It means death. Or rather, the absence of being. Something terrible is coming, it has to be. Otherwise..."

"What?" prodded Cas. "What else could it mean?"

"That – that you're not the Foretold," stammered Cecil, stumbling over the words. "But that's even more ridiculous."

Cas wasn't sure which was worse: not being the Foretold or dying as the Chosen One.

"The Oracle confirmed that you *are* the Foretold, which means the only option left is..."

"The Master is going to kill me. I'm not going to defeat him like everyone thinks."

Cecil didn't need to reply. Out of nowhere, Cas felt unable to breathe. His heart was falling, tumbling out of his chest...

"Wait!" Cecil burst out in a whisper, hanging fast to

Cas as if he was afraid he might leave. "Hang on, you and the girl…"

"Warrior."

"You're moving away from the Master. I can feel your warmth, your light, your hope … it's rolling off you both in waves. That coldness and emptiness … it must've been from the Master of All… You *are* the Foretold and you *are* going to succeed. Although, *hmm,* that's odd … those words are still echoing everywhere. *The balance is not the equal. The balance is not the equal.*" The Oracle-in-training retracted his grasp completely, letting Cas go. "Does that mean anything to you?"

Heart still thundering, Cas shook his head. He had no idea what those words meant. No idea what any of this meant, except maybe that being the Foretold wouldn't be as plain sailing as the real Oracle's prophecy made it seem.

"What did the Master look like?" queried Cas, wanting some concrete proof that he would be able to succeed in beating him. He desperately needed to know what he might be up against.

Cecil concentrated harder, a bead of sweat racing down his cheek. Maybe if the Master was on his knees, sobbing and begging for mercy, or stuffed in manacles, then Cas would feel better.

"I'm not sure," said Cecil. "I mean, I assume it was him. I could only sense someone lurking on the edges of my vision… I couldn't fully see him, but he gave me an awful feeling."

"Have another go," said Cas, pitching forward on his seat. "Describe him to me." He shoved his arm closer to Cecil's face, as if waving his limb around like a television aerial would somehow fine-tune the boy's mental image.

"Well, he's tall," said Cecil, taking hold of his arm. "With a dark soul … he's wearing a long purple cloak … and his face is covered, obscured by…"

"A hood? A mask?"

"Shadows. Like he's keeping to them, hiding in them. *Belongs* to them. He doesn't want to be found or seen. There's that hollow emptiness … it feels like something there but not entirely there. I can't explain it very well, but it must be coming from him. The waves of brightness and hope are definitely rolling off you and that girl…"

This was slightly more encouraging – however, it was still annoyingly woolly and vague.

He couldn't lie: he'd hoped that allowing Cecil to read him would give him some clue about how to be the Foretold and fulfil his destiny.

Instead, it had done the opposite.

"Sorry," Cecil mumbled, drawing his hands back and turning away. "I knew it wouldn't work. I never get clear, straightforward visions. No wonder the Grand Council hasn't taken me on yet. I wouldn't be surprised if they never do."

"Don't be silly," Cas fibbed. "Thanks for trying. You did great."

Cas knew his attempt to cheer Cecil up was flimsier than a wet paper towel, but he was too preoccupied to try harder. Who was right about him and his future? His own doubts and the Du Villaines'? Or the original Oracle's prophecy? Was there any truth – good or bad – in Cecil's prediction? And if so, what part of it should Cas believe?

Before he could figure it out, the bell rang for classes. They both grabbed their things and Cas invited Cecil to join him and the Abnormies at lunch.

"You don't know how much longer you'll be stuck at Wayward," Cas chuckled, only half joking. "It might be nice to have a few friends."

Cecil mustered a feeble grin. "I'd love to."

But Cecil Igwe never turned up to lunch.

As Cas and the Abnormies were leaving the dining hall – with Warrior belching out the alphabet after guzzling down five plates of fritters – Cas spotted Cecil being whisked away by a brigade of orange-clad wardsmen.

"Cecil!" Cas called out, wanting to know why the boy had never joined them. "Cecil, over here!"

Yet as Cas was swallowed by the streams of students shoving their way down the hall, Cecil was equally engulfed by the wardsmen's carrot-coloured uniforms. In a tangerine-tinged tsunami, they swept Cecil out of the grand entrance.

Cas never found out which of Cecil's predictions the Oracle must've sensed was true. Whether it was the shepherd's pie, or the homework-eating hamster, or his confusing vision about Cas and the words *the balance is not the equal*, the mystery lingered over him like a dark cloud.

Part of Cas wondered if he would ever see the Oracle-in-training again.

CHAPTER 10
THE LAST DEATHMAKER

THE GHOST OF CECIL'S WORDS CONTINUED TO haunt Cas for the rest of the day. He had hardly uttered a word to the Abnormies over lunch. His maybe, not-quite-sure, looming doom wasn't the kind of thing he felt like sharing over sandwiches. But by the time he slipped into his seat beside Warrior in Order Studies, he couldn't take it any more.

He told her everything.

"Who cares what kooky Cecil has to say?" said Warrior, sitting with her legs thrown up on the desk. "Igwe told you himself that his predictions are unreliable."

Cas's revelation meant Warrior was ignoring everything else going on around her – including Madame Aster taking the register and repeatedly calling her name. Cas coughed loudly as, with a sharp flick of her wrist, Madame Aster sent a rain-cloud which had been drizzling away in the corner of the room speeding towards them. With a huff, Warrior clocked it and kicked her feet off the desk.

It didn't take a genius to figure out this was Aster's unique way of punishing troublemakers.

The rain-cloud retreated.

"But there was that hollow emptiness," Cas went on. "And those words, *the balance is not the equal* – I still don't know what they mean." He raised his hand when Madame Aster called his name to avoid her wrath. "What if Cecil was wrong about being wrong? What if it does mean—"

"That you're going to fail and die fighting the Master?"

"Exactly."

"A noble way to go out, in my opinion."

"Warrior, please. Take this seriously."

Warrior huffed again. "All right – all right. But it's poppycock. There's more than one way to interpret a vision."

"Yes, but if Cecil wasn't talking about me failing, then that must mean—"

"That you're not the Foretold?" She rolled her eyes. "Please, that's insane." Warrior scooted her chair closer and stared Cas dead in the eyes, her hair tips turning a suspicious shade of forest green. "Are you suggesting the Oracle, the *real* Oracle, the one who's been trusted by the Grand Council for decades, is wrong?"

"No, I'm not," said Cas, "but—"

"And are you telling me that you didn't bring that raven back to life in the curiosity shop?"

"I *think* I did."

Warrior glared at him. "*Did* you?" she repeated. "Because I didn't. And I didn't see anybody else do so."

"I must have, then."

"And don't you trust my stellar, flawless, wonderful, no-way-I-can-ever-be-wrong judgement?"

This was the scariest question of all. "I trust you."

"See, it's settled," she said, throwing her hands up exuberantly in the air. "You *have* to be the Foretold. You *will* defeat the Master of All. There's no other way it can be. *The balance is not the equal* just sounds like a rip-off of the prophecy the Oracle already made. *Only someone with power equal to, or greater than, the Master's can stop him. Greater than* is more than *equal*, isn't it? So *the balance is not the equal* simply means that you're more powerful than the Master, you just might not realize it yet!"

It was this outburst that pushed Madame Aster over the edge. She scowled, her thin lips poised ready to bite their heads off. She rose from her desk and stalked towards them.

"Mademoiselle Bane, Monsieur Darkbloom," Aster cawed. "I assume that you're discussing how you've completed all the assigned summer reading."

"Naturally," lied Warrior, not missing a beat.

"*Bon,*" Madame Aster spat at them through gritted

151

teeth, throwing down a stack of what looked like surprise exam papers onto their desk. "This will make up half of your grade for the term."

The whole class groaned.

"There will be no talking!" scolded Aster when she caught Warrior muttering unpleasantries under her breath. Begrudgingly, Warrior passed the stack of exam papers to the next student to hand around. "*Un* mark shall be deducted for every word you utter. Begin!"

Madame Aster spun on her heel and returned to the front of the room. Everyone bent their heads low and started scrawling on their tests as soon as they received them. Meanwhile, Warrior took the opportunity whilst Aster's back was turned to whisper, "Besides, I heard that Cecil Igwe's dog *did* eat his homework. The dog ate the homework-scoffing hamster, so technically it still counts."

There were no two ways about it. When Warrior set her mind to something, she didn't stop until she got what she wanted – even if that was convincing Cas that Cecil Igwe was wrong.

"I believe in you," she added discreetly, narrowly avoiding Aster's gaze as it raked across the classroom.

Warrior looked down at her exam paper.

Predictions be damned, thought Cas. If Warrior and the real Oracle thought he was the Foretold, then he could be. If nothing else, he would just have to train hard at

Wayward School and make sure that he was ready to face the Master of All when the time came.

But a moment later, Cas found his new determination challenged.

Glancing down at his own exam paper, every question made him draw a blank.

It's fine, he tried to reassure himself as he re-read the first few questions. *You're new to this world. You'll have plenty of time to pull your grade up. This test is just a chance to see if there's anything you already know.*

But to say the Order Studies test was brutal was an understatement. By the end of the lesson, once Madame Aster had marked all of their tests, Cas had been awarded a big, fat zero. He didn't have a single tick next to any of his questions, only answers scribbled in the margins.

Question 1: On 6th September, the ending by Others of which disastrous event in the Normie world is celebrated by everyone in Balance London prancing through the streets, drinking Kindlin' Koola and waving orange streamers?
Answer: The Great Fire of (Normie) London, 1666

Question 2a: Which supposedly fictional character in the Normie world was actually a renowned Reader (someone who can read minds, but cannot interpret a person's soul or future like an Oracle) and lived at 221B Baker Street?

b: And which Order did he belong to?
Answer a: Sherlock Holmes
           b: None. He was an Abnormie

Question 3: Which other allegedly fictional figure belonged to the Deathmaker Order and had to be imprisoned in Nowhere Prison by the Grand Council after he reanimated a monstrous corpse and wreaked havoc on a small town?
Answer: Dr. Frankenstein

Question 4: Name the delicacy that the Airscapers Freyja and Frankel Fairweather are credited with inventing.
Answer: The Bubble Fritter

Question 5: List the different days of the year when the following Orders' powers are most intense:
     a: Lifemakers and Deathmakers
     b: Earthshapers
     c: Firetamers
Answer: a: New Year's Eve
           b: Spring Equinox
           c: Summer Solstice

"*Tut-tut,* Monseiur Darkbloom," Madame Aster took pleasure in crooning at him. "Being the Foretold, I would have assumed you'd be more familiar with the world you are supposedly destined to protect."

"Well, he basically didn't know we existed before this week," Warrior said defensively.

After his disastrous first week, Cas was more motivated than ever to work hard and make the following ones better.

For the next few weeks, his classes thankfully passed without any more unusual happenings or ominous predictions, and his mind gobbled up information more greedily than Headmaster Higgles at an all-you-can-eat breakfast buffet. It also helped that, day by day, he felt like he was getting stronger now that he was in the Balance Lands. His body felt sturdier, his mind sharper and his memories remained intact. As he lay in bed at night, Cas let the memories whizz through his mind like miniature films before he went to sleep, wishing they would keep replaying when he closed his eyes – from every laugh he shared with Paws and Fenix, to every time he had to elbow Warrior under the desk to prevent the teacher catching them talking.

Despite Madame Aster's attempts to dissuade him, Order Studies soon became Cas's favourite lesson.

No amount of nit-picking at him for silly things – like not sitting up straight enough or chewing on his pencil too loudly – could distract him from the amazing traditions and secrets the Balance Lands held.

In one fascinating lesson, they learnt about Elementies: magical creatures who had powers like the Others' own.

"Some believe that originally each Elementie was created to be a perfect counterpart to a specific Other," Madame Aster told them. "Known as Other Halves, the Elementie and their Other were said to be woven from the same threads, meaning they were destined to be loyal companions. Just like us, Elementies belong to Orders. These magical animals and beings mirror us, in the same way the Balance Lands mirror the Normie world – another way the universe is kept in perfect balance."

"I wish I could find my Other Half," sighed Warrior dreamily later that afternoon. "You know, an Elementie made especially for me."

They were sitting in the library, slaving away over Aster's homework. The students had been tasked with writing a one-page essay on an Elementie of their choosing. Fenix had chosen one of the Firetamers' many species of firebirds, whilst Paws had bucked the trend and gone with something outside her Earthshaper Order: the Wavebreakers' scaly water snake (it turned out, there was a famous one living in a loch in Balance Scotland. According to Paws, the creature used the loch as a waygate to visit the Normie world, where it was called Nessie). Warrior was supposed to be writing about the Airscapers' grotesque-looking wyverkeys, but instead she kept gazing longingly out of the window, no doubt imagining flying around between a pair of the wyverkey's leathery wings.

Cas busily rifled through a children's picture book called *Earthy Eddie's Easy Encyclopaedia of Eclectic Elementies*, trying to decide between the Deathmakers' banshee crow and the Lifemakers' caladrius. It was the only beginner's guide to Elementies on the shelves. Apparently everyone else had grown up knowing about these creatures; they were woven into everything from bedtime fairy tales to campfire horror stories, in the same way Normie children were told about Cinderella or the Bogeyman.

"You have to actually belong to an Order to have one of those, Riff-Raff," Lucille Du Villaine heckled nastily from a nearby table.

"You know, I think I can hear a kind of buzzing," said Cas sarcastically, as Warrior stuck out her tongue. "But I don't know what it is. Sadly, we don't speak whiny brat."

"She's wrong, anyway," said Paws, laying down her pen and pulling a snoozing Mogget into her lap. "Other Halves don't *have* to be Elementies. At least, I don't think they do. I'm pretty sure Mogget is mine."

Cas smiled, but Warrior grimaced.

"No offence, but I'd rather have one of these ugly wyver-thingys—"

"Wyver*keys*," corrected Paws, who was naturally an expert on the subject.

"Wyver-whatevers," said Warrior, waving dismissively, "than a boring old cat."

Paws raised her eyebrows as if to say *beggars can't be choosers*. "Don't listen to what old meanie Warrior says," she cooed, fussing over a sleeping Mogget, who didn't have the faintest clue what was going on.

"Actually, um, Paws is right," chimed in Fenix, not looking up from where he had already written double the required length of the essay. "You stand a better chance of finding your Other Half in an ordinary animal. There are hardly any Elementies left."

"How come?" asked Cas.

"Hunting, poaching or, um, wandering into the Normie world and dying out." Fenix tapped a picture in Cas's book without taking his eyes off his homework. It was a long-forgotten Earthshaper bird. The label below read: DODO (EXTINCT).

"Some Elementies are kept as pets, even though their owners aren't their perfect Other Halves," said Paws. "My parents run a rehoming emporium for injured or captured ones. They've got a much better chance of surviving in a loving family than fending for themselves."

"But most Elementies merely run amok these days," finished Warrior, eyes fixed out of the library's window. "Wild, untamed and free."

In the end, Cas's favourite part of Order Studies wasn't the Elementies, or the different Orders' traditions, or even the famous figures. It was seeing the different Orders' magic in action. Every few weeks, the class would get to watch one of their peers' Special Studies lessons, and it was these sessions that excited Cas the most.

One time, they wandered down to the Wavebreakers' boathouse to observe students like Quinnberley Crestbourne moving puddles from spot to spot, and the Wavebreaker teacher, Professor Oxbow, cleaving a dry path through the water of the lake. On another occasion, they trundled down to the Kiln, a sweltering brick basement below the school where the old Firetamer dorms were located, to see Professor Vulcan (assisted by the Airscaper teacher, Professor Breezy) demonstrate how to make simple fires levitate into flickering orbs and candle flames jump from wick to wick.

"Vulcan used to be a top Flameball champion," Fenix told Cas, briefly describing the sport, which sounded a lot like dodgeball except with balls of fire. "That was, er, before all the Lifemakers died out and there was nobody to heal the life-threatening burns and scalds that the players got."

The only Special Studies lesson Cas didn't enjoy as much was the Earthshaper one.

Traipsing behind Madame Aster to a far wing of the school, the class was confronted with a plain wooden door. From the outside, it looked like an entrance to nowhere – there was no room, ceiling, floor or windows on the other side. Instead, once they had all squeezed over the threshold, they found themselves standing in a canopy corridor made entirely from tree tops. Out of thin air, a gigantic lion made of crisp, fiery autumn leaves appeared in front of them and let out an almighty roar. Then it disappeared in a blazing cascade and the class picked their way along the corridor, which sloped down and out of the side of the school, leading to the homely Earthshaper cabins in the woods. Standing to greet them was Professor Everglade, a waify, willowy woman with wavy blonde hair down to her ankles. She wore a long white dress and nothing on her bare feet.

"Welcome, welcome," she chimed softly.

The teacher looked like an extension of the leafy corridor. Creepers and flowers wove around her arms and legs.

Enchanted, Cas sat down with the others outside Professor Everglade's cabin, desperate to discover how she had done the trick with the lion.

Unfortunately, Everglade had other ideas.

Digging out her guitar, Professor Everglade poured them each a mug of nettle tea and serenaded them as they spent the afternoon chipping their teeth on rock-hard boulder cakes.

Warrior clucked her tongue. "All this incredible magic and we waste our time singing silly songs."

Cas agreed.

Just as he was about to brave his third jaw-shattering confection, he noticed something. The birds that had joined in with Everglade's tune had stopped singing. Suddenly, Cas was overwhelmed by the skin-prickling sensation of being watched. He swivelled around, but there was nothing but towering trees in every direction. He knew Wayward School's forest extended far beyond the boundary of the protective wards, but they weren't in that part of woods now. Still, Cas couldn't help imagining someone out there, spying on him between the pines.

But they're not, Cas told himself sternly. *You're safe. Wayward is safe.*

By the time the lesson ended, he wished he had convinced himself that it was true.

The only downside to watching other people's Special Studies lessons was that Cas longed to begin his own.

The hiccup was that Dr Bane kept cancelling Cas and Warrior's lessons.

"Don't take it personally," Warrior told Cas for what felt like the umpteenth time. "Dr Bane often goes away on business. If he's not busy representing Headmaster Higgles and Wayward School at the confederation of this-or-that, he helps the Grand Council track the Master of All. He's basically obsessed with it."

This did nothing to quell the queasy feeling in Cas's

gut. How was he supposed to learn to defeat the Master if Dr Bane was never around to teach him?

"Where does he think the Master is now?"

Warrior shrugged. Her answer changed from week to week. After one such cancellation, she told Cas that Bane was acting on reports the Master had been spotted in Balance Budapest. Another time, some threadologist scholars had allegedly disappeared in Dijon. Though the places sounded far away, Cas knew that only a waygate separated them.

"So, does Dr Bane *officially* work for the Grand Council?" he prodded one evening.

"Ha! Not a chance," Warrior scoffed. "The Grand Council is too proper and … *restrictive* for him. Dr Bane gives them the information he gathers, but he prefers to work solo. Don't get me wrong, the Grand Council are great at handling disasters in the Normie world. Give them a landslide or tsunami and they'll sort it out in a jiffy. It's just that all the High Councillors have to agree on something before they can do it – and you've seen yourself how much they argue. Bane doesn't believe in that. He wants to act *now*."

"And has anyone ever succeeded," Cas asked, "in catching the Master?"

Warrior's expression turned grave. "Not yet. He always manages to slip away. Although he likes to leave his Heretics behind to finish off whoever dares try."

Cas swallowed the lump in his throat, bile burning his stomach. Just what kind of evil Other was he up against? How many more people were at risk of disappearing – or worse – if he didn't stop him?

"Bane doesn't have Grand-Council-level ambitions, anyway," added Warrior, sensing Cas needed a change of subject. "I think he's only interested in running Wayward School."

Cas stared at her, confused. "Why doesn't he just take Headmaster Higgles's job, then?"

It was no secret that Helpless Higgles was exactly as useless as his name suggested. If he wasn't napping or lingering about whenever something delicious was wafting out of the kitchen, Higgles only ever emerged from his office to parade Cas around the school like a shiny trophy.

He was half surprised Higgles hadn't tried tackling him with a duster or shoved him in a display case yet.

"Being headmaster of Wayward School would mean the Grand Council is always watching. That's probably why Dr Bane recommended Hapless Higgles for the job. This way, Bane is still important to Wayward School but he can come and go as he pleases, without anybody paying too much attention."

Despite how interesting Warrior's insights into Dr Bane were, it wasn't what Cas yearned to learn from the Deathmaker. Just when he thought he'd never experience his own Special Studies class, Cas was bopped on the head between classes one October afternoon by a crisp envelope, transported on an Airscaper's wind:

Tomorrow. 3pm. My office.

Don't be late.

Dr B, the note read.

Cas's chest swelled with relief.

He was finally going to get a chance to practise his Order powers. How fitting it would be on the most haunting day of the year too.

Halloween – or, as Cas liked to call it, *Hallow'tween* – was an odd celebration at Wayward.

According to Warrior, the festivity had begun in the Balance Lands as something called Mourners' Morn. It was a Deathmaker celebration to honour the departed. People used to *ooh* and *aah* at the fifth Order's talents in midnight marvels, where they demonstrated how they could rob the breath from your lungs and even speak to the dead. But at some point, the celebration had crossed over into the Normie world and become Halloween, a day packed full of fancy dress and sweets, before crossing back – except various bits of it seemed to have got wondrously warped on their way through the waygate.

When Cas met Warrior in the dining hall for breakfast that morning, she was dressed head to toe in traditional Mourners' Morn garb: a thick black veil and long black dress. The ends of the skirt pooled around her short legs so copiously that she had to kick the hem out of the way when she walked to avoid tripping up.

Everyone else appeared to be in some form of confused fancy dress. There was a one-eyed cyclops hag. A werewolf in a wizard's hat. A mummified gargoyle. A grim reaper with fairy wings. And a zombie with fangs in a high-collared cape. Even Paws and Mogget were dressed up as pumpkins, with Paws sprouting matching cat's ears and whiskers. Fenix was wearing a fluffy s'mores costume with devil horns, so that whenever he accidentally set himself ablaze, he looked like some kind of satanic marshmallow.

Only the Du Villaines and the Snouts seemed to understand how to do Halloween properly. They rampaged through the halls dressed as ghoulish bats, ransacking bags of chocolates and leaving a trail of empty wrappers in their wake.

"What a load of rubbish," Warrior scoffed, as she shoved past a Wayone dressed as a schoolboy with a strange squiggle on his forehead. Cas had no idea what he was supposed to be – maybe an Aurelius Academy student? "Doesn't anyone celebrate Mourners' Morn properly any more? It's supposed to be about séances and memorials, not this piffle. Halloween's just an excuse to stuff your face with sweets and look like an absolute fool – I mean, why do we have to dress like the Normies do? After all we've done for them, you don't see any of them dressing like us!"

After everything he'd heard about the two forms of the holiday, Cas liked Wayward's version best. It wasn't the old Balance Lands' Mourners' Morn or the new Normie Halloween – it was something different. Something special. Something in between.

It was *Hallow'tween*.

Cas felt slightly dejected that he was one of only a handful of people who wasn't in costume. He'd been too anxious waiting for his first Special Studies lesson to think about it.

When the clock bells chimed three, Cas and Warrior were already standing outside Dr Bane's office.

The door inched open with an ominous creak.

"Ah, my two prodigies," said Dr Bane, greeting them with a wry smile. "Please, come in."

Dr Bane's office was a gloomy and curious place. Grand iron cabinets lined the firefly-lantern-lit walls, and a twisted steel staircase spiralled up to his sleeping quarters above. There was a high-backed chair set behind a dark mahogany desk, which was reached by climbing a set of smaller stone steps. Chains, crossbows and numerous pearly white animal skulls hung on the walls. But it was the contents locked inside the cabinets that fascinated Cas the most.

Each cabinet emitted a different coloured glow, the light seemingly coming from the objects within. A greenish hue came from one cabinet containing jars of shrivelled heads and bony fingers. A silvery sheen came from another that held the strange, luminous dish Cas had made react during the Order Trials. Meanwhile, a bronze tinge bloomed from a separate one containing a small, glowing orb surrounded by spinning metal rings. It was about half the size of Cas's palm. The rings spun faster when he pressed his face against the cabinet's glass.

"Intriguing, isn't it?" said Dr Bane, peering over Cas's shoulder. Today he was wearing a silver-grey suit with brass buttons beneath his purple cloak. "I could tell you all about these weird and wonderful artefacts, of course, but that would take up our entire lesson…"

Reluctantly, Cas let Warrior pry him away.

They both took a seat at Dr Bane's desk, whilst Bane himself sat in the high-backed chair on the other side.

"This," he said, pushing a very heavy, leather-bound tome towards Cas, "contains everything you could ever want to know about being a Lifemaker or Deathmaker."

Awestruck, Cas ran his fingers over the chipped gold script on the cover. "What is it?"

The book's title was written in an ancient language he didn't understand.

"The Book of Skulls and Skin," said Dr Bane, pressing his fingers together and nodding towards the tome. "This is how the Master of All began his quest for the Orders' powers. This is how he learnt to take another's Lifemaker abilities for himself."

A chill ran over Cas and he snatched his fingers back.

"What's such a dangerous thing doing here?"

The corner of Dr Bane's mouth quirked up in a secretive smile. "There are many strange and powerful things kept at Wayward," he said. "Wonder and danger often go hand in hand. But this particular object was gifted to us by the Grand Council. Once the Master claimed those Lifemaker abilities, and all the fifth Order's powers began to disappear, they no longer had any use for it. Why guard an object containing the fifth Order's most archaic instructions and incantations when the Master has already exploited its secrets for his own gain, and there are no new Lifemakers or Deathmakers who could possibly do the same?"

"But you still have some of your powers, don't you?" said Cas bluntly. The words escaped him before he realized it was a very personal, and perhaps rude, question to ask.

Gratefully, Dr Bane chuckled.

He reached below his desk and pulled out a potted plant with black-spotted leaves. With one sweep of his hand, the leaves on the plant curled up, withered and died, his skin barely touching its surface.

Cas blinked in amazement.

"Do you know why you have the movement condition with your leg, Cas?" said Dr Bane, slipping the plant back into his drawer before Cas could get a second look.

Cas shook his head.

"Because you're special," explained Dr Bane, pointing a finger towards Cas's chest. "You've been directly touched by the threads of power. They don't just run through your veins; they specifically made you. And whoever the threads touch, they leave a mark on. No doubt you've realized that some of your friends are the same with their unusual abilities. But the difference with you – what makes you unique – is that your uncontrollable movements are caused by the energy of your powers wanting to get out. This book" – he nodded towards the tome again – "and I can teach you how to harness that power. How to let it break free and use it for good."

Cas was captivated by Dr Bane's words. It was like he could feel the threads of power that made up Bane and the book calling to him.

"Teach me," Cas begged.

"*The Book of Skulls and Skin* is good for a number of things," said Dr Bane, standing up and moving around the desk to where Cas and Warrior sat. He leant against the polished mahogany and manoeuvred the book closer. "It has a chapter that taught Warrior how to craft and shape her illusions, and that is what we'll be starting with today: *anatomy*. Both Lifemakers and Deathmakers control how the body works. In time, you will be able to heal with a single touch … or kill with a single stare."

Cas balked. "I – I don't want to hurt anyone."

For a second, Dr Bane looked like he had to check himself. "Of course not, my dear boy. Regardless, those things are years away from where you're at now. First, you must learn to visualise and direct your power. There are several tricks that I can teach you to help." He flipped to a page with a sketch of the human body. "Such as memorizing these labels."

Hiding his disappointment at not being able to try practical magic straight away, Cas spent the rest of the lesson pouring over anatomical sketches in *The Book of Skulls and Skin*. It wasn't easy. He struggled not to be distracted by Warrior, who had already learnt this chapter, as she spent the time perfecting the intricacies of her illusions. Cas couldn't stop himself from sneaking glances as she created a fearsome smoky jaguar who prowled around the room on six legs and a huge rat with three eyes, and gave Hobdogglin even scalier legs, which gleamed in the dim light with an emerald sheen.

All of her illusions had the same striking violet eyes.

As Cas was getting ready to pack up his things at the end of the hour, Dr Bane stopped him. "Have you memorized at least half of the labels?"

Cas nodded.

"Then let's give your powers a try." The corner of Bane's mouth twitched ambitiously. "Look at me and only me." Dr Bane drew an invisible line from Cas's eyes to his own. "Now, I want you to make me blind."

Instinctively, Cas faltered. The joy drained from his face as he thought about the Oracle and Cecil.

"No, not *actually* blind," Dr Bane clarified, noting his concern. "Although with time, that is a real possibility," he muttered under his breath. "I want you to make me temporarily blind, so that I can see nothing but black. Invisibly blindfolding someone can be a good way to subdue them if you don't want to knock them out."

Cas breathed a sigh of relief, narrowed his eyes and focused on the Deathmaker.

"Concentrate," commanded Dr Bane, sensing that Cas's attention wasn't all there.

Cas focused as hard as he could. *"Okuli,"* he murmured through clenched teeth, remembering the label for *eyes* in the book. He imagined a thick, black curtain falling over Dr Bane's eyes. He envisioned the light and colour being sucked out of his world as he fell into an endless dark pit.

"Believe, boy. You've got to do more than just *want* to do it – you have to trust that you actually can."

I can. I must. I will, Cas thought, straining with every fibre of his being.

I can. I must. I will.

Momentarily, Dr Bane's eyes widened and his lips parted in terror. Then, "Bravo! Huzzah, huzzah! You've done it."

The sudden noise knocked Cas's concentration and the

invisible blindfold on Bane slid off. Dr Bane strode over proudly and clapped Cas on the back.

"My boy," he said. "Do you see? Self-belief is the halfway point to any goal. *Think* is step one, *want* is step two, but believing you can, that'll see it through. We'll make a damn good Foretold of you yet. Just wait, the Master of All will have no idea what's coming."

CHAPTER 11
THE MINT
EXCHANGE

THE LAST DAY OF TERM BEFORE CHRISTMAS BREAK was a festive feast of special treats. Classes were cancelled for the day, so Cas, Warrior, Paws and Fenix squirrelled themselves away by the cosy, roaring fire in the library, buried deep in the comfort of the brightly patterned armchairs, nibbling on mince pies and drinking smooth, fudgy hot cocoa. While Paws wiled away the morning fashioning a tinsel tuxedo for Mogget, Warrior scribbled out drawings for new, fantastical illusions in her sketchbook and Fenix gathered as many books as he could carry to take home for the holidays. This was an entertaining but arduous task, as the books themselves had a mind of their own. They liked to jump about from shelf to shelf and flap around the library like large paper birds, making them very hard to catch.

"Whenever an Other writes a book, they leave behind

a piece of their soul – essentially some of their threads of power – giving it life," Mrs Crane told Cas, as she handed Fenix a net. They watched and giggled as Fenix leapt around the library, trying (and often failing) to catch the swooping books.

Cas was grateful for the distraction.

Despite initially making excellent progress, his last Special Studies lesson with Warrior and Dr Bane had ended on a particularly trying note.

In his first few lessons, Cas had felt like he was mastering his powers at an exceptional rate. Dr Bane had been right; learning to believe in himself truly was half the battle. Whenever Cas was struggling with something, he would take a steadying breath, clear his mind and switch his attention from focusing on the actual move to believing that he could do it.

Once, Dr Bane had released an entire cage of banshee crows, and Cas had been able to freeze them in mid-air, still flying, by only whispering, *"Muskuli."* He had imagined their tiny black wings keeping them airborne, whilst their bodies became statue still. Another time, Bane unexpectedly dropped a gigantic rattlesnake on Cas's head to teach him to deal with the element of surprise. Cas hadn't had time to doubt himself and instead had instinctually focused hard on the snake. Within seconds, it had flipped onto its back, offering its belly to Cas to tickle like a dog.

But yesterday, Cas had been given the task of trying to make Dr Bane unconscious. It sounded simple enough, but there were so many elements to think about. Sight, sound, touch, smell – actually knocking Bane out wasn't the problem, but to keep him down, Cas had to block out all of these senses and more. Unable to trust that he could control more than one body part, Bane kept dropping to the floor like a limp marionette and then springing awake again.

"Don't worry," Warrior had reassured him on their way back to the Attic. "Learning to control your abilities is obviously going to take time. There's no point beating yourself up about it."

Maybe Cas hadn't been hiding his disappointment as well as he thought. Warrior seemed to know exactly what he was thinking.

"All right for you to say," Cas grumbled bitterly. He couldn't help himself. While his progress was tempered by how quickly – or slowly – he could memorize *The Book of Skulls and Skin*, Warrior's powers seemed to double in strength with every session. Her only limit was her imagination.

And it seemed like it was endless.

Warrior had sighed.

"Look," she said comfortingly, jostling his shoulder in a playful manner. "It's just the crusty old *Book of Skulls and Skin* that's bogging you down. It is useful, yes, but also packed full of gobbledegook. I'm so glad I don't have to go back to reading it. I found it really hard."

"*The Book of Skulls and Skin is* hard."

"Yes, but it's not just *The Book of Skulls and Skin*," she went on, growing quiet and serious. "I mean … I find reading *anything* hard. I think that's why I'm so good at my illusions."

Cas's mind flew to the walls of the Attic. Every spare centimetre of wall was covered with Warrior's sketches of makeshift beings – usually on the back of homework sheets she was supposed to hand in.

"Don't get me wrong," Warrior continued. "All the teachers want to help, even crones like Madame Aster. Most adults will, as long as you're brave enough to ask. But I can see pictures so clearly, whereas words … they're like infuriating squiggles that squirm and jump around on the page.

"We all have our differences, Cas. Our unique bits. Our quirks. But that's what makes each of us special. That's what makes us strong."

Cas was brought back to the present reality by a frosty breeze sweeping through the library. The Du Villaines and their cronies had arrived, undoubtedly coming to ruin the Abnormies' fun.

"It's freezing outside," announced Sam Du Villaine, strutting over and jabbing a finger towards the windows, where a flurry of snow was falling outside and coating the courtyard like a thick layer of marzipan.

"It's our turn to sit by the fire," Lucille wailed. "It's not fair. You've been hogging the armchairs all morning!"

It wasn't hard to tell that the pale twins were just trying to stir up trouble. Both Sam and Lucille were covered head to toe in thick, furry white coats, the same shade as their silvery bone-coloured hair. On their left, Maxwell Snout was so big and beefy that he was walking around in a T-shirt, oblivious to the cold. On their right, his older sister, Aubria, was sporting a pair of hideous lime-green earmuffs. The only one who looked remotely chilly was Quinnberley Crestbourne. She stood shivering behind them, her teeth chattering a million miles a minute. From the longing looks she shot her, it was clear Aubria had stolen Quinnberley's mittens and hat.

Mrs Crane started towards the Du Villaines, staring them down with her hands on her hips. "Those seats are reserved for Gollywabbles only," she said in her sternest voice, stepping in front of Cas and his crew like a defensive mother hen.

The Du Villaines screwed up their faces in disgust and confusion.

"Gollywabbles?" spat Lucille.

"There's no such thing!" moaned Sam.

Mrs Crane waggled a disciplinary finger at them. Her tree-shaped tweed earrings swung ferociously as she shook her head. "Yes, there is. Everyone knows that it goes: Perfects, Student Order Heads, Headmaster's Apprentice, Gollywabbles."

"Perfects?" whispered Cas, unsure he had heard her correctly.

"Normies call them Prefects," hissed Warrior, clearly annoyed. "Yet another thing they stole from us and muddled up. Originally, here in the Balance Lands, they were called Perfects. As in, *perfect* students."

"And what's a Gollywabble exactly?"

Warrior struggled to stifle a snicker. "Nothing…" She lowered her voice so the Du Villaines couldn't hear. "A made-up word… Mrs Crane uses it to keep other people off our seats."

"It's their own fault really," said Fenix, dumping his mountainous stack of books on the floor and collapsing into a chair. "If they read the Wayward School handbook, they'd know that Gollywabbles don't exist."

Warrior lifted an eyebrow. "Who reads the school handbook?"

"Well, erm, me," said Fenix timidly. "You know, for fun. Or if I want something easy to read before bed."

Cas glanced at the teetering stack of books beside the Firetamer. After Fenix had been banned from the library for a while last year – a freak accident had resulted in half the stacks going up in smoke – Mrs Crane now took the time to painstakingly coat each book he wanted to borrow in a gloopy fireproof substance. Apparently, there was nothing Mrs Crane wouldn't do for her students.

Cas turned his attention back to the librarian just as

she was shooing the Du Villaines and their minions away.

"All settled," Mrs Crane declared, smacking her hands together satisfactorily. "Now, who's for another mince pie?"

But by lunchtime, the situation with the library's armchairs was very much *not* settled.

"Blithering banshee crows, those absolute snitches," swore Mrs Crane, walking over with a thunderous face. Cas had never heard her speak so poorly about a pupil before. "The Du Villaines' parents have sent a letter in. According to them, I'm giving you four 'unfair treatment'. If we don't give up the chairs, they're going to have a stern word with me and Headmaster Higgles later."

"Don't worry," said Paws sweetly. "It's fine. Thanks for trying, Mrs Crane."

Warrior sniffed. "Yeah, but I know we haven't heard the end of this. I overheard Tweedlemean and Tweedlemeaner telling the Snouts to make our lives hell earlier. There's still half a day left before we're free of them for Christmas."

"Don't worry your little cotton socks," said Mrs Crane. "I'm going home to spend winter break with my folks. A Bane family tradition—"

"You're related to Dr Bane?" Cas spat out his cocoa.

Mrs Crane looked highly amused. "He's my brother, though he doesn't always act like it when he abandons me at family gatherings. I often get left to squabble over the cranberry sauce with Cousin Melandra alone. Anyway, as I was saying, even though I have to go home for Christmas,

I'm still going to give you four the best last day of term you've ever had. C'mon."

After putting on their snuggest coats and cloaks, Mrs Crane escorted the group of them through the entrance hall and straight out of the front doors.

"Where do you think you're going?" squawked Miss Grimbly when she caught them leaving.

"Into town for a few bits and bobs!" Mrs Crane called out over her shoulder, not bothering to look back. "Tell Dr Bane we'll be back by the end of the day."

"Do you have Headmaster Higgles's permiss—"

But the rest of what Miss Grimbly said was drowned out by Mrs Crane, who began singing a Christmas carol at the top of her very out-of-tune lungs.

"*Do* we need permission to leave?" asked Fenix, gnawing on his bottom lip like a chewy toffee.

"Permission pish posh," said Mrs Crane, shrugging the matter off as she helped to steer Paws's wheelchair safely down the icy hill. "There hasn't been a break-in or anything odd going on for months. We're perfectly safe in Wayward Town as long as we stay inside the wards."

When they reached the bottom of Wayward School's hill, Cas's eyes filled with wonder.

Wayward had changed location again overnight. For the past few weeks, it had sat precariously on the edge of the Balance Grand Canyon. Cas had felt incredibly sorry for any poor soul who tried to waygate there and was faced with climbing the stomach-churning yellow rock face to reach the boundary. But today Wayward had moved to the middle of the Serengeti. Sunny brown-green plains spotted with herds of wildebeest, giraffes and elephants, as well as prides of lions and even a lightning-fast cheetah, stretched far into the distance. It was in stark contrast to the cold, frigid weather inside the town. Wayward had its own weather and seasons, and in the icy grip of December, the town looked like a beautiful, jarring Christmas painting in comparison. Crooked, tiled roofs of colourful slanting shops were coated in an icing-sugar dusting of snow. Glistening icicles hung from every window and awning. The fountain that many Others used as a waygate was frozen and out of use, although people were still flooding through the wards, using portals outside the boundary to enter, and disappearing into the many mirrors propped outside buildings to leave.

It was what lay inside these shops that stoked Cas's excitement the most, though.

"Welcome to the Classic Quarter," said Mrs Crane with a flourish, as she and the Abnormies entered the oldest part of town. "It's a bit old-timey, like me, but everyone knows the old-fashioned things are the best. Over there, we have Sylphie's, a market shop where you can buy all your food and drink. Oh, and next to it is Ondine's Oddities and Essentials … and that's the Gnome's Garden pub, perfect for a party. And there's Mr Mander's Museum of

Mundane Monstrosities. Mr Mander's is where we keep all the useless artefacts from the Normie world that we Others either can't use or have no use for." Through the museum's large windows, Cas spied cars, boats and train carriages on display (Others didn't need transport when they had waygates), alongside computers, mobile phones and cameras (the threads of power were so strong in the Balance Lands that they made anything electrical go on the blink).

"Yada, yada…" squawked Warrior, highly unimpressed. "The Classic Quarter is only the best bit of Wayward if you're as old as the threads themselves."

Striding ahead, she steered the group down a narrow alley until they came out on a shiny, wide street lined with modern shops. "Newbusy Avenue is better. It's the newest, coolest part of Wayward. There's Gladys Raggety's Glorious Garbs" – Cas gawped at a group of giggling girls twirling around in a selection of outrageous fashions, inside a shop with a flared roof shaped like a tutu – "and then there's The Diddly Squattery." Warrior indicated to a tiny, teetering shop that seemed the complete opposite of Ondine's, apparently only selling the most pointless objects – chocolate teapots, umbrellas with holes in them, and even jumpers with dead-ended arms.

A deliciously sweet smell drew Cas towards the window of Captain Caeli's Cakery, a bakery and café whose shopfront was lined with every mouth-watering delicacy under the sun. From coal cookies to chocolate cheesecake clouds; bright blue, salty sea scones to fat, greasy bubble fritters; pink coral cupcakes and bubbling foam frothies to cans of zingy Kindlin' Koola in whizzpoppin' watermelon flavour.

On their tour, they passed the Legacy League, an exclusive country club for hoity-toity families like the Du Villaines, where nobody was welcome, at the opposite end of town to The Terranical Terrace, a glassy hotel with foliage spilling off the balconies, where everyone was. The most ancient building in Wayward, the gloomy Paracelus Shadow Puppet Theatre, sat adjacent to the newest one, The Arcadia – a big, arched gallery of Normie shops which had sprung up out of necessity ever since the Master of All took away the Life and Deathmakers' powers. Doctors, opticians, dentists and even a shady market stall where you could buy poisons for a penny were located there.

A handful of people in scruffy, torn Lifemaker and Deathmaker cloaks were begging outside The Arcadia, rattling cups of change.

For the first time, Cas was confronted with exactly what the Master had taken from these people. He hadn't just stolen their powers. For many, the loss of their magic must've meant the loss of their jobs and their homes.

And now he wanted to do the same to the other Orders too.

He had to be stopped.

"Can we swing by my parents'?" asked Paws, as they returned to the central square with the fountain to make their plan of attack. "I'd love to surprise them."

"Of course," said Mrs Crane cheerfully. "The Grover-Rosales Animal Hospital and Elementie Emporium, isn't it?"

Paws nodded.

"We'll just grab a few things on the way," said Mrs Crane. "Plus, there's somewhere I need to take Cas first."

Mrs Crane winked at him.

"There's no point coming to Wayward Town to do some Christmas shopping if you haven't got any pocket money. Luckily for you, I know just the place."

"Is it a bank?" Cas asked.

"Not exactly," said Mrs Crane.

"Is it a sweet shop?"

Mrs Crane and the Abnormies stood outside a huge, bottle-green establishment shaped like a gigantic sweetie. Judging from the outside, the building could've easily been either. It was made entirely of glass and the words THE MINT EXCHANGE glittered above the door in an emerald glow. A doorman in a teal-and-white pinstripe suit ushered people inside with a polite tip of his bowler hat.

"You'll see," Mrs Crane replied, tapping her nose and smiling, before shooing them inside.

They entered the building onto a green-and-white-striped trading floor. Despite what Mrs Crane said, The Mint Exchange certainly looked like a bank. Clerks in teal-and-white pinstripe blazers sat behind desks, serving Others and jotting down numbers in notepads as they weighed things in strange brass contraptions. Mrs Crane and the Abnormies spotted an empty desk across from a man with a fluffy, cloud-shaped moustache, and Cas was promptly shoved into the customer seat.

Mr Moustache instantly broke out into the world's widest grin.

"Welcome to The Mint Exchange!" he squealed in a high-pitched, chirpy voice. "Where we've been mint-exchange-minting since 1671! What can we do for you today?"

Cas blinked at the man in befuddlement. He was making about as much sense as the Oracle. "Um—"

Mrs Crane passed Cas a heavy, jangling money bag. Except to Cas's surprise, when he tore it open, it wasn't full of money. Odd knick-knacks and trinkets lay inside, everything from rubber bands to paper clips, shiny bits of jewellery to old ticket stubs, a broken pencil and even a couple of glimmering rubies and diamonds. Cas handed the bag to the clerk, who spilled the contents out into a dish on one side of the strange brass weighing contraption, as if such a random collection of objects was perfectly normal.

On the other side of the device, a number scale began to climb upwards from the hundreds into the thousands. Cas glanced around and saw many other patrons having their goods weighed too – except, he realized, the contraptions didn't seem to be measuring weight.

They seemed to be measuring value.

But value against what? Or for what?

"Five hundred gubbins and seventy-five doobries," Mr Moustache happily bellowed, sliding the empty bag back towards Cas. He tipped the contents from the scale into a brass tray, which he handed to a runner.

Another pimpled clerk sprinted away with the jingling tray as Warrior, Paws and Fenix gasped beside Cas.

"What are gubbins and doobries?" Cas queried.

Mrs Crane patted his shoulder. "Our version of money, dear. Like how Normie London has pounds and pence. There are one hundred and twenty doobries to a gubbin."

Warrior snorted. "But *five hundred gubbins* just for Christmas shopping? You could buy the whole town."

"I – I don't understand—" Cas began.

Warrior tapped a seal stamped on the side of the money bag. "The Grand Council have special provisions in place at Wayward School for exceptional students like you. And seeing as you're the Foretold…" She let out a long, low whistle. "It looks like they've raided the Chambers' vaults."

"Shh," hissed Mrs Crane. "It's not wise to go about blasting Cas's identity like a foghorn."

Sure enough, at the sound of Warrior's exasperation, a couple of nearby patrons whipped round and stared.

At that moment, the runner returned with the jingling tray.

Only this time, the knick-knacks and trinkets were gone.

"Here you are, young man," said Mr Moustache, smiling even more widely and sliding the tray towards Cas.

In place of the trinkets, there were large, bright green coins and small, dark purple ones. Gubbins and doobries. Cas held one of the coins up to the light, inspecting it. It appeared he had swapped the objects for money…

No, the money was *made* from the objects.

There, he could see them: the old ticket stubs, the rubber bands, the broken pencil, the rubies and diamonds … they had been pressed down and *minted* into coins. He had exchanged the unspendable value of the things in the money bag for a spendable one.

A perfect balance.

The Mint Exchange. At once, it made sense.

"And here's your mint," said Mr Moustache, thrusting a glassy green boiled sweet into Cas's palm. "Enjoy your day!"

Cas was still mesmerised by The Mint Exchange as they wandered into Ondine's Oddities and Essentials on their way to Paws's parents' shop. Mrs Crane wanted to grab some last-minute Christmas presents while Fenix finished up in Bibbity Bashety Books – a bookshop where the shelves were arranged like an obstacle course and flying books ran wild, so you had to scale the stacks or leap from shelf to shelf to catch the ones you wanted.

Weaving between the shelves at Ondine's reminded Cas of being in Mrs Crane's curiosity shop. Ondine's sold a rather unpredictable, eclectic mix of goods – everything from Order clothes to lavish portraits, exotic plants to training aids that claimed to help struggling Others enhance their powers.

"These things are like training wheels," scoffed Warrior as they trudged down one such aisle, poking and prodding at the various Order offerings.

"There's nothing wrong with wheels," said Paws faintly.

Warrior didn't hear her. "You'd have to be really hopeless to be looking at stuff like this."

Cas veered away from Warrior and Paws to look at a stack of tabloids and magazines. A rich-looking couple, with very familiar scowls and silvery hair, seemed to be plastered on the front of every one. Publications such as *The Oracle's Eye* ("*We predict tomorrow's news before it's even happened!*") and *The Threadly Times* reported on the millionaires like they were celebrities:

LIFE ON CLOUD NINE: EUPHOLOUS AND YVAINE DU VILLAINE SPILL WHAT IT'S LIKE TO BE ONE OF THE MOST INFLUENTIAL AIRSCAPER FAMILIES IN THE BALANCE LANDS

DU VILL-FAME: OUR SUPER-SECRET SECRETS TO SUCCESS

Shuddering, Cas quickly stuffed the publications back onto the stack and returned to the others. He refused to let the thought of the Du Villaine twins spoil his day.

Yet to his dismay, Warrior and Paws were gone when he retraced his steps.

"Hello?" Cas called, venturing along the training aids aisle to find them.

He passed by everything from Firetamer sparkshooter bracelets (which had an eye-wateringly high price tag), to leather blinkers (designed to block out any distractions) and pink-purple crystals (which claimed to attract dirt and soil towards an Earthshaper's power and even detect precious metals in the ground).

Cas knew that last claim was codswallop.

In one of their Order Studies lessons, Madame Aster had told them that such a feat was only achievable by an Elementie creature, though Cas couldn't remember which one. He was just attempting to rack his brain for the answer when he rounded a corner and smacked straight into a mess of white fur and long, pale hair.

189

"Watch where you're going, Freak Mould," a voice snarled.

Cas staggered back, knocking over a black-spotted pot plant (with a sign which read: *Tactillus Morticus – The Death Plant; dies with a single touch*), and found himself staring into the bright green eyes of Lucille Du Villaine. They widened in shock, before narrowing in fury.

"What are you doing here?" they both said at the same time.

Cas glanced around the shop, but Lucille was alone. "I thought you were up at the school stealing our seats."

"I was – I mean, I am… I'm going back to…" Lucille stammered. Cas was surprised to see her so shaken. She hastily moved away from the display case she had been looking at. "My parents brought me into town to shop for my Christmas present. They're at the Legacy League having afternoon tea with my grandma."

Cas looked sideways to see what Lucille had been examining, but she hastily grabbed a fistful of his cloak.

"Don't tell anyone I was here," she ordered, her eyes transforming into venomous slits. "Or I'll make you regret it, Darkbloom."

In spite of her threat, Lucille's voice sounded pleading. "O-OK," spluttered Cas.

He was more knocked off-kilter by seeing the cool and callous Lucille Du Villaine so flustered than he was by her words. She gave the fistful of his cloak an extra tug for good measure, then flounced off. The tinkling of the bell above the door was the only sign that she had ever been there at all.

"What are you doing?" said Warrior, reappearing from behind a rack of red leather Firetamer cloaks, Paws wheeling her chair ahead of her.

"Nothing," said Cas a little too quickly. He jerked his thumb at the display cabinet. "Just looking."

"Are you an air-headed Airscaper in need of extra assistance?" Paws read the card propped up against a basket of twisted wooden staffs. *"Try one of Articus Arroweather's Airy-Fairy, Not-So-Quite-Contrary Airscaper Staffs today. Only nine gubbins and fifteen doobries."*

"Why are you looking at Airscaper staffs?" said Warrior suspiciously.

Cas knew he should tell the others about seeing Lucille lurking near the training aids, but something stopped him. In the nick of time, Mrs Crane staggered around the corner, stooping under the weight of the shopping bags filling her arms, and Cas leapt at the chance to help before Warrior could ask him any more questions.

"Everyone ready?" called Mrs Crane, counting their heads to check that they were all present. Fenix had reappeared too, equally laden with bags. "Super. Off to the Elementie Emporium we go!"

CHAPTER 12
THE ELEMENTIE EMPORIUM

THE GROVER-ROSALES ANIMAL HOSPITAL AND Elementie Emporium was a small, wonky, fuchsia shop with peeling gold letters above the arched door. Every steamy window was crammed full of cages and tanks – some apparently empty, where the Elementies were hibernating or hiding, while others were full to bursting with the most bizarre and fascinating creatures Cas had ever seen.

As they stepped into the pet shop, the grin on Paws's face grew so wide that Cas thought she might explode. He had never seen someone look so happy, so at home. His chest ballooned and then gave a small twinge when he realized that he had never felt like that. At least, not that he could remember. Maybe somewhere, out there in the Balance Lands, he had a home and a family like Paws did. Parents and siblings who were missing him. Or maybe he was an orphan like Warrior.

That was more likely.

In all the weeks Cas had been at Wayward, there hadn't even been whispers of anyone looking for a lost child.

But when Warrior smiled at Cas, a warm, fuzzy feeling flooded his stomach. *Perhaps I don't have a home like this,* Cas thought, *but I have Warrior. And Paws and Fenix. Mrs Crane and Wayward.*

And he supposed that was good enough for now.

A wave of heat rushed to greet them. Soon, Cas understood why. As well as offering up the odd Normie cat or dog for rehoming, the Elementie Emporium was mainly home to, *well*, Elementies. In a large tank by the frosted windows, red, gold and orange-speckled salamanders shot in and out of a miniature crackling fire. On the counter, a preening peacock gave a great shiver and its fire-coloured feathers shuddered into a flaming plume. A snoozing basket of half hedgehog, half pig-like creatures sat by the back door. They looked like enormous boars with dangerous, prickly spikes on their backs. *Thickethogs.* Cas identified them as the gemstone-sniffing animals he had been trying to remember before.

In a far corner of the shop, a lone, roomy cage held thirteen three-headed chickens with chains around their scaly feet.

Are you experiencing a security problem? an advertisement above the cage read.

193

Or do you have something precious to protect? Do you want a creature that will guard your possessions like the entrance to the Underworld?

Then Cerberoosters are the bird for you!

Don't delay, grab your three-headed Deathmaker chicken today!

Enraptured, Cas drew closer, dying to get a better look. No sooner had he pressed his face against the cage's bars than the three-headed birds lunged. They squawked, flapping their skeletal wings and baring their tiny, toothpick-sharp teeth. Fenix yanked Cas out of the way as they collided with the cage, gnashing at the bars. Fenix nodded towards another sign above the cage which said: *WARNING!! Risk of pain, injury or dismemberment. Licensed cerberooster rehomers only.*

Moving away, Cas squirmed. The prickling feeling of being watched scuttled over the skin on the back of his neck – but when he spun around, the cerberoosters were busy pecking away at their grits and there was nobody outside the shop's windows. Shaking off the sensation, he peered into another nearby habitat. This one was muddy and humid, with leaves, sticks and soil. It housed mudwellers the size of his palm and fluffy, sand-yellow moles with ridiculously long, droopy noses.

"Amalia!" an excited voice squealed as someone emerged from the back room.

Cas straightened up to see a lady who looked strikingly

like Paws. She had the same olive skin and unkempt, scraggly brown hair, which she pushed out of her face as she entered carrying a squirming tea towel bundle. She almost dropped it at the sight of her daughter.

"Mum! The sand snoots!" Paws shouted quickly. The woman reacted just fast enough to catch the falling bundle before it hit the floor.

"Andromeda Crane," said Paws's mother, hurrying over to deposit the armful of baby sand snoots into the tank beside Cas. "Gosh, I don't think I've seen you since before the summer. How are you?" She pulled Mrs Crane into a long, hearty hug, then leant down to plant kisses on Paws's cheeks.

"Diana Rosales," said Mrs Crane. "Long time no see indeed."

"Hopefully it won't be that long again," Diana continued cheerfully. "I'm planning on coming up to the school soon."

"Oh, are you joining us for the Mini Questial?" Mrs Crane clapped her hands in delight.

"We wouldn't miss it for the world," replied Diana. "Sorry, it's just me out front today. Artemis is in the animal hospital operating on a thickethog." She pointed towards the young thickethoglets, fast asleep in their basket. "Poor babies almost lost their mother last night. She got caught in a poacher's trap. It's disgusting what some people will do to these innocent animals just so they can make a pretty penny from their abilities – thickethogs are like a get-rich-quick scheme on trotters."

"Well, it's wonderful to see you, my lovely," said Mrs Crane, glancing at the clock above the counter. "But we can't stay long. I promised I'd have these rascals back at school before the end of the day. Although…" She trailed off, elbowing Paws mischievously. "I suppose there's no harm in letting this one stay so she can start her Christmas break early."

Paws's face glowed. "Really?"

"I won't tell if you don't."

Diana Rosales hugged her daughter, before throwing her arms around Mrs Crane again.

"Whilst I'm here, I wondered if you had any advice," Mrs Crane managed to ask through a mouthful of Diana's hair. "*Pfft…* We've got a terrible whatsit problem in the old Lifemaker dorms above the Nurse's Quarters—"

"Copper wire and pink Himalayan salt," said Diana, knowing the answer to Mrs Crane's question before she had even asked.

"Brilliant." Mrs Crane nodded. "And we're also having a bit of a problem with, erm, *leishis*" – she spoke the word very quietly, evidently hoping Cas and the others wouldn't hear – "sneaking in past the wards by burrowing in underground."

"What are leishis?" Cas asked Fenix out of the corner of his mouth.

"Well, um, they're really quite nasty," said Fenix. "They're these hideous … no, that's really cruel, I shouldn't judge … *less-than-conventionally-pretty* Earthshaper gremlins who are renowned for kidnapping children and taking them back to their lairs to tickle them to death."

"And they can get in under the wards?"

"Nobody's died at the school yet," said Fenix, gesturing wildly at Cas's alarm. "Besides you can always, you know, escape and confuse them by going into the woods with your shoes on the wrong feet. Or turning your clothes inside out."

"Wonderful," said Cas sarcastically. "I'll be sure to remember that if I'm on the brink of—"

BOOM.

At that instant, Cas was interrupted by a loud crashing sound from outside. Within seconds, orange-clad wardsmen were hurtling past the windows, their heavy boots thundering on the cobblestones.

"What on earth?" cried Diana Rosales, who was midway through bottle-feeding the baby sand snoots. She paused, with the lid of the tank still open.

Warrior stuck her head out onto the street to see what was going on, just as another woman with short, spiky hair peeked around the door leading out to the back. "What's happening?" she said, wiping blood from her hands onto a surgeon's gown. Her face went white at the same time Paws sensed something. "Diana, my love—"

"Mum, watch out! The tank—"

197

Too late, Paws's mother noticed what was happening. The baby sand snoots had climbed up the side of the tank, desperate to reach the milk bottle she was dangling centimetres out of reach. Before Diana had a chance to react, the weight of the animals toppled the tank sideways, pouring crab-like mudwellers and fluffy, yellow sand snoots onto the floor.

"Everyone stay calm! Stay calm!" Diana Rosales panicked.

The Elementie Emporium descended into chaos.

"Sweetpea, it's all right!" Paws cooed, as the flame-feathered peacock ignited in a *whoosh* of terrified flames. This set off Fenix, who went up in his own blazing glory, startling both Mogget snoozing on Paws's shoulders and the young thickethoglets, who squealed like dying pigs and struggled to escape from their basket.

To Cas's left, the cerberoosters began going berserk. They turned their razor-sharp teeth on each other, grappling viciously. All of them except one, who was pecking away at the padlock on the cage in a frenzy.

"*NOOO!*" Mrs Crane lurched forward to stop the chicken, but before she could, the padlock snapped.

The cerberoosters broke free.

"Cas, Fenix, Warrior, Paws. Into the stockroom. *NOW!*" Mrs Crane bellowed, grabbing hold of Paws's wheelchair as Diana Rosales desperately tried to round up some of the escaped creatures. "*WARRIOR – SHUT THAT DOOR!*"

As Warrior started to close the front door, Cas spotted a yellow dot streaking out through the entrance and onto the street.

"Baby sand snoot!" he shouted, hobbling past Warrior as speedily as his funny leg would carry him.

Breathing hard, Cas chased the surprisingly quick yellow blur deeper into the heart of Wayward Town. He pursued it down one twisting cobblestone side alley, round a sharp turn, and then down another, plunging into the labyrinthine maze of Wayward's back lanes until he was wildly lost. Finally, the baby sand snoot stopped to sniff at a pile of rubbish in a passage alongside a café. The sun was dipping low behind the horizon. Everything in Wayward was beginning to close.

Knowing this might be his last chance to catch the animal before dark, Cas approached the sand snoot slowly, tiptoeing as silently as he could. He was three paces away … two paces … one…

He lunged.

At the same time, something large burst from the shadows, knocking Cas sideways and snatching up the sand snoot instead.

Stars speckled Cas's vision as he fell, knees cracking against the curb. It took several moments to blink them away so he could glance up. Relief washed over him when he spotted the sand snoot safe and sound in another pair of human hands.

199

"Thank you," Cas gasped, scrambling unsteadily to his feet. But when he reached out to retrieve the sand snoot, the pair of hands that had captured it pulled away.

"Help me," a voice panted, gruff and trembling. "You have to help me … there's Heretics at the wards … trying to break in…"

Cas's stomach plummeted with dread. *Heretics.* His gaze flew back vaguely in the direction he had come. He had to find the others. But as he stared at the figure before him, he knew he couldn't just leave the sand snoot's saviour behind.

The hunched man wore the same scruffy purple cloak as the beggars outside The Arcadia. He reeked of rubbish, sweat and something stale. Something rotting. The unmistakable Deathmaker scent of despair and decay. Cas couldn't see much of the young man's face from where it was obscured by the sunset's shadows, but his terrified amber eyes bore into Cas's very soul.

"Please," the man pleaded. "Help me."

For a heart-stopping moment, Cas hesitated.

It was getting late. He was completely and utterly lost, and nobody knew where he was. Yet the thought of the petrified man in front of him, a forgotten soul who had had everything taken from him by the Master…

The sound of thumping boots from the next alley over made the man cringe in fear.

"Over here," said Cas, taking the sand snoot from

the homeless stranger and leading him further down the passage at the back of the café. It was a dead end. Thinking fast, Cas directed the man to crouch down against the wall and threw the threadbare cloak over his figure to disguise him.

Then, he tucked the sand snoot safely into his pocket and dashed round to the front of the building. With a start, Cas realized that he was back at Captain Caeli's Cakery, on the other side of town.

"Hey, you! Yes, you!" Cas shouted loudly at no one. "Why are you running? There's nothing but The Mint Exchange that way!"

The smattering of onlookers on Newbusy Avenue regarded Cas warily, but at the sound of his words, he heard the pursuing boots in the next alley over skid to a halt and change direction, running the opposite way. Cas sagged against the alley wall as the footsteps departed.

They were safe. *For now.*

Cas rushed back to the man. Now that he had time to stop and think, he supposed the boots he had heard could have belonged to the wardsmen, rather than the Heretics. But seeing as both Cas and the Deathmaker stranger were in danger if it *was* the Master's followers, could he really afford to take that risk?

Cas held out his hand to help the man up. He took it, and for a long moment Cas and the man stared at each other, unblinking.

"Thank you," the homeless man said. This time when he spoke, his voice was less raspy, more human, than before.

"Don't mention it," said Cas. He would've done the same for anyone. "But I think it's best if we split up and hunker down somewhere safe until we know what's going on."

The man nodded.

There was just one hiccup in Cas's plan. He had no idea how to find his way back to Mrs Crane and the others. They were likely going out of their minds with worry.

As if he'd conjured them up, the most welcome sounds to Cas's ears bounced down Newbusy Avenue to greet him.

"CAS!"

"Casander!"

"Where are you, Cas?"

It was the Abnormies.

"Cas," the man mused, regarding him ravenously. An unsettling feeling stirred in Cas's gut, telling him that the stranger's hunger had nothing to do with the end-of-day scents wafting out from Captain Caeli's Cakery. "Is that short for Casander Darkbloom? The Foretold boy from up at Wayward School?"

Cas immediately felt the hairs on the back of his neck stand on end.

"Erm, well, yes, that's me," Cas half stammered, half chuckled, rubbing the nape of his neck.

He realized too late what he had done.

Cas wasn't stupid. He knew that the news about the Foretold, and inevitably his identity, would leak out of Wayward School eventually – despite every precaution Dr Bane and the Grand Council had put in place. But it still struck him as odd that the homeless man was so quick to assume that was who he was. Had Warrior been overheard calling him the Foretold in The Mint Exchange? Or had Lucille referred to him by that name in Ondine's?

Either way, Cas had just confirmed it. It suddenly hit him exactly what being the Foretold meant. He was someone very famous and very valuable, alone, in Wayward Town.

He had to find his friends.

"Wait."

The man gripped Cas's hand fiercely as he turned to leave, pinning him in place. Cas froze. The homeless man was stronger than he looked. Much stronger.

"What's the rush?" the man cajoled, trying to coax Cas down a darker, shadier side street that Cas hadn't even spotted in the gloom. "Let me pay you back for helping me. You're our saviour. There's something I want to show you … to give you … right down here."

"No, really, I'm fine," protested Cas, trying to wriggle free.

Icy panic washed over him. With one last tug, Cas wrenched his arm from the man's hold. "I'm here!" he yelled over his shoulder, chancing a glance down the street.

203

At that moment, the figures of Mrs Crane, Fenix and Warrior stampeded into view.

"There you are," Mrs Crane heaved, barrelling to a stop beside him. Pink-faced and puffy, she leant against a firefly lamppost to catch her breath.

"What happened with the Heretics at the wards?" Cas asked urgently.

"Nothing," puffed Warrior. "Nobody got through. The wardsmen captured a couple of them, but we think the rest were scared away."

She knitted her brow, bobbing around Cas to glance at the space behind him.

"What are you doing down here?" Her hair flickered between a suspicious green and a serious shade of grey.

Cas pivoted back towards the man, ready to introduce him, but in the split second he had been distracted by Warrior, the mysterious figure had slipped away.

"Nothing," said Cas, casting a final look around for the homeless man.

But he was gone.

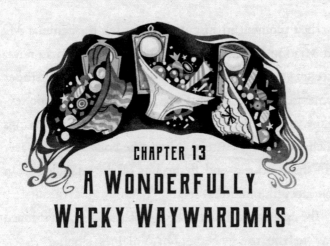

CHAPTER 13
A WONDERFULLY WACKY WAYWARDMAS

THE NEXT DAY, WAYWARD SCHOOL FELT LIKE A gaping hollow without the other students. Cas was loath to admit it, but amongst the ghostly silence of Christmas Eve, he even almost missed the Du Villaines' cruel taunts.

Rumours about the twins' pre-Christmas reign of terror rapidly pushed the encounter with the homeless stranger to the back of Cas's mind. He had intended to tell the others about it, but when they arrived back at Wayward School with Mrs Crane, he was too distracted by the swarm of students spilling out of the *WS* gates in a blizzard of crestfallen faces and tear-stained cheeks. Whilst Maxwell Snout had allegedly run around handing out ice wedgies like they were going out of fashion, Aubria had been under strict orders from the Du Villaines to ruin every Christmas gift exchange in sight.

They pitched up just in time to see the famous Mr and Mrs Du Villaine pick up their vile sprogs in a grand, wheelless wyverkey-drawn carriage. The Airscaper Elementies looked like part-wyvern, part-monkey-donkey-turkey things. They had slimy, scaly grey skin and wings which were attached to a chimp-like body, but their feet were sharp hooves and fleshy bits of skin dangled from their faces like wattles.

The carriage had soared high into the air and swooshed away to the tune of the Du Villaines singing *"Jingle bells, Darkbloom smells."* But Cas would've paid good doobries to hear the twins' caterwauling shatter the empty eeriness now.

Even if only so he could yell at them for being such show-offs; Others didn't need vehicles when they could waygate from place to place in the Balance Lands. The Du Villaines simply rode about in a carriage to prove they could.

Fenix, like the rest of their peers, had gone home for the holidays. So had most of the staff – except Dr Bane. Just like Mrs Crane had predicted, Dr Bane insisted he had to stay behind for work, leaving her to face their family alone. However, Cas suspected this was only because Warrior had declined Mrs Crane's invitation for her and Cas to join the Bane family gathering too, and they couldn't very well be left at Wayward School alone.

"Oh, no," said Warrior, when Cas asked about it.

"Dr Bane won't be here tomorrow. He always goes gallivanting off."

They were sitting by the frozen lake, skimming pebbles across the glittery, glacial surface. Every now and then, a creature that looked like a hairy, chubby bay pony crashed through the ice, shaking its seaweedy mane and whipping its pinwheel-like tail. It was Puggle the Nuggle, a Wavebreaker Elementie who lived in the boating lake. He was renowned (and avoided) for chasing unsuspecting students into the watery depths as they wandered past the lake between classes. Fresh-faced Wayones were Puggle's favourite. He liked to nip at their buttocks, herding them into the shallows until they fell in the water, spluttering. But Puggle the Nuggle was harmless really; once he'd got a few good screams out of someone, he always left them alone. Seeing as neither Cas nor Warrior fancied taking a dip in the freezing water today, though, they were tossing the cheeky pony stale bread crusts whenever he appeared.

Their tactic seemed to be working.

"Where does Bane go?" asked Cas.

Warrior sighed. "It's always the same. He goes after the Master of All. Even the Grand Council have plans at Christmas, so there's nobody to stop him. Bane can track the Master as closely as he likes."

"Why didn't we go with Mrs Crane, then?"

Warrior chuckled darkly. "Because, trust me, you don't

want to go to a Bane family Christmas. It always ends in a duel with turkey legs at dawn."

"Surely it's got to be better than being stuck here."

The idea of a family Christmas, no matter how manic, sounded very nice to Cas.

"No way. You're just saying that because you haven't met the Banes. There's nutty Great-Uncle James, who insists every member of the Grand Council is really a chicken–lizard hybrid in disguise. Then there's Great-Great-Granny Megs, who never fails to drink herself into a sherry stupor by two o'clock. Oh yes, and let's not forget Cousin Radford, who's so rude about those *namby-pamby, wishy-washy Earthshapers* that you can't take him anywhere in public without getting dirty looks. Believe it or not, Mrs Crane is one of the sensible ones."

Somehow that seemed unlikely.

"Well, she is if you don't count the fact that she always starts a food fight over the cranberry sauce."

Cas stifled a snort. "OK, fine. Maybe Dr Bane won't stick around this year, but maybe he will. I'm the Foretold. He wouldn't leave me at Wayward unprotected, would he? Plus, you're his adopted daughter."

"*Adopted.*" Warrior rolled her eyes. "That's exactly why he won't be here."

"What do you mean?"

She paused, considering what to say next. "I think…" Warrior began, before her words quietened to nothing.

She watched Puggle the Nuggle trotting across the lake's icy surface, tossing his head and demanding more bread crusts, before she pressed on. "I think Dr Bane is my father. My *real* father."

Cas wasn't sure what to say.

"No, I know he is. And he knows that I know too." She turned to face Cas fully. "Of all the places, in all the Balance Lands, my mother dumped me here. On Wayward School's doorstep. With a note specifically addressed to Dr Bane."

"Perhaps your mother and Dr Bane were friends?"

Warrior shook her head. "Bane doesn't have friends. He has family, students, people he answers to and people he's responsible for. That's it. His life's mission is to find and stop the Master of All. Nothing else matters. So why would he, a man as important and busy as he is, take in me, an abandoned baby? An Abnormie, of all things. Why didn't he just ship me off to Wayling Orphanage? Or leave me to freeze to death in the cold? Why didn't he send me to live with one of his relatives, if he really felt sorry for me? Great-Great-Granny Megs has about a billion cats. I'm sure Bane could've dressed me up in a furry jacket and collar and I'd have fitted right in."

Cas took a moment to let this sink in.

"Bane doesn't hang around at Christmas because he shoots off to track down the Master of All," Warrior continued. "But he also doesn't hang around because there's a chance I might start asking questions."

"Questions he doesn't want to answer."

"Questions he *needs* to."

"Because sometimes you just need to know," said Cas thoughtfully.

Warrior nodded. Like she so often did to him, it felt like Cas had read her mind.

It was at times like these that Cas felt as though they were the same person. He wondered if it was because he had spent so much time with Warrior since he came to the Balance Lands. They had been stuck together like glue from day one. Even in his first Thread Theory 101 class or when he had chased after the sand snoot, it had turned out Warrior had been keeping an eye on him through a crack in the wall from the room next door or was merely steps behind.

"You don't need Bane," said Cas. "Or any of his whackadoodle family. You've got me."

Warrior's lips curled up. "And you've got me."

For the first time he could remember, Cas felt it. That feeling he had been dying to feel ever since he had seen Paws at the Elementie Emporium.

He was home.

Christmas morning broke not with the chiming of bells or tinkling of carols, but with the sound of "Get up! Get up, you lazy oaf!" echoing across the Attic.

Cas groaned and shielded his eyes against the bright sunlight streaming in through the window, gilding the creaky floorboards. He pulled the bed covers over his head, only to have them roughly ripped away.

"Warrrrior," Cas drawled, burying his head under his pillow. "I thought we were having a lie-in. You said that was your Christmas present to me."

"Warrior Bane!" a voice that was very much *not* Warrior's scolded. "How dare you. If I've told you off once, I've told you off a hundred times for fobbing people off with rubbish Christmas presents. You've at least got to give them something with a bow!"

Cas's eyes flew open. He yanked the pillow off his head and saw that it wasn't Warrior who had shaken him awake. Another culprit with wild, untameable hair, giant jam-jar spectacles, and a tweed poncho decorated with rainbow-coloured baubles sat at the end of his bed.

"Mrs Crane?"

"Oh good, you're up," said Mrs Crane sweetly. She tapped the top of Cas's head, as if to knock the last dregs of slumber out of him, then shuffled over to Warrior in her fuzzy tweed slippers to wake her up too.

Even in her dozy state, Warrior put up a good fight. She clung on to the bed's headboard for dear life as Mrs Crane struggled to pry her free. Even Hobdogglin joined in, appearing out of nowhere to *yip-yap* at Mrs Crane's heels in protest. But eventually Mrs Crane won. She heaved

Warrior to her feet and tugged two hideous tweed knitted jumpers over Cas and Warrior's heads. Warrior crossed her arms and scowled at Mrs Crane over the top of the big green tweed Christmas tree that adorned her jumper. It wouldn't have looked so bad, except the Christmas tree had a face. And the face had pointed eyes made from a bright red herringbone, making it look devilishly sinister.

Meanwhile, Cas wore a jumper sporting a tweed cat, which resembled a grumpy version of Mogget, pouting under a party hat.

Mrs Crane stepped back, her eyes twinkling admiringly.

"Perfect," she breathed, shoving a reindeer-shaped slab of white chocolate into each of their mouths to complete the look.

"Gree twaught twoo were gwoing home fur dee holidways," said Warrior through her mouthful, white chocolatey goo dribbling down her chin.

"Change of plan," said Mrs Crane, humming merrily as she made their beds. "I saw Dr Bane packing his trunk on my way out yesterday. I'm not a monster. I couldn't just leave you both here over winter break, especially on Cas's first Christmas with us, no matter how hard I tried."

"You should hab twied harder." Warrior glanced longingly at her tightly tucked-in bed.

"Don't speak with your mouth full, Warrior," said Mrs Crane disapprovingly. "It's very unladylike. Or at least, if you do, pack your gob full so it looks impressive."

Warrior swallowed her chocolate with a gulp. "Dr Bane's not gone," she insisted, pointing out of the window. Glancing outside, Cas saw a solitary, Dr Bane-shaped figure sitting in the courtyard, riffling through papers and enjoying the morning sunshine with a cup of tea.

Mrs Crane waggled her finger at Warrior. "I'm not a fool either, missus. I know my brother will have run off somewhere in the next hour."

Warrior couldn't deny this; she had told Cas as much yesterday.

For this reason, they had already planned out their entire gloriously adult-free day together:

7 o'clock: Realize it's too early to be awake and go back to sleep

12 o'clock: Have a late brunch of biscuits from Headmaster Higgles's special secret stash, followed by hot chocolates and as many mouldy toffees as they could pilfer from Miss Grimbly's desk

1 o'clock: Stair banister slide racing

2 o'clock: Ice skating on the boating lake

3 o'clock: Snow-angel-making and whatsit-baiting above the Nurse's Quarters

4 o'clock: Christmas dinner sandwiches from any leftovers they could find (likely more biscuits and sweets)

*6 o'clock–Midnight: Scary Christmas stories, Kindlin'
Koola and crashing into bed thoroughly
exhausted, ready for another lie-in the next day*

"Besides," Mrs Crane continued, "fat lot of good Dr Bane would be if he stayed. Claudius wouldn't know Christmas spirit if it smacked him in the face with a pair of antlers."

"But what about your family?" said Cas guiltily. "We can't ruin your fun."

"Yes, and you can't ruin ours," said Warrior. "We were going to put pine needles in Madame Aster's seat cushion and everything."

Mrs Crane swept over and enveloped them both in a rib-shattering squeeze. "*We're* family. And families stick together. Plus, if you're going to do that, someone needs to be around to teach you that whoopee cushions are much funnier than pine needles."

"*Help me,*" Warrior wheezed, trying to claw her way free from the hug.

Cas noticed she didn't struggle too hard, though. Deep down, she seemed to be enjoying it.

"Right." Mrs Crane clapped her hands, releasing them. "Seeing as you layabouts have slept in until almost lunchtime, we may as well spend the rest of the day with full bellies. How does Christmas dinner in one hour sound?"

Cas's stomach answered for them. Food was never a bad idea as far as he was concerned.

Enthusiastically, Cas began pulling on his jeans as Warrior flopped dramatically back onto her bed. Mrs Crane disappeared down the spiral staircase, humming all the way to the bottom, where she broke out into a very out-of-tune Christmas song.

Maybe the Sydney Opera House had been right to ban her for life.

"Have you really never had a Christmas before, Cas?" said Warrior.

Cas shook his head. "Not that I can remember."

"Well, I suppose a traditional Wayward Christmas isn't bad for your first. Most of our festivities these days come from the Normie world, so I'm sure it won't be that different to one you've had before, even if you could remember it."

"So, Christmas didn't exist in the Balance Lands first?"

His mind jumped back to the whole Halloween–Mourners' Morn debacle.

Warrior's face soured. She was clearly thinking about the same thing. "Not exactly. Years ago, we used to celebrate something called Wynterfest, but that was mainly about going outside in the snow naked and dancing around trees or something. A couple of Earthshaper families still do it. But almost everyone in the Balance Lands celebrates Christmas now. We've taken on most of the Normie traditions but put our own spin on them. Wayward, in particular, has its own special way of doing things."

"Brilliant!"

Cas couldn't wait.

"Speaking of." Warrior leant forward and dug around under her bed. "Here you go." She tossed Cas a single, crisp envelope. "Happy Waywardmas!"

Furrowing his brow, Cas snatched the envelope out of the air and shook it.

"What's this?"

"Duh, your Christmas present. What else?"

Cas opened his mouth to thank her, but Warrior gave him a very odd, wide-eyed look.

"Oh, right. Yeah." Cas rummaged around blindly in the trunk at the end of his bed. "Here's yours. Happy Waywardmas too!"

When he handed it to her, Warrior's visage became even more scrunched up.

"What's this?" she demanded, pinching the present and holding it out like a smelly sock. She tilted her head from side to side, examining it with a mixture of bamboozlement and repulsion.

Cas felt his cheeks heating. "Your Christmas present."

"Is this it?"

Despite how hard he tried to squash the feeling, Cas immediately felt wrongfooted. Looking down at the envelope in his lap, he realized their gifts couldn't have been more different. Whereas Warrior's present to him was plain, small and flimsy, barely big enough to contain a scrap of paper, Cas's present to her was hefty and bulky, trussed up in old newspaper and gold tinsel. If anything, he should've been the one who was unimpressed.

"I know we exchanged presents with Paws and Fenix like this before they left," elaborated Warrior. "But this isn't traditionally how you're supposed to hand someone their present at Waywardmas, Cas."

"It's not?" said Cas, even more lost.

Before they had both returned home, Paws had given Cas a scratchy, hand-crocheted bobble hat and Fenix had gifted him a light-up Christmas ornament of Wayward School, soldered using his own flaming hands. Paws and Fenix had similarly swapped gifts with each other. She had bought him a pair of leather fireproof gloves and he had redesigned the pulley system that Paws used to get up and down the stairs from the Attic. Now, Paws was able to whizz over the spiral steps twice as fast as before, something she had demonstrated countless times before a motion-sick Mogget had spewed up a hairball into her lap.

Warrior sighed. "No. Didn't you hear me? We might borrow our Christmas traditions from the Normie world, but they all have a Balance Lands twist. People in the Normie world give each other Christmas gifts, so naturally, in the Balance Lands we hide them."

She pointed towards the envelope.

"That's what that is. Your first clue."

Cas pitched forward eagerly, all thoughts of embarrassment and small presents gone. "Like a scavenger hunt?"

Warrior groaned as if to say, *Obviously.* "This" – she shook the box-shaped present Cas had given her – "takes all the fun out of…"

Warrior's words dwindled and her eyes grew wide as she figured out what was bumping about inside. She dropped the present onto her lap and ripped off the paper ferociously, until only a frenzied mound of shredded confetti remained at her feet.

"It's wonderful!" she gasped, clutching the unwrapped object to her chest.

Cas beamed. He had bought her the most expensive set of watercolours and drawing pencils from Ondine's that gubbins and doobries could buy. They went perfectly with the brand-new sketchbooks Paws had given her and the bedside firefly lantern Fenix had made, so that Warrior could draw late into the night.

"Your turn," she said. Warrior's face shone almost as brightly as the joyful yellow tips of her hair.

Buzzing with anticipation, Cas tore open the envelope. Inside, there was a single slip of paper:

Dear Cas,
Welcome to your first Wayward Christmas!

Seeing as you haven't done this before (or not that your terrible memory can recall), I thought I'd keep the clues easy for you this year. We've got so much planned that I don't want your pea brain poking around Wayward School looking for your present for too long or we might miss out on all the fun.

Hope you enjoy this Waywardmas scavenger hunt!

Warrior

Grinning more widely, Cas flipped over the paper to find the first clue:

In order to find your Waywardmas gift,
Search low and high, but do be swift.
For clue two, seek the lady who never moans,
Amongst the rows of spines, but none with bones.

Cas frowned.

"Any ideas?" said Warrior, still hugging her art set.

"How many clues are there?" asked Cas.

"Three, so you'd better get a move on. If you're not done by the time we're supposed to be booby-trapping Madame Aster's classroom, I'm going to dunk you in the boating lake and leave you to the mercy of Puggle the Nuggle."

Cas re-read the clue. *Seek the lady who never moans. Amongst rows of spines, but none with bones.* Who was

Warrior talking about? Who never moaned? And what kind of spines didn't have bones?

Cas thought long and hard. *Spines … bones…* The only place that came to mind was…

"It's not in the mausoleum," said Warrior bluntly.

Cas supposed he should have known. Of course Warrior wouldn't stow it there, given her rather unpleasant history with the place.

Rows of spines, but none with bones…

What else in Wayward School came in rows, except rows of tombs … classrooms … windows and doors … bookcases…

Books had spines but no bones.

"The library!"

Warrior applauded slowly to let Cas know that he was correct.

Here you'll find the lady who never moans…

Mrs Crane.

Without another word, Cas and Warrior darted down the spiral staircase. He supposed they could have taken the trap-door slide, but when they barrelled out into the corridor, Cas was glad they hadn't.

The Waywardmas scavenger hunt wasn't the only topsy-turvy thing about Christmas in the Balance Lands. In the same way that the Normies seemed to decorate their Christmas trees with everything, Mrs Crane had decorated everything at Wayward School with Christmas trees. *Ouch*-ing and *ooh*-ing, Cas and Warrior picked their way barefoot across the second-floor corridor, which was strewn with prickly holly leaves and conifer branches. Bundles of mistletoe hung from every wall, lantern and ceiling, entangled with the normal climbing ivy and dangling bunches of poinsettias.

When they reached the library, Cas burst through the doors and sprinted over to where another envelope was waiting on Mrs Crane's desk:

> *With swathes of green,*
> *And bark like a dog,*
> *You'll find clue three*
> *Where glade sleeps like a log.*

He turned the paper over. There was nothing on the back this time. He ran the clue over repeatedly in his brain. *Swathes of green ... bark like a dog ... glade, glade...*

There was Professor Everglade. At once, it clicked.

"The Earthshaper cabins in the woods!"

Still half-dressed and holly-pricked, Cas and Warrior raced up to the treetop corridor in the far wing of the school, which led down to Professor Everglade's cabin in the forest. As they did so, they hurtled past another peculiarity of Christmas at Wayward: rows of brightly patterned, voluminous underwear hung from every doorknob, stuffed full of sweets.

The Balance Lands' version of stockings.

Picking their way carefully along the icy canopy corridor at a snail's pace, they emerged, shivering, into the woods. Propped up on the porch of Everglade's cabin was a soggy envelope dusted in snow:

> *A place of learning and getting things done,*
> *Of glowing objects but not much fun.*
> *In the clash of teacher and death-bringer air,*
> *You'll find your present hidden here.*

It took Cas less than a second to solve this final clue. *Teacher and death-bringer. Glowing objects.*

He laughed. "This one's obvious. It's Dr Bane's office."

Warrior lazily half shrugged. "I thought I'd be nice to you. It is Christmas Day, after all."

Heart thrumming, Cas took off like a bullet back up the hill towards the school, stumbling slightly as his funny leg was jolted into action. Still barefoot, he skidded and slipped up the stairs leading to Dr Bane's office. A present with a large, sparkly ribbon sat proudly outside the door, which Cas and Warrior were surprised to find ajar.

"Bane must have forgotten to lock up," said Cas, nudging the door open with the tip of his toe.

There was no one inside.

"Open it then," said Warrior, thrusting the present at Cas.

Cas turned back to her and took it. He peeled the wrapping open hastily.

"Mismatched trainers!" he cried.

Warrior flushed, the ends of her hair turning a faint shade of petal pink. "Just like the ones you were wearing the day I found you outside the curiosity shop."

Once again, it was like Warrior knew Cas better than he knew himself. Cas dropped to the floor and squeezed his feet into the trainers. He loved them. Ever since he had been forced to wear the standard-issue black leather shoes that were part of Wayward School's uniform, he'd been longing for a pair like these. Cas could never understand why someone would ever want to wear two shoes that were the same.

In his opinion, two different shoes were twice as fun as one.

Cas wiggled his new trainers appreciatively. One was off-white and patterned with Christmas puddings, the other periwinkle blue with silver crows.

"Funny," Warrior muttered, her face falling as her gaze strayed to Dr Bane's open door. "For a moment, I thought he might've stayed."

Cas's heart sank as hers did.

"Let's go," she exhaled, spinning on her heel to trudge back down to the dining hall. "Mrs Crane will have dinner ready soon."

But as Cas looked at the door, a bright idea sparked inside him.

"Hang on," he said, catching Warrior's elbow. "You've got me such an awesome present and all I got you was that lousy art set. Come on, if Dr Bane isn't going to be here, the least I can do is help you get some answers. Don't you want to know where he might've gone?"

Warrior hesitated for a moment, but Cas didn't wait for an answer.

Warrior Bane was attracted to mischief like a magpie to tinfoil. He knew she would consider it a personal insult if hijinks and hooliganism were afoot and she wasn't somehow involved.

Together, they pushed open the door.

CHAPTER 14
THINGS BEST
LEFT FORGOTTEN

D R BANE'S OFFICE WAS TWICE AS EERIE AND OMINOUS
when it was empty.

The gloomy stone walls seemed to climb higher, the
cabinets glowed brighter, and the polished, bone-white
animal skulls lining the walls seemed to follow Cas and
Warrior with their black, empty sockets as they slunk
across the room. They headed straight for Dr Bane's desk.
The gleaming mahogany surface was spotless, save for
a blank piece of paper, a letter opener and an ink pen. All
three sat flawlessly aligned as if ready and waiting for Bane
to return.

"His sleeping quarters look locked," commented Cas,
glancing up the staircase leading to the loft room above.

Warrior rattled each of the desk drawers in turn.
"These are all locked too."

But Cas wasn't prepared to admit defeat so easily.

He should've known that even if Bane had left his office unlocked, he wouldn't have been stupid enough to leave anything valuable or informative lying around. Yet the drive to help Warrior and his own burning desire to find out where the Master of All was gave him a burst of inspiration. Grabbing the sharp, pointed letter opener off the desk, Cas started jamming and twisting it into each of the drawers' keyholes, trying to wiggle one of the locks free.

It was a lot easier in theory than in practice.

"Forget it," said Warrior frostily. "It's useless. Let's go."

"Hang on," heaved Cas, wrenching this way and that. "Keep an eye out – in case anyone comes by. I'm … I'm almost in…"

A satisfying *click* pierced the air.

"Forget what?" he teased, dragging a large, leather-bound bundle of artefacts out of Bane's desk. The stack contained a bunch of portraits and letters that Cas held up to the light. "These?" He splayed the documents on the desk and divided them into two piles, one for each of them.

Eagle-eyed, they began to riffle through.

"Look at this," said Cas, jimmying one of the coloured portraits out of his stack and pushing it towards her. "Who do you think this is?"

Warrior squinted at the picture.

Since it wasn't possible to use cameras in the Balance

Lands, people had drawings and portraits done of them instead – though these drawings were vastly different to any in the Normie world.

The picture was of a young Dr Bane. Amongst the other figures in the portrait, he was easily recognizable by his wiry beard and younger, silver-thread-free auburn hair pulled back in a bun. Not only that, but Cas could sense it was him, in the same way one could sometimes discern a powerful Other's Order simply by the scent or sensation they gave off. As he studied Dr Bane, Cas could feel the familiar cold, creeping sense of Deathmaker magic – *Bane's* Deathmaker magic, captured at that moment in time. He felt the air being momentarily snatched from his lungs and smelt the faint scent of something withering into decay. Dr Bane was standing in front of the Eiffel Tower in Paris – but because on the face of it Normie Paris and Balance Lands Paris were identical, it was hard to pinpoint which world he was in. Bane had his arm wrapped around a pretty young woman standing next to him. She had dark hair that flowed down to her elbows in shimmering waves, and the most amazing, piercing amber eyes.

"Do you think that could be…" Cas trailed off, side-eyeing Warrior, unsure whether he dared say what he thought.

The feeling rolling off the woman was completely opposite to Bane's. It reminded Cas of light and happiness. Of rebirth and fresh air. He could feel his lungs expanding again to the fullest they had ever been and his heart beat louder, more bravely, in his veins.

She was a Lifemaker.

Warrior bit her lip, brushing her fingers over the miniature canvas. "My mother?" She clucked her tongue and laughed. "Not likely, we barely look the same."

She's right, thought Cas. They both had the same snow-white skin and dark hair, but the similarities ended there. If anything, the woman looked more akin to someone like Madame Aster, all graceful lines and high cheekbones. But there was something unique about her too. Her eyes.

Cas was sure he'd seen them before.

"I do know who this is," said Warrior, pointing to another figure in the picture – a lady with unruly sandy-blonde hair, sporting a tweed beret and singing into a baguette. *Mrs Crane.* "And this." She jabbed at another person, who was unmistakable as a young Headmaster Higgles, about two-metres tall with long limbs and munching on a croissant.

So that's how Dr Bane knew which buffoon to recommend for the headmaster's job.

"Look here," said Cas, inching something else out of his stack. He tossed a pile of crumpled letters knotted with frayed string onto the desk.

As he began to spread them out, he froze.

A single name was repeated numerous times, scrawled on letters dated from twelve to seventeen years ago:

Aeurdan Darkbloom.

"The Master of All went to Wayward School, like us," Warrior reminded him, peering over. "These must be letters and notes he sent to Dr Bane while he was here."

Cas plucked out one of the letters and began to read:

Dear Dr Bane,

I feel silly writing this, but I don't know what else to do. I have nobody else to talk to. Ever since I came to live at Wayward School, I've felt lost, so very lost, and you are the only person I can turn to. I'm sorry, at first I was angry. Confused. Bewildered and just ... I didn't understand why I had to be here. But you tried to talk to me, to explain everything, and though I didn't want to hear it then, I want to listen now. My only living relative, my grandmother, has stopped writing to me. Nobody has heard from her for months. It seems that she doesn't just want nothing to do with me, but she's moved away so that I can't find her. I suppose this means Wayward School has to be my home now.

Please, Dr Bane, if you're reading this – please come and talk to me again. I will listen this time. I want to stay here. I want to learn.

I want to be the most powerful Other I can be.
Yours,
Aeurdan Darkbloom

They both jumped as a bell chimed outside.

It was lunchtime.

Mrs Crane would be looking for them soon, but neither Cas nor Warrior were ready to abandon the new evidence yet. What if they were on the cusp of an answer, teetering on the precipice of everything they wanted to know?

Hurriedly, they skim-read the other letters as quickly as possible before they were caught.

Warrior picked up the next note, dated two years later:

> *Dear Dr Bane,*
>
> *I know you're avoiding me. You're supposed to be my Deathmaker tutor, but you always seem to be away when I stop by your quarters after class... Mrs Crane says that you're away on Grand Council business – but you're not one of them...*
>
> *The Grand Council are too restrictive, aren't they? I know you think so too, because you and I are the same... Nature has always existed with a little chaos in it; disorder to balance out the order....*
>
> *I want to do more in our Special Studies lessons together – something to really push the boundaries of my powers, of everything.*
>
> *Please, Dr Bane, I promise I won't tell...*

If Cas and Warrior thought the Master's second letter sounded frantic, it was nothing compared to the third.

This one had been written mere months before the Master of All left Wayward School at sixteen years old:

> Bane,
> So, this is how it's going to be, is it?
> This'll probably be the last you'll hear from me. I've outgrown this wretched school, the silly Grand Council, the rules of nature they're stupid enough to protect. You know who I am, what I am, what I aim to achieve...
> Don't try to stop me.
> If you involve the Grand Council, you'll have to explain the part you played ...
> I will tell everyone your secret. The one you're willing to do anything to protect.
> Aeurdan

Stuffed behind this last letter were news articles and magazine clippings of the Master of All's succeeding attacks:

MYSTERIOUS MURDER OF TOP-SECRET GRAND COUNCIL ARTEFACT CURATOR: 107-YEAR-OLD ALBERTICUS ENIGMA FOUND DEAD

THREE MORE SCHOLARS KIDNAPPED ON KAHO'OLAWE ISLAND

Madman Or Monster: Threadologist Monks in Nepal Disappear in Violent Circumstances

As the foreboding final bell tolled, Cas roughly shoved the letter and clippings back into the stack. Warrior's papers were more of the same. A timeline of the Master of All's stint at Wayward, from a scared Wayone, to an overly enthusiastic, dewy-eyed Waythree, to a threatening Waysix who left the school to terrorise the Balance Lands. Crumpled in front of them were also notes from other teachers about Aeurdan; glowing progress reports about his incredible talents, with no idea of what he would one day become.

Sadly, there was no indication where Bane had gone this time.

Unsettled, Cas stuffed everything back into the drawer and resolutely slammed it shut. He had changed his mind. He didn't want to think about the Master of All after all. Every time he did, his chest tightened and the walls closed in around him. He felt himself spiralling at the thought of everything the Master had done: murdering his own mother and robbing everyone in the fifth Order of their powers – and what the Master was still doing: wreaking havoc and kidnapping people who he thought could help him learn how to steal the remaining powers.

The only way this horror would end was if Cas could stop him.

But Cas didn't know how. He didn't know if he could.

"Let's eat," said Warrior, seemingly as equally spooked as he was. As they passed by the strange, glowing cabinets, Cas couldn't help casting a final glance at the object he was still most drawn to: the small glowing orb with the spinning metal rings.

Down in the dining hall, any lingering thoughts of the Master of All melted away when Cas saw the splendid spectacle that awaited them.

Surprisingly, the table in the middle of the room wasn't set for three. Instead, all of the tables in the room had been shoved together in a mismatched hotchpotch, and almost every teacher and several students and their families sat crowded around them.

"Happy Waywardmas!" Mrs Crane called, practically buoyant with excitement. "I invited a few friends!"

A pleasant feeling like hot honey flooded through Cas as he looked around the table. Fenix was spending Christmas in Balance Ireland, but Paws and her mothers sat grinning at them from one end of the table, whilst Professors Everglade and Breezy sat perched under the mistletoe at the other end, pecking each other like chickens. Madame Aster was there, swigging a large glass of whisky as sour as her demeanour and talking to the Earthshaper High Councillor. And next to them were Neerja and Akash

Gill, chatting animatedly to Quinnberley Crestbourne, her younger siblings and her father, who was on a pair of crutches.

"Happy Waywardmas, Dewey!" Cas called as he passed the Earthshaper boy.

Dewey Cricket gave a massive bucktoothed grin. "And a happy Waytide to you too, Casander!"

As Warrior went to say hello to Bracken Moonstrike and Ellie Green, Cas settled himself down at the table, his eyes bulging in delight.

This, he decided, had to be his favourite Balance Lands tradition.

All the elements of a typical Christmas feast were laid before him, but not in the ordinary Normie fashion.

There was a centrepiece of a fat chocolate-orange turkey, surrounded by stuffing-filled satsumas and vanilla ice cream, roast chicken jelly and sprinkles. Steaming bowls of buttered toffee potatoes in glistening, gooey caramel sauce sat astride plates of peppermint broccoli, marzipan prawns, gingerbread peas and sugar cookie paté. There were savoury batter puddings stuffed like mince pies and mince pies stuffed with sprouts. Jars upon jars of whipped bread sauce, pourable eggnog and fudgy hot cocoa lined the perimeter. Nearest Cas, there were dishes holding chestnut-coated candy canes and gravy drizzle tart beside a rainbow-coloured cheeseboard. When he snaffled a few morsels, he discovered each wheel of cheddar and brie tasted like a different variety of sweets – sherbet lemons, strawberry laces, rhubarb and custards, liquorice and wine gums.

Within minutes, everyone had tucked in.

"Happy Waywardmas, Cas," whispered Mrs Crane, sidling up to him after his fifth slice of gravy tart.

Cas wiped his gloop-stained mouth. "And a Happy Waytide to you too."

He realized this was the proper reply.

Mrs Crane quirked an eyebrow. "Where did you and Warrior disappear to earlier?"

The lump of tart became lodged in Cas's throat. "Oh, um … nowhere." He choked. "Warrior was just giving me my present on a Waywardmas hunt."

Cas felt awful for lying to Mrs Crane, but technically it was the truth. They *had* been looking for Cas's Christmas present. He had simply omitted that they had gone poking around Dr Bane's office, too.

"Well, this clue might lead you to a certain something hidden under your bed," said Mrs Crane conspiratorially, slipping him a lumpy envelope under the table.

Cas glanced up at her. "But that's not – I haven't—"

"Oh, shush. Don't for even a second think about refusing it because you haven't got me a present. This Christmas with you is the happiest I've ever seen our Warrior. That's gift enough for me. Don't go and open it now. Later. Warrior can see, but I don't want anyone else getting jealous."

Later that evening, after the dinner plates had been scraped clean and everyone's hearts (not to mention their stomachs) were full, Cas snuck upstairs to the Attic to open Mrs Crane's gift.

Dear Cas, its label read.

> *Merry Waywardmas!*
> *Well done for surviving your first term at Wayward School! I hope you like your gift. I made it from one of Dr Bane's old Deathmaker cloaks and my old Lifemaker one. I used to wear it all the time as the school nurse – but you have more use for it than I do now.*
> *Wear it proudly!*
> *Your friend,*
> *Mrs Crane*

Cas delicately drew out the soft gift. A velvety half purple, half white cloak slid between his fingers. The symbol of the fifth Order – a snow-white bird and jet-black raven entangled mid-flight – was sewn onto the breast pocket.

Cas balked.

Purple-and-white cloaks were the signature look of the Master of All and his Heretics. He couldn't wear this.

But then he noticed a tiny tweed heart hand-stitched on the inside of the cloak. And, whereas the Heretics' cloaks were mainly purple with white thread running across the fabric in swirling patterns, one half of Cas's cloak was solid purple, while the other half was solid white.

Mrs Crane had fashioned him his own look. A way for Cas to reclaim the identity that the Master had stolen from all of the Lifemakers and Deathmakers.

A second realization hit then.

Mrs Crane used to be a Lifemaker.

How had he never thought about her Order before?

He supposed Mrs Crane being an ex-Lifemaker nurse made much more sense than her being a librarian who just happened to keep a stash of candy-flavoured cough syrup behind her desk during flu season.

Slipping it on, Cas buttoned up the new cloak beneath his old, tatty Deathmaker one and returned to the festivities below.

Christmas dinner at Wayward had turned into a full-on Waywardmas shindig now, with everyone jigging and jiving to Professor Everglade on the guitar and Professor Breezy bellowing out renditions of "O Come All Ye Wayful".

Feeling lighter than if he had been borne aloft by an Airscaper's wind, Cas joined in.

CHAPTER 15
THE MINI QUESTIAL

THAT NIGHT, CAS WENT TO BED MORE TIRED AND content than he thought possible.

As he drifted off, he could think of nothing but continuing the festivities the next day. Warrior had told him that Boxmas (the Balance Lands version of a cross between Waywardmas and Boxing Day) involved twenty-four fantastic hours of stuffing their faces with leftovers and slouching about the Attic in their comfiest pyjamas, seeing who could move the least.

But by the next morning, the happy illusion had been shattered to smithereens.

"Cas, come quickly!" shouted Warrior, bursting into the Attic in a frenzy and shaking Cas awake. "Nurse's Quarters! Now!"

Before she could explain, Warrior launched herself

down the secret slide leading to the library, Cas scrambling in hot pursuit.

Instantly, his mind flew to the worst possible conclusions. Who was in the hospital? Fenix? Paws? Mrs Crane? Had Dr Bane been injured tracking the Master?

His heart simultaneously swooped and sank at the sight of Dewey Cricket's strawberry-blond head poking out from behind a drawn bed curtain in the Nurse's Quarters.

The airy room was so fraught with tension that Cas could have sliced it with a knife. Upon entering, Cas and Warrior nimbly nipped behind the bed hangings. Mr and Mrs Cricket sat pale and grave on either side of Dewey, but neither looked anywhere near as pale as their son. Dewey lay curled on the bed, shivering feverishly under a mound of blankets. Even his brightly coloured hair seemed to have dulled with shock.

"What happened?" Cas gaped.

Mr and Mrs Cricket remained silent, stroking Dewey's clammy hand, whilst Mrs Crane sponged his forehead. They were all still wearing their nightclothes and Mrs Cricket was missing one of her slippers.

Warrior thrust a copy of *The Threadly Times* towards Cas. "The newspapers are already reporting on it."

With a sickening wave of dread, Cas scanned the front page:

O Violent Night: Wayward Woes as Heretics Attack

He didn't even need to read the full article to get the gist.

According to the newspaper, a bunch of merry revellers had been stumbling home from a late night spent celebrating at the Gnome's Garden pub, when they had witnessed another breach on the wards around Wayward Town. Their accounts were all the same. A troupe of purple-and-white-hooded figures, led by one man in a silver mask, had attacked a patrol of wardsmen on the east boundary between shift changes. The guards had been ambushed, bound and gagged, before the Heretics ravaged and rampaged their way down Newbusy Avenue, setting fire to The Arcadia and vandalizing The Terranical Terrace. Five wardsmen were seriously injured. Two were now missing.

But by the time the Grand Council and reinforcements had arrived, the Heretics were gone. Whether deeper into or out of Wayward Town, nobody knew.

Cas's heart fluttered wildly. The whole room danced and he felt his forehead sweat as much as Dewey's. He glanced from Warrior to Mrs Crane, seeing his own panic reflected on their faces.

As if he could sense Cas was about to look at him next, Dewey Cricket spoke.

"He found me," Dewey gasped in a voice less than a ghost, less than a whisper, of his usual bubbly tone.

Cas didn't need to ask who he meant.

"He – he had hair like soot and eyes of flame. He s-sounded like a hungry wolf when he growled my name. He wanted to leave a message with someone who went to Wayward School. So he knew it would get to the right person: *Tell him. Tell him there's nowhere to run. He's mine.*"

Cas's mind flashed back to the homeless stranger he had met outside Captain Caeli's Cakery. To the ominous feeling of being watched in the Earthshaper woods. To the wards going off on his second night.

Despite everyone's best efforts, it seemed it was no longer a secret that Cas was at Wayward School.

This time there was no denying it.

The Master of All was coming for Cas.

Fear dogged Cas's steps all week – but it wasn't just him who had been scared by the latest breach.

New Year's Eve in Wayward was a much quieter affair than usual. Normally, Warrior informed him, the streets were buzzing with bright colours and the shrieks of laughter from Life and Deathmaker celebrations. But this year, a new curfew had been put in place. Everyone had to be in their homes by sundown and more wardsmen than ever were brought in to patrol the empty streets by dusk. The Wayward residents were forced to settle for watching an extravagant Firetamer display high above the town from their windows. Cas and Warrior observed the bangs and whistles of exploding rockets from the Attic, occasionally *ooh*-ing and *aah*-ing as two Firetamers made a great flaming cat chase a tiny glowing mouse across the black canvas of the night sky.

Up in the Attic, the Master of All felt very far away.

But everything changed when school started again.

The Grand Council had decided it would be safest for all of the Wayward School students to start boarding in the dorms once more, claiming that they would be much safer all grouped together within the school's wards.

"It's just a precaution," High Councillor Hephaestus announced.

Only Cas wasn't stupid. He and everyone else knew what the Grand Council's actions truly meant. They were scared too.

Trunk-laden students started flooding through Wayward School's wrought-iron gates in droves. Security was tightened. Wardsmen were deployed to monitor the school's boundary and a few were stationed in the odd hallway or corridor. Even Mrs Crane took to sleeping on a camping chair outside the Attic's entrance, armed with her trusty firefly lantern and feather duster.

Yet rather than being concerned with missing their parents, or the fact that any of them could be harmed – or Cas could be, you know, *killed* – all anyone seemed to be worried about was whether the Master's attack would mean something called the Mini Questial would still go ahead.

"What's the Mini Questial?" enquired Cas, sitting down at breakfast with the others. It had been less than a day since Wayward School had turned into one gigantic sleepover, but he was already sick to the back teeth with hearing about the mysterious event and not knowing what it was.

He was surprised when Warrior answered. Since she had seen the Du Villaines' butler lugging their suitcases up the entrance hall's stairs, she had sworn she was going on silent protest for the next week and homework protest for the next two.

"Dits swimple weally," said Warrior through a mouthful of jammy toast. "The Questial is a big, global competition in the Balance Lands that the Grand Council puts on once a decade. There's a ballot and each country selected can put forward a team of school students to compete. It consists of a series of challenges in a race across the world, designed to test competitors' wit and Order abilities, with prizes up for grabs. Plus the usual tosh, such as honour, fame … blah, blah, blah."

"But the real reason the Grand Council organizes it," Paws chipped in, "is because they use it as a way to seek out the most powerful, up-and-coming Others who they might want to join their ranks in the future."

"The Mini Questial, on the other hand," added Fenix, "is a smaller version of the Questial. Wayward School holds it once a year. It's, erm, like a special sports day. There's one relay race with four sections – each containing a challenge relating to one of the main Orders: earth, air, water and fire – and anyone can participate if you have a team of four to compete. We, um, use it to practise until the next real Questial comes around. Teachers can figure out who they might want to put forward and parents come along and watch."

"Awesome," said Cas, his eyes shining. "How do we enter?"

Warrior spat out her next bite of toast and Fenix choked on his juice.

"We," said Paws in a small voice, "don't."

Cas couldn't believe his ears. "Why not?"

"Firstly," said Warrior, listing off the points on her fingers, "the Mini Questial's relay consists of four challenges based around earth, air, water and fire. Therefore, it only makes sense that the four members of your team are an Earthshaper, an Airscaper, a Wavebreaker and a Firetamer."

"OK," said Cas, mulling this over. "We've all still got powers, though. We'll just have to think outside the box."

"Secondly, Lifemakers and Deathmakers have never really been allowed to compete. Others belonging to the fifth Order are rare. The teachers don't want to risk any of them drowning or being burnt to a crisp."

"Not to mention, um, when there were Deathmakers and the like in seventh year, they could, well, almost kill people," said Fenix, taking another tentative sip of juice.

"It's fine. I'll persuade Hopeless Higgles to let me join

in," said Cas. "Besides, there's no risk of that, Fenix. I can't even knock someone out cold, let alone kill them!"

"And thirdly—" Warrior started to say, before she was rudely and snootily cut off.

"You don't stand a chance." The malicious, snarky tone of Sam Du Villaine's voice split the air behind them.

Cas, Warrior, Paws and Fenix swung around in their seats to face him.

"Don't tell me they're thinking about entering?" scoffed Lucille, appearing at her brother's side. She tossed her long, silver hair over her shoulder and covered her button nose to suppress a snigger. "You embarrass yourselves enough on a daily basis by being Abnormies."

"We don't need you lot turning the Mini Questial into a freak show."

"Not to mention you'd lose anyway."

They both howled with laughter as they took their breakfast trays over to their table, the one furthest away from where the teachers ate, so that they couldn't be caught flinging toast crusts at the back of Wayones' heads.

"That's it," said Cas, slamming his spoon down on the table. "We're entering."

Warrior's hair flashed the angriest shade of red Cas had ever seen. She ripped off a bite of bread like a rabid animal in agreement.

"I don't care if we come last," Cas said. "Or don't finish at all. We're doing this. I'm not going to sit on the sidelines and watch the Du Villaines win because we were too scared to enter. Whatever it takes, we're going to prove them wrong."

The Mini Questial took place exactly three weeks later.

On a crisp February morning, the whole school marched down to the boating lake, where towering stands full of seats for parents and staff were packed to the brim.

Entering hadn't been easy.

It had taken Cas an entire day and a half to persuade Headmaster Higgles to let him compete. Only after plying Higgles with persuasive phrases like "think how good it will look to show off the Foretold to the parents after the latest attacks" and "how can I hope to defeat the Master if I don't compete in the Mini Questial?" and "yes, sir, of course I'll come and sing at your birthday party next weekend" were they in.

Cas, Warrior, Paws and Fenix submitted their entry as a team of four to Madame Aster with one minute to spare before the deadline.

For once, she didn't give them a snooty remark or smug smirk. She looked positively thrilled.

"Probably thinks at least one of us will get offed in some way," Warrior muttered bitterly.

Yet as Dr Bane and Mrs Crane escorted the Abnormies down the sloping lawns towards the steadily swelling crowd, Cas couldn't help thinking Aster might not be wrong.

For the past few weeks, the Wavebreakers' boathouse and the Earthshapers' woods had been out of bounds, meaning all Special Studies classes were postponed. Cas wasn't sure who this had upset more: the Wavebreakers, who had to sleep with the Firetamers down in the sweaty Kiln; the Mini Questial competitors, who could only wildly imagine what tasks lay ahead; or Puggle the Nuggle, who, deprived of his usual pranking ground, had taken to paddling around the moat surrounding the school and bucking out at the ground-floor classroom windows in protest.

Cas himself had worked extra hard in his last few Special Studies lessons with Dr Bane, determined to hone his powers as much as possible. It felt like the contents of *The Book of Skulls and Skin* was practically plastered onto his eyeballs.

But would it be enough? What if he failed as the Foretold in front of all these people? Or let the other Abnormies down?

"Take care out there," said Dr Bane, eyeing them all with the greatest concern in the world. "Especially you, Cas."

"And make sure you whoop the other teams' buttocks!" cheered Mrs Crane, punching the air excitedly.

Dr Bane and Mrs Crane took their seats in the front

row and Cas felt the vice-like grip on his stomach loosen slightly. The Abnormies hugged each other, wishing one another luck.

We aren't doing this to win, Cas reminded himself. *We're doing this for everyone who is like us. Everyone who is different, who doesn't think they belong.*

"Are we clear on the plan?" said Cas, as they gave each other one last squeeze.

They nodded, broke apart and split off to their respective start lines.

The exact nature of the Mini Questial tasks had been kept secret until today, but the order of the legs of the race had been released to the competitors last night.

Like Fenix had said, the Mini Questial was a relay race with four stages. Each one consisted of a different Order challenge.

The first leg was a twenty-metre sprint over hot coals. The aim was for the Firetamer in each team to extinguish the flames heating the coals so they could pass the relay baton on to the second team member.

The second leg consisted of an open-top passage with Professor Breezy standing at the far end. It was Breezy's job to manipulate the air to create a blustery wind tunnel. The second team member would either have to struggle through or bend the air away from them, thus freeing up their path to pass the baton to the third team member.

The third leg was the Wavebreaker one: the third

team member had to somehow cross the lake to reach their fourth teammate, who would be standing ready on a pontoon.

Once the fourth team member had the baton, they would have to loop back towards the original start line at the boathouse and complete the fourth task: scaling a smooth, steep hill, before sliding down the other side and crossing the finish line. The idea here was that the Earthshaper in each team would speed up their ascent by using their powers to create hand and footholds in the mud.

Fenix would go first, followed by Cas, Paws and finally Warrior.

Cas took a deep breath and readied himself at the Airscaper post.

"I can't wait to see you fall flat on your face, Freak Mould," drawled Sam Du Villaine, limbering up beside him.

Cas gritted his teeth. "Not if you fall first."

Sam was the only Du Villaine taking part. A quick glance around revealed that Maxwell Snout was the Firetamer in Sam's team, whilst Quinnberley Crestbourne was the Wavebreaker and Aubria was the Earthshaper. Lucille was sitting stiff as a rod in the stands between her parents. They were being jostled from side to side by the chattering crowd, who were enraptured by today's commentator, Professor Vulcan, regaling them with tales of his glory days as a famous Flameball player.

"I played sniper for the Wayward Whimsies, you know," Professor Vulcan told them. "Fifteen times unbeaten Balance Lands Flameball World Champions. After that, I coached the Wayward Whippersnappers Junior Division. Of course, I understand why they banned the sport when all the Lifemakers lost their powers—"

Behind them, Cas spotted Paws's parents waving a brightly coloured, hand-painted sign bearing the words: GO WAPAWFENCAS!

Cas snorted as Professor Vulcan stood and cleared his throat into a megaphone.

"Competitors," Vulcan addressed them. "Take your positions!"

All of the competitors lined up on their start lines. The crowd fell silent. Headmaster Higgles, Dr Bane, Mrs Crane and even a reporter covering the event for *The Threadly Times* leaned forward on the edge of their seats.

"On your marks," Professor Vulcan boomed. "Get set…"

The whistle blew.

"GOOOO!"

Like lightning, the six Firetamers, one from each team, shot off the start blocks and headed towards the hot coals.

"And they're off!" Professor Vulcan narrated. "Five of our first team members have already reached the first obstacle, *the callous coals*." He spoke in a particularly sinister voice. "And they're now attempting to quell the flames. Who among them will succeed?"

Every Firetamer except Fenix skidded to a stop where the stretch of coals began and proceeded to whirl their hands around in strange motions, painting invisible shapes in the air. "Nice wrist movement from McClusky," said Vulcan. "He's really working well to control those flames; so is Snout ... not so much Tsang ... but what's this—"

After a moment of stage fright, Fenix erupted in a roar of flames and tore past the others onto the track.

"We've got a rogue one!"

Dashing like he'd been fired out of a slingshot, Fenix ran across the scorching surface, completely immune to the heat at his feet. The hot, sooty rocks were nothing compared to the licks of red and gold that flickered on his skin.

"I don't believe it, Embershade has taken the lead!"

Cas grinned widely as he realized that the fire from Fenix's human-torch-like powers was *refeeding* the fire beneath the coals, giving them a gigantic head start, as the other Firetamers had to work twice as hard to calm the inferno.

"Embershade has come from the back and is ahead, five skips in front, ten skips, twenty ... that'll really take some catching up to beat..."

Fenix slapped the relay baton into Cas's outstretched hand before two of the Firetamers had even started across the coals.

They were in *first place*.

Cas launched himself into the wind tunnel, but Breezy's

gust was so strong that it immediately pushed him back out again. Cas shielded his face with his arm in a useless attempt at a buffer, but as he tried to surge forward again, his funny leg threw itself into a spasming action.

Helpless, he watched Maxwell Snout hand the baton to Sam Du Villaine, who pushed back Professor Breezy's onslaught of air with a single swish of his hand and ran through the tunnel to hand the baton to Quinnberley.

"In a heart-pounding turn of events, the lead has been stolen by Du Villaine," Vulcan declared. "Darkbloom will have to do better than that…"

Do something, Cas thought, as yet another Airscaper streaked past him, curling Professor Breezy's wind around them with ease. *But what?*

"Zunter slips into second!" cried Professor Vulcan.

Think, Cas. Think.

Cas's powers were useless against an Airscaper's blustery gale. Not to mention, the only thing that he had confidently mastered was temporarily taking someone's sight away.

Ah-ha! he thought. *But I only need to distract one person.*

Cas lowered his arm and focused all his attention on Professor Breezy, who raised his own arms, ready to send another mighty gust of wind Cas's way.

"Okuli," he murmured, imagining a dense black blindfold covering the professor's eyes.

It worked. For a split second, Professor Breezy faltered.

252

"My sight!" whined Professor Breezy, rubbing at his face. "I can't see anything!"

"Oh, look. What's this?" Professor Vulcan's deep voice speculated, as the crowd gasped in surprise at Cas's unexpected move.

The wind died just long enough for Cas to escape the tunnel and slap the baton into Paws's hand.

"Darkbloom's back in the game!"

Cas smiled wider, glimpsing Professor Breezy over his shoulder and returning his vision in time for Breezy to throw another bombardment of air towards Cas's rivals. Two lagging Airscapers became trapped in the wind tunnel once more.

"Your turn, Paws," said Cas, panting.

The girl nodded.

Cas had never seen Paws use her powers in person before. He jumped in shock when her eyes rolled back in her head and she slumped forward, utterly still, in the seat of her wheelchair. But suddenly Mogget, the mangy cat sleeping around her neck, leapt up on all fours and waved her paw at Cas.

"See you at the finish line," said Paws through Mogget's mouth.

Inside the cat's body, Paws picked up the baton in her gummy mouth and dived into the lake.

"Crestbourne is charging ahead," Vulcan called. "Look at that Wavebreaker go!"

Cas observed Quinnberley Crestbourne running across the lake's surface as if it was solid ground. But Mogget was unexpectedly fast as she paddled through the water, edging towards Warrior on the pontoon.

"Ha ha!" chuckled Vulcan. "It looks like a soggy moggy has entered the race! Who's carrying the cat kibble?"

"*Ew!* I'm allergic to cats!" squealed one of the Wayfive Wavebreakers, spotting Mogget swimming on the wave above where she was cleaving a dry path through the lake. The distraction caused the Wayfive to break her focus and the parted water came crashing down, soaking her where she stood.

"*ASSISTANCE!*" Vulcan shouted loudly, as the Wayfive spluttered and flailed, suckered into the squelchy lakebed.

"Kids these days," grumbled Madame Aster, striding down from the stands to cleave the water away, before dragging the Wayfive to safety.

"And it looks like the moggy has reached the pontoon!" Vulcan returned to commentating on the race.

Cas whooped when he saw Paws transfer the baton to Warrior.

"Only Snout and Heatherby are ahead of Bane … it's going to be a tight one…"

They were in third place.

They only had the Earthshaper challenge to go.

Warrior reached the smooth, steep hill in front of

the boathouse a long time after the other two. Both of the Earthshapers were ripping chunks of soil out of the mound to create footholds by clenching their fists in mid-air. Aubria Snout was almost at the top, with the other Earthshaper about halfway up.

"Do something!" Cas called over to Warrior. "Use your powers. Think outside the box!"

Bewildered blankness crossed Warrior's face for a second, before her eyes sparkled with a devilish new idea. She squinted and concentrated hard on the hill, the ends of her hair turning the mischievous shade of orange that meant something brilliant and terrible was about to happen.

The hill gave a great shudder.

Aubria was caught off guard and one of her hands lost its grip, but somehow she managed to cling on. The hill shuddered again. This time, three ginormous holes opened in the earthy surface as clumps of mud and rock plummeted to the ground. Two eyes and a hungry mouth appeared as the hill grew a terrifying face.

Warrior smirked. Picking the edge of the hill furthest away from its mouth, she started to climb.

"What an interesting turn of events!" exclaimed Vulcan.

"It's not real, Aubria!" yelled Sam from his place next to Cas by the lake. "It's just another one of her silly, useless illusions!"

But Cas wasn't so sure.

He knew that some of Warrior's illusions were nothing more than imagination and vapour, but some of them felt real. They *were* almost real. They could think and feel and physically interact with the real world themselves. They simply didn't possess a "real" body.

As Cas watched the hill's wide eyes latch on to the struggling Earthshaper boy halfway down and its mouth open to gobble him up, he hoped it was the former. From what he had seen of Hobdogglin whenever Warrior tossed him the odd boiled sweet or crumpled-up homework sheet, if the hill devoured the Earthshaper, the poor boy would simply disappear from existence.

Poof!

Gone for ever.

Cas held his breath. The Earthshaper tried to scramble away from the hill's hungry mouth, before letting go in a panic and falling to the ground. Cas's heart soared in relief, but then took a dramatic nose-dive when he saw the dangling Aubria use her long, narrow frame to swing herself up. She reached the top of the hill and slid down the smooth far side at the same time as Warrior.

They were neck and neck.

Both girls threw themselves into a run, scrabbling and grappling with every body part they could...

"C'mon, Warrior!" encouraged Cas.

They were both ten paces away from the finish line … eight … six…

A thunderous round of applause exploded as the winner was crowned.

"Aubria Snout has done it. Team Du Villaine wins!"

Aubria threw her arms in the air triumphantly. Meanwhile, the dust cleared to reveal Warrior sprawled on the floor, nursing a kicked ankle, barely two paces behind. Gobsmacked and furious, she hauled herself across the finish line.

Cas supposed he should have felt the same way, but he didn't care.

They had come *second*!

With a start, he noticed the crowd weren't actually applauding for the winners. They were chanting the Abnormies' names. They were cheering for *them*.

The Du Villaines might have claimed the Mini Questial, but the Abnormies' victory was much better.

Against everyone's expectations, they had done the impossible. They had shown that they could do what everybody thought they couldn't. It was better than any placing or ribbon. For as long as Sam and Lucille lived, Cas knew they wouldn't forget this:

The Abnormies had only lost by a hair.

CHAPTER 16

THE FORBIDDEN SCUFFLE

"CHEATS!" ACCUSED THE DU VILLAINE TWINS, storming over to where Cas, Warrior, Paws and Fenix were celebrating with their supporters.

They stood huddled in a gaggle of beaming grins and giggles. Artemis Grover and Diana Rosales had raced down from the stands at the sound of the final whistle and smothered Paws in kisses, whilst Warrior was being spun around in circles by Mrs Crane, and Cas was doing a high-kicking jive with Mogget. Even the usually reserved Fenix stood on the edge of the crowd, smiling shyly and whooping.

"It's not fair!" said Sam Du Villaine angrily.

"It is too!" retorted Warrior once Mrs Crane had stopped spinning her about. "If anyone cheated, *you* did. Aubria tripped me at the finish line!"

"There's nothing in the rules that says I couldn't," Aubria spat.

"Well, there's nothing in the rules that says I can't now," growled Warrior, lunging forward.

Cas reached out and pulled her back.

"You freaks should've never been allowed to enter," snarled Lucille poisonously, glowering at the Abnormies from behind her brother. "Why do we deserve to be placed next to the likes of *you*?"

Something snapped inside Cas. "Get lost, both of you."

"Language, Casander!" reprimanded Mrs Crane, pretending to clout him on the ear.

"Sorry, Mrs Crane. Get lost, both of you, *please*."

Mrs Crane smiled. "Much better."

"Enough!" said a low, throaty voice as Headmaster Higgles blundered into view. He was hotly tailed by Mr and Mrs Du Villaine, looking furious, as well as Dr Bane, numerous spectators and the squat, spotty-faced reporter from *The Threadly Times*. "What's going on here?"

"It's them, sir," said Lucille vehemently, jabbing her finger towards the Abnormies. "They cheated. They shouldn't have been allowed to compete. It's a disgrace to the school!"

Warrior balled up her fists again, but suddenly Fenix's voice broke through the clamour.

"There's, um, nothing in the Mini Questial rules that says an Earthshaper, an Airscaper, a Wavebreaker and a Firetamer have to compete," he said, wringing his hands. "I've read the handbook cover to cover. Technically we haven't done anything wrong."

Everyone considered Fenix uncertainly for a moment, but Cas grinned warmly at his friend.

Of all the people to stand up for the Abnormies in the middle of the chaos, it was Fenix. Quiet, placid Fenix. Peacekeeping Fenix.

The King of Handbooks and Rules.

"See," said Cas, gesturing to the Firetamer boy. "We came second place, sir, fair and square."

"*Not* fine," growled Mr Du Villaine, his fingers digging so hard into his son's shoulder that Sam Du Villaine looked on the brink of tears. "Being what you are … *Abnormies* … you had an unfair advantage out there, an edge nobody else could match. Such a close result is embarrassing for our children. We demand a rematch."

"Fine." Warrior sniffed. "As long as you don't mind that we might beat you next time."

The Du Villaines froze. They clearly hadn't considered this.

Cas shot a glance towards Fenix. When Eupholous Du Villaine had used the word *Abnormies,* Fenix had shrunk back. He was hanging his head in shame, like he thought they didn't deserve their second place now too. Like he also thought he had cheated by gaining the Abnormies their massive lead in the first leg.

Cas glared at Mr and Mrs Du Villaine, his blood boiling.

He had never hated anyone more.

Mr and Mrs Du Villaine stared back at Cas and his friends with a predatory gaze. They reminded Cas of their sabre-toothed wyverkeys. *Except, no,* Cas thought, *that isn't right. They aren't like the wyverkeys; they are the sabre teeth.* All paleness, sharpness and harsh, cutting angles, from their silver hair and alabaster skin to their pointy elbows and cheekbones hewn to slice ice.

Eupholus Du Villaine was a rapidly balding man with a long, kinked handlebar moustache, whilst Yvaine Du Villaine had slick, greasy hair the colour of moonlight cascading down to her hips.

"Let it go, Eupholous," said Dr Bane defensively, stepping forward to place a fatherly hand on Warrior's shoulder. Cas recognized that the gesture wasn't simply an act of protection. Bane was holding Warrior back.

"We didn't cheat," she said again, huffily.

"We didn't, sir," concurred Cas, changing tack and looking at Headmaster Higgles imploringly. "Fenix is right. We read the rules and earned our placing. I'm the Foretold, why would I lie?"

The Du Villaines couldn't make Headmaster Higgles take their victory away. They just *couldn't*.

"Yeah," another voice joined the fray. Dewey Cricket's strawberry-blond head bobbed into view as he stepped out from the spectators that had gathered from the school. "Cas is right. I've read the rules too."

"And me," said Bracken Moonstrike.

"And me," agreed Neerja Gill.

"Me too," chipped in Laula Spinks.

Too many other *"and me"*s echoed out for Cas to count. Their fellow students were supporting the Abnormies' claim to second place. Clearly they wanted to see the Du Villaines knocked down a peg as much as Cas did.

Headmaster Higgles let out a bellowing belly laugh, as if this had all been one big jest. "Of course I believe you, my man." He slapped Cas hard on the shoulder. "I just had to indulge the Du Villaines' complaint for formality's sake. Well done on second place!"

The crowd around them cheered. Headmaster Higgles smacked his hands together and declared, "Now who wants to wander back up to the school for a spot of tea and some boulder cakes? I hear Professor Everglade has prepared some specially."

As one, the gathering of teachers, students and parents departed, until only Cas, the Abnormies and the Du Villaines remained.

"Despicable." Mr and Mrs Du Villaine shot a filthy look at their children, before tilting their chins haughtily and flouncing off, *The Threadly Times* reporter scrambling in their wake.

For a moment, Cas nearly felt sorry for the twins.

Then Sam opened his mouth.

"You're … *Abnormies*," Sam sneered. "It's embarrassing. We didn't deserve to win next to the likes of you. The Mini

Questial isn't for *your* kind; it's for us – *proper* Others."

"What was the point of this?" said Lucille. "They aren't going to let people like you compete when the next real Questial comes around."

"A once-in-a-decade event," mused Cas, tapping his chin. "Sounds exactly like something I'd love to be a part of. Maybe we'll even end up on a team with you."

It went without saying that the thought of doing anything with the Du Villaines made Cas want to be sick. But he knew his comment would rile them.

"Today we proved we're just as worthy as you," he concluded, before they could get another malicious word in edgeways.

Sam scoffed. "You didn't prove anything. The Snouts and that ridiculous Crestbourne girl were slowing me down."

"Why weren't *you* competing?" said Warrior, turning her attention to Lucille.

Lucille blanched. Cas still hadn't told anyone that he had caught her staring at the Airscaper training aids at Christmas, but as her eyes flashed to his, he knew they were both thinking about it.

"Th-there was only one Airscaper spot, Abnormies," stammered Lucille.

"I'm sure you could've been creative," said Warrior. "We were. Or are you Airscapers by name, air-headed by nature?"

This seemed to strike a nerve.

"I want a rematch," said Sam, moving so he and Cas were facing off against each other. "Tonight. Meet me in the Airscaper training room in the Sky Tower. Nine o'clock. Riff-Raff can be your partner, unless you'd rather replace her with Furball or Phoenix Boy over there."

"My partner?" said Cas, trying not to sound too puzzled.

"I challenge you to a Scuffle. A double Other duel."

Paws and Fenix gasped. Even Warrior sucked in a sharp breath.

"You can't," whispered Paws, tugging on Cas's sleeve. "Scuffles are forbidden, even outside of Wayward."

Cas shook her off. "You're on."

He refused to back down to Sam, who smirked. "Let's settle who the real winners are, once and for all."

Waiting for the clock tower bells to chime nine that evening felt like an eternity.

Cas wasted away the hours pacing the length of the Attic, trying to stay firm about not wimping out. He didn't know what a Scuffle was exactly, but it must be some kind of fight as Sam had called it a "duel".

Paws and Fenix weren't helping matters.

"Don't do this," urged Paws. "What's the point? We've already proved ourselves to everyone today, including the Du Villaines. They're probably just trying to get you in trouble."

"There are wardsmen patrolling the corridors now," said Fenix. "Even if they don't catch you in the middle of a, erm, dangerous Scuffle and throw you in Nowhere Prison, you might still get caught out of bed after hours."

"Getting expelled will only make it easier for the Master of All to find you."

"No Wayward, no wards. No protection."

"What good will that do the rest of us, then?"

But when the bells tolled, Cas stopped repeatedly fastening and unfastening his new cloak and looked at Warrior. "Ready to go?"

She nodded. "Beating the Du Villaines will feel like Waywardmas has come early this year."

The second-floor corridor was eerily deserted when they emerged from the spiral staircase. An eight o'clock curfew for students to be in their dorms was in place, so stalking along the hall in the shadows felt like entering a sinister spectral plane. There wasn't another soul to be seen. They crept past a snoozing Mrs Crane and stuck close to the walls. The stone floor was ice cold beneath Cas and Warrior's bare feet. They had taken their shoes off so their footfalls wouldn't be heard, but every now and then the looming shadow of a tree branch or the howling wind rattling the windowpanes made them hold their breath, waiting to be caught.

Cas hoped that if they were, he wouldn't be expelled. He was the Foretold. That had to count for something.

But he also knew that relying on being the Chosen One to offer him any kind of protection was extremely arrogant.

They crouched in a sliver of impenetrable gloom outside the Calligraphy and Cartography classroom and waited until one of the wardsmen had passed, before sneaking down the marble steps to the entrance hall. From there, they headed east until they reached the Sky Tower: a tall turret that disappeared into the cloudy night sky above. The unlocked door groaned open with a gentle shove. After putting their shoes back on, Cas and Warrior headed towards the training room.

Without warning, something moved in the blackness.

"Quinnberley?"

Cas jumped as the Wavebreaker prodigy appeared out of thin air. Dressed in a periwinkle cloak, she held a firefly lantern up to her face and pressed a trembling finger to her lips. "What are you doing here?"

Quinnberley Crestbourne didn't say anything for a moment, as if she was warring with herself about whether she should. Then at last, she murmured, "I came to warn you."

Cas sucked in a quick breath. "Warn us? About what?"

"Nothing," said Warrior scornfully, swatting the girl's lantern down. "Can't you see it's a trick? She's one of *them*."

But Quinnberley shook her head, panic and fear swelling in her glassy, tear-filled eyes.

"No, please, listen," she pleaded, her voice splintering. "Don't go in there. It's a trap."

"Trap?" said Cas, confused. "It's not a trap. We agreed to meet Sam and Lucille for one of those things. A Scuffle."

Quinnberley kept shaking her head. "It's not just them," she choked out. "They've got Maxwell and Aubria with them ... they think *The Threadly Times* are going to write something awful about them after the Mini Questial, so they want to make you pay ... they tried to get me to help too..." She burst into tears, her gulping, snotty sobs echoing around the room. If the Du Villaines hadn't known Cas and Warrior were already here, they certainly must now. "I – I don't want to hurt you ... it's not a fair fight ... you're going to lose..."

"Don't worry," said Cas soothingly. "We won't tell them you warned us."

Warrior caught Cas's eye. "Yeah, thanks, Quinnberley," she muttered. "But we're doing this. You should lay low for a while, stay away from the Du Villaines and the Snouts."

Quinnberley swallowed hard, sniffling and blowing her dripping nose on the corner of her sleeve.

"Good luck," she whispered, finally stepping back from the entrance. Then, just like an ocean tide ebbing away, Quinnberley was gone.

Warrior swore. "Those whatsit-munchers," she said,

once they were alone in enemy territory once more. Hobdogglin appeared from nowhere at her side, growling.

She was ready for a fight.

Cas couldn't even bring himself to sigh. He should've expected as much from the Du Villaines.

They nudged open the training room's door.

"Ah, well, well," crooned Sam Du Villaine's voice, "the Abnormie freaks have arrived at last."

The Airscaper training room was a circular room, with padded mats on the floor, as well as targets and faceless dummies set up for practice.

Lucille took one look at Hobdogglin and cringed. Cas knew that the quirky illusion was a sore spot for her. Many times, Warrior had sent the creature nipping at the twins' heels between classes, and he supposed that kind of torture was hard to forget.

"You're late," said Lucille pettily, pretending Hobdogglin wasn't there.

"And you're pathetic," said Cas, gesturing towards Maxwell and Aubria Snout cracking their knuckles beside the twins. "Scared to face us without your cronies? Four on two isn't exactly a fair fight."

"We can still beat you, though," said Warrior, making sure they knew.

A muscle twitched in Sam's jaw.

"We only brought them along as back-up," said Lucille, jumping in to defend her brother. "In case you decided to pull any tricks on us. We know what you Abnormies are like."

But Warrior had heard enough.

"Look, it doesn't matter how many minions you have," she said. "You can have the whole Airscaper Order behind you for all I care. Are we doing this or not?"

Sam and Lucille exchanged a stony look, as if speaking some secret telepathic twin language only they understood.

They stepped forward and readied themselves, waving the Snouts back.

Cas and Warrior did the same.

Sam Du Villaine begrudgingly stuck out his hand.

"Shake it," said Warrior, elbowing Cas. "It's proper Scuffling etiquette."

Cas screwed up his face. "I actually have to *touch* him?"

Nevertheless, the boys shook hands. Both of them withdrew sharply after three shakes, as if they had touched something slimy in the kitchen sink.

Not taking their eyes off their opponents, the duos strode backwards five steps.

"Are you ready?" whispered Warrior. "On three, we attack. One ... two..."

"Are we going *on* three or *after* three?" Cas hissed.

Before he got an answer, his body was hit by an enormous rush of wind that sent him flying into the stone wall. He slammed against it and slumped to the floor.

"Three!" shouted Warrior.

She threw her hands forward and Hobdogglin lunged, teeth bared and yapping at the twins. Sam waved his hand almost lazily and blew Hobdogglin aside with another whip of air. The imaginary creature vanished through the back wall in smoky, mist-like wisps.

"Is that all you've got, Freak Mould?" taunted Sam.

Cas's bones ached but he pushed himself to his feet. "You wish," he said. *"Okuli."* He narrowed his eyes and focused on slipping the invisible blindfold over the pale boy.

For a moment, it worked. Sam stumbled back a few paces, grappling at his eyes, whilst Lucille fussed over him, trying to help. But as Cas stepped towards them, ready to capture Lucille under his power too, the fuzzy, tingling feeling started up in his leg and spread to his arm. He couldn't control his movements. His knee buckled and he threw his hand out against a dummy to brace himself.

His funny leg made Cas's concentration slip and Sam broke free from his spell.

"Why, you—"

Lucille flung her hands towards Cas, who felt nothing more than a gentle breeze curl around his ankles, feebly trying to bring him down, before Sam pushed her aside and redirected his attention to Warrior instead. The flimsy targets pinned to the training room's walls fluttered as the air rose and swirled around Sam in a vortex. With a flick of his wrist, he sent the whirlwind barrelling towards

Warrior. It snatched her up and she rose several metres off the ground, spinning wildly.

Just then, Hobdogglin reappeared through the far wall and sank his teeth into Sam's leg.

"Get off!" hollered Sam, shaking his limb.

Hobdogglin didn't let go. The creature growled and pulled Sam to the floor, pinning him in place. Sam's focus broke and Warrior dropped to the ground as the miniature hurricane died. Aubria and Maxwell sprang forward to help, but Cas's funny leg had stopped and he focused his attention on them.

"Muskuli," he muttered under his breath, directing his power.

The Snout siblings froze like stone statues, their muscles rigid. The only one still standing, Lucille's gaze flew between Cas and Warrior.

"Give up," said Cas, regaining his stability and walking over. "We've won."

Sam, though, wasn't prepared to admit defeat. "Do something, Lucie!" he shouted. *"Now!"*

But Lucille's hands were shaking. A weak breeze whipped about their ankles again, then she exploded into tears and ran crying from the room.

He didn't know what made him do it, but Cas took off after her.

"Casander!"

Cas ignored Warrior's cries as he charged up the rickety

wooden staircase leading to the Airscaper dorms. Despite their new snoozing inhabitants, cobwebs still glistened from the ceiling. Only one dorm room door was slightly ajar, and he headed towards it, expecting Lucille to be inside.

She wasn't.

The spare dorm was vacant apart from three beds covered in dust sheets and a balcony that overlooked the whole school. At first, Lucille was nowhere to be seen – but when Cas edged towards the balcony, he saw her sitting cross-legged, weeping, in mid-air.

"Lucille!" he yelled.

The girl was perched on nothing, suspended on the other side of the balcony's railing. She craned her neck around when she heard his voice, her long silver hair fanned out behind her, but then her concentration broke. She had just enough time to let out a small scream before she fell.

Without thinking, Cas leant out and grabbed her.

His sweaty fingers closed around the cuff of Lucille's blazer, as she dangled from the Sky Tower, a hundred feet above the ground. A look of surprise passed across her face before the terror set back in. Cas used all of his strength to haul her up, but as he did so, she became lighter than air and floated upwards until she was safely on the other side of the railings.

Together, they stumbled into the dorm. Cas's jaw dangled open, speechless.

"Don't tell anyone you saw that," sobbed Lucille, clutching her arms protectively around herself. "I'll – I'll … make your life a living hell."

Her threat was meagre at best.

"You can fly," breathed Cas, amazed. He knew from his Order Studies lessons that Airscapers weren't supposed to do that.

"Float," Lucille corrected him. "But I told you not to say anything."

Cas held up his hands in surrender. "I won't," he promised, "but not because it's wrong, because you have nothing to be embarrassed about."

"Embarrassed?" said Lucille, swallowing her tears. "I'm an Airscaper who's terrible at air magic. I can't even generate a good wind. Instead, I have this stupid power – this useless, Abnormie gift – that I don't know what to do with. I don't even want it!"

Cas wanted desperately to say something. Despite their differences, he knew what it felt like to feel strange, out of the ordinary, an oddball.

But Lucille beat him to it.

"GO!" she shouted, burying her head in her hands and descending into tears again. *"Just GO!"*

Unsure of what else to do, Cas left the dorm and lumbered down the Sky Tower's stairs.

Warrior was waiting for him at the bottom, looking hurt and furious. "Where did you go?"

273

"Um, nowhere," Cas lied. "I tried to find Lucille to finish her off, but I lost her."

Warrior's hair turned from a gentle lobster red to crimson. "I didn't say you could do that." Her voice sounded more outraged and wounded than ever.

After what he had just seen, Cas ground his teeth. "I didn't realize I needed your permission."

Warrior hesitated, her face flashing ghostly white. She opened and closed her mouth like a goldfish, as if she was about to spit back something harsh, but then decided against it. This was the first quarrel they'd ever had. Cas wondered if she felt as sick to her stomach about it as he did.

"I... I..." Warrior trailed off.

Moodily, they stalked back to the Attic in silence, dodging any wardsmen they saw along the way. The uneasy quiet that filled their journey made their victory against the Du Villaines feel hollow. Cas was aching to speak to Warrior and breach the void, but she couldn't even bring herself to look at him. Was she really that mad at him? Had chasing after Lucille truly been such a terrible thing?

They reached the library and the passageway that led to the Attic, and skidded to a halt.

Mrs Crane was gone. Her empty chair lay on its side, her feather duster discarded.

"Do you think she's gone to look for us?" asked Warrior, shattering the tension.

Cas shook his head, a suspicious sixth sense kicking in. "Something's wrong."

Forgetting their fight, they pressed their eyes against the library's keyholes, wondering if Mrs Crane was inside.

At once, their blood ran cold.

Mrs Crane was inside all right. Pressed fearfully up against the library's counter, her knees knocking together, she cowered in front of the purple-and-white figure in front of her. The figure spun around and glanced towards the door, their face obscured by a silver mask.

Only one person wore that look.

It was the Master of All.

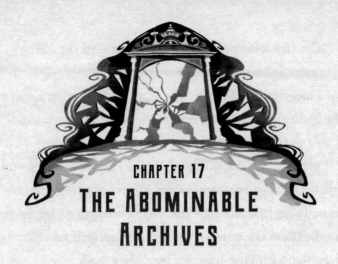

CHAPTER 17
THE ABOMINABLE ARCHIVES

"WHAT DO WE DO?"

At the sight of the Master of All, Cas and Warrior leapt back from the keyholes and shrank down against the door. They waited for a second, wondering whether by some unfortunate miracle the Master had seen them, before slowly pressing their eyes against the openings once more.

They could see and hear everything that was going on inside the room.

"We have to get help," whispered Cas urgently, his heart stuttering a jackrabbit beat in his chest.

But as he spoke, the Master of All turned back to face a cornered Mrs Crane. Cas and Warrior pressed themselves harder against the door to listen.

"You know what I seek. Where is it?" the Master of All demanded. His voice was much smoother and deeper – more human – than Cas expected.

He didn't know why, but for some reason the Master had always been a hulking great ugly monster in Cas's head. Instead, the villain he saw standing before him was nothing more than a man, an Other like anyone else in the Balance Lands.

Or at least, for a second, so he thought.

Without warning, the Master of All let out a roar and punched out his clenched fist. With a mighty invisible force, he upended an entire bookcase, ripping it free from the wall and flinging it across the room. It smashed into pieces above Mrs Crane's head.

"I don't know, I don't know," Mrs Crane wept, trembling on all fours.

"He's looking for me," hissed Cas, leaping up to enter the library. He had to surrender himself to save Mrs Crane. But Warrior tugged him back down.

"No, listen," she said in a hushed tone.

"WHERE IS IT?" the Master of All bellowed.

Mrs Crane shook like a leaf. "Please, I don't know," she wailed, clutching the desk for support. "I truly don't."

The Master of All used his unnatural power to shatter another bookcase, before hovering his hand over Mrs Crane's heart. His body relaxed into a deep sag of concentration. Gut-twisting dread flooded through Cas; he knew that look.

"We can do this the easy way," said the Master, smirking horribly. "Or the hard way." He narrowed his eyes, using his Deathmaker powers to gently squeeze Mrs Crane's heart. Mrs Crane covered her chest protectively, cringing in pain.

"Do your worst," she blubbered, her face defiant and brave even though she was snivelling. "But I'll never give up the Foretold. I'll never give you the boy you seek." Her tear-streaked visage was the most courageous face Cas had ever seen.

The Master of All's eyes bulged. He let out an irate cry and slammed his hands together. Mrs Crane toppled over sideways. Her head hit the floor with an ear-splitting *crack*. For a split second, Cas's own heart stopped.

Was Mrs Crane dead?

But as she lay on the floor, her body faintly quivered as the Master howled. He strode across the library, tearing apart everything in his path.

"The Foretold, the Foretold," he raged, upturning chairs and desks with a single swipe, toppling carts stacked high with tomes and tearing yet more bookshelves free from the walls. "*THE FORETOLD!* As if I still seek that worthless boy, when my informant tells me that Wayward School hides something much more valuable."

He slammed his fist against an old woven tapestry hanging on the wall, knocking it loose. A corner curled back, revealing a concealed entrance. Eyes alight, the Master of All yanked the tapestry down. Hidden behind it was a heavy, solid metal door. It looked like some kind of vault.

Or an escape route.

"The Abominable Archives," the Master of All snarled. Cas barely heard him.

He had already leapt to his feet and was rattling the library door. He had to get to Mrs Crane. He couldn't let the Master of All go free.

"Help!" Cas yelled when the door refused to budge. Before he could worry if the Master of All had heard the noise, he was sprinting away to find the nearest wardsman. *"HELP!"*

Cas barrelled haphazardly around one corner and then the next. Blinded by panic, he ran slap-bang into a solid mass of black. It was Dr Bane. Bane was pressed up against the corridor's wall, his ashen face illuminated by the moonlight, whilst the rest of his body melted into the shadows as if he was one with them. He looked stunned that Cas had discovered him.

"Dr Bane—" Cas began.

But Dr Bane gripped Cas firmly and levelled his gaze. "Where is the Master?"

Cas spluttered out the words. "Library," he said. "He's got Mrs Crane. He's looking for something."

"Andromeda," Dr Bane murmured quietly, his features turning even paler in despair. "Get to safety, Cas!" he commanded as he took off running towards the scene of the crime.

Just then, an entire patrol of orange wardsmen

279

thundered past Cas, their boots slapping against the marble floor as they followed in Dr Bane's footsteps.

Despite Bane's strict instructions, Cas dashed after them. But when they all reached the library, the doors had been blown off their hinges and the Master of All was gone.

Only Mrs Crane remained, shaken, tearful and barely conscious, in a curled-up ball by the vault-like door. Warrior was crouched at her side. The sole waygate mirror in the library lay smashed about her feet, brightly reflecting the Abominable Archives' once-concealed entrance, now exposed for everyone to see.

"What are the Abominable Archives?" wondered Cas, as he and the Abnormies sat huddled in the dining hall the next morning.

Cas and company had to keep their voices down as they spoke; no one was talking much over breakfast.

"No idea," said Warrior, munching on her cornflakes. "I didn't even know there was a secret room in the library."

The feud over their fight with the Du Villaines had seemingly been pushed aside in light of more pressing matters. Paws and Fenix were equally clueless.

Whatever the Abominable Archives were, or held, nobody knew.

The mystery of the Archives wasn't the only thing making the air in the dining hall charged with apprehension. Since the attack last night, it was like the world inside Wayward School had gone even more topsy-turvy. More wardsmen than ever patrolled the halls now, and some had even taken to tailing anyone they thought looked remotely suspicious between classes. The Du Villaines and their cronies were actively avoiding the Abnormies, not – as Warrior believed – because she and Cas had beaten them in the Scuffle, but more likely because Cas had discovered Lucille's secret. And the only reason most parents hadn't removed their children from the school was because the Grand Council had decided to keep the whole incident hushed up.

Nobody except the Abnormies knew the real reason why everyone was suddenly being escorted to and from their lessons by a teacher. But the students at Wayward School weren't daft.

They could tell something was wrong.

Madame Aster had just arrived to take them to their first class of the day when Warrior said, "What I would like to know is how the Master of All even got into Wayward without setting off the wards in the first place? He might've left through the library's waygate mirror, but you can only journey here through its twin in the Grand Council Chambers. And I highly doubt he came from there."

Cas, Paws and Fenix puzzled over this for a moment, pushing their scrambled eggs around their plates, dithering for as long as they could.

"Are you sure nobody with evil intentions can get through the school's wards?" said Cas, shovelling a forkful of lukewarm eggy gloop into his mouth.

"Positive," affirmed Fenix, nudging his crooked glasses up the bridge of his nose.

Cas levelled his gaze at the Firetamer as an idea took hold. "How about *under* them?"

It took a moment, but then Fenix's eyes widened in understanding.

"The leishis," they chorused together.

"Leishis?" mimicked Warrior, completely perplexed.

"Oh, leishis are terribly misunderstood," piped up Paws. "They're a little tricky at times, but—"

"That day we went into Wayward Town at Christmas, Mrs Crane said the school had been having problems with leishis burying under the wards," said Fenix, uncharacteristically butting in.

"Which means the Master could have got in," said Cas, "if he went *under* the wards instead of *through* them."

Warrior tutted. "I doubt the Master of All brought a little spade and dug himself a tunnel last night."

"Maybe not, but where does the toilet waste go?"

Warrior looked at Cas, revolted, and Paws appeared very concerned.

"Well, I'm guessing it doesn't just go into the Wavebreaker lake."

"It goes out of the school via the pipes, and

empties somewhere west of the town… OH, BY THE THREADS!" Warrior exclaimed, slapping her forehead as the thought occurred to her too. "The Master of All got in via the sewers."

Paws slowly spat out the mouthful she was chewing. "That's gross," she said, cereal milk dribbling down her chin.

"Someone must still be helping him, though," said Fenix. "How else would the Master know where the sewers are to get in?"

"Well, he was a student here," suggested Paws.

"But the sewers are like a never-ending labyrinth under Wayward Town. You'd get lost down there unless you knew the way in and out," said Warrior. "Can you remember what he said in the library, Cas? He has *an informant*. It must be someone with access to Wayward School's plans. Again, I can't imagine the Master waltzing up to the Grand Council and asking for the blueprints himself."

"The Du Villaines have family in the Grand Council," Cas offered.

Warrior shook her head. "Too proud. The Du Villaine family would never help someone who could rob them of their precious powers. But Madame Aster has ties to the Grand Council too."

"Unless it's Hopeless Higgles. He would be privy to such information," speculated Fenix worriedly.

Cas pondered this. He wouldn't put it past Hapless

Higgles to have unwittingly left a plan of the school grounds lying around for the Master of All to find. Or even handed it directly to one of the Heretics themselves, if they'd come knocking on Wayward School's front door claiming to be the Balance Lands' Most Magical Map Collector or something equally ridiculous. However, that wasn't the question currently buzzing around his brain.

"I'm less interested in *who*," said Cas, "and more interested in *what*. Now that we know how the Master got in, we need to figure out what he's looking for. It doesn't matter who's helping him if he gets whatever it is. It isn't me. The Master of All kept asking Mrs Crane where *it* is, not *he*."

Cas had tried to tell the Grand Council as much last night. They had arrived shortly after the wardsmen to take in the scene, but for all the good Cas's words did, he may as well have been talking to a brick wall.

"Nonsense," High Councillor Brooks had said, twiddling his plaited beard so hard his fingers chafed. "The Foretold is the only thing the Master is after."

"Yes," said High Councillor Aster, his ears growing redder by the minute. "He's been seeking you relentlessly since before you came to Wayward."

"But maybe he's not any more," Cas had insisted. "Maybe we've got it all wrong. The Master said there was something more valuable than me at the school. Whatever it is, it's hidden inside the Abominable Archives."

Mrs Crane had been out cold at the time, so she couldn't vouch for Cas's story, and even if she had heard or seen anything, she wasn't in a fit state to tell.

"Abominable Archives? We don't know what you mean," said Aster.

"There's no such thing," supported Brooks.

"Wretched, silly boy," High Councillor Du Villaine had snarked, "making up stories because he's unhappy with the new rules we're bringing in to try and keep him safe. I say we should leave your ungrateful hide to the Master."

"It's for your own good, Casander," High Councillor Hephaestus had told him gently.

Silly boy. Making up stories.

The words made Cas bristle even now. Not only did they not believe him, but he had a funny feeling they were playing dumb about the Abominable Archives too.

"Cover for me in Order Studies," he said, turning to Warrior. She had grown silent once more. Even though they had been talking only moments ago, something still felt off between them. "I need to pay Dr Bane a visit."

Despite the new security measures, it was surprisingly easy for Cas to sneak away from class.

He had one secret weapon nobody was counting on: Warrior Bane.

While Warrior distracted Madame Aster by leaping out from behind various columns and statues on the way to their lesson, scaring the other students by pretending to be the Master, Cas quickly slipped away and headed up to the first floor.

He was surprised to find Bane's office vacant and locked. After last night's attack, Dr Bane had made it clear to Cas that his door would always be open if Cas wanted to come to him with any fears or concerns.

Figuring that Dr Bane must have momentarily popped out, Cas changed direction and headed towards the Nurse's Quarters instead. Bane had said that Mrs Crane needed rest and wouldn't be accepting visitors, but Cas needed to get out of the open in case anyone spotted him wandering around unsupervised. Besides, he figured he could still wave through the window or slip a get-well-soon note under the door.

The Nurse's Quarters were located in a glass-roofed wing at the rear of the school and Cas had to take the long route around the outside of the building to avoid detection. He had just slipped back inside and was walking down the final corridor, scribbling a heartfelt message on the back of his History of the Balance Lands homework, when the sound of raised voices floated down the hall to meet him.

"For you to think that I could have possibly – *unimaginably* – had anything to do with that break-in last night is absurd, Dromeda…"

Cas dropped his homework sheet and stilled.

He had found Dr Bane.

"Do you *really* doubt me, sister?" Cas heard Bane ask, as he pressed himself flat against the corridor's wall, listening keenly.

"Do I have a reason to, Claudius?" shot back Mrs Crane.

At odds with how broken and bruised she had looked last night, Mrs Crane's voice sounded strong, resilient … and, most worryingly, accusing.

"We both know what will happen if the Master gets hold of what he seeks," she said.

"Chaos. Catastrophes. Calamities—" Bane listed off.

"And just about every other terrible thing that doesn't begin with the letter C," remarked Mrs Crane, thoroughly agitated. "If the Master succeeds and acquires all the powers, the balance of nature will be disrupted beyond repair. It will be ruined, ripped apart and destroyed. The very threads that hold our world and the Normie one together will unravel. You can't blame me for asking, brother. We both know your personal ties to him."

A loud bang echoed out as Dr Bane slammed his fist against something. "Ties I mistakenly made," said Dr Bane. "Ties I have tried to sever. Ties I have lived to regret."

"Oh, please—"

"Let's not forget the part you've played in all of this, Andromeda," said Dr Bane, cutting Mrs Crane off.

A moment's silence passed between them. Cas imagined them both catching their breath. "Remember, I keep your secrets and you keep mine."

Before Cas could hide or run, the sound of footsteps stormed closer and the doors to the Nurse's Quarters flew open. Cas stood, looking as innocent as possible, in front of a very tense and flustered Dr Bane.

"Casander," said Bane, looking as startled as Cas felt, before rapidly regaining his composure. The concerned crinkles around his fox-like eyes smoothed and he pulled his tight lips into a wavering, welcoming smile. "I thought I might be seeing you today."

Dr Bane moved forward, letting the doors swing shut behind him. Cas managed to sneak a quick peek at a dishevelled Mrs Crane, sitting on one of the many empty hospital beds in a frilly tweed dressing-gown, before the doors closed.

"I was just coming to give Mrs Crane this," he said, scrambling around on the floor for his get-well-soon homework sheet. "But I was actually hoping to talk to you, Dr Bane."

"Of course," said Dr Bane, "though I suspect I know why you're here."

The Deathmaker tutor wrapped his arm around Cas's shoulders, steering him back along the corridor in the direction of his office. Dr Bane didn't elaborate until he and Cas were safely back in his quarters, with the door firmly shut and Cas cajoled into a seat. Bane himself didn't sit down, forgoing his high-backed chair and instead leaning casually against the desk on the same side as Cas, as if they were equals.

"I can assure you, Mrs Crane is perfectly all right," Dr Bane said. "A little shaken and bruised, but that's to be expected – she's simply confined herself to the Nurse's Quarters to avoid any unnecessary attention. If anyone knows how to look after herself, she does."

"I know," Cas told him, shuffling to get comfy in his chair. "She used to be a Lifemaker."

The corner of Dr Bane's lips twitched. "And I know you know," he confessed, gesturing to Cas's outfit. "Don't think I don't know who gave you that cloak."

Cas hugged the purple-and-white cloak tighter around himself, holding the small tweed heart sewn on the inside close to his own. He had started wearing the cloak openly after the attack last night. Everyone else at Wayward was too preoccupied with the new security measures to pay much attention.

"Dr Bane," said Cas, choosing his words delicately. He picked at a chip in the wooden arm of his chair. "Why were you hiding from the Master of All last night?"

Cas suspected this was what Mrs Crane had been questioning Bane about in the hospital. If it had been anyone else, the answer would have been obvious. But as someone who had been tracking the Master for over a decade – and the last Deathmaker alive with any of his powers still intact – Cas would've thought Bane was the most qualified person to take on the Master of All. Even more so than Cas himself.

Dr Bane raked his fingers through his shaggy mane of silver-threaded hair, his pewter rings catching the light thrown from the glowing cabinets. "There are many complicated things in this world that you don't understand yet, Cas. That you may never understand."

"But there's a reason, isn't there?" said Cas boldly, undeterred. "A reason you keep leaving to find him, so the Grand Council can catch him. A reason why you sent Warrior to the Normie world to find me, but don't want to face the Master yourself."

Dr Bane let out a deep, sorrowful exhale. "Yes," he said, although his words cracked, as if it pained him to speak them. "Last night, I was hiding from the Master of All because I thought that if he hadn't come to Wayward for you, then he had come for me."

"You knew him when he was a student here, didn't you, sir?"

"Aeurdan Darkbloom." Dr Bane said the Master's old name heavily. "I didn't just know him as a student here. I was the one who brought him here. I discovered him in the Normie world a mere seventeen years ago, shortly after he had killed his mother and taken her Lifemaker powers. I … I did it anyway, knowing what he had done."

Out of nowhere, Cas felt very cold. Goose pimples rippled over his skin and his muscles froze with rigor.

"When I found Aeurdan in the Normie world," said Dr Bane, pacing the length of his office, "I thought I could help him, shape and change him. For a while, it worked. He was a talented and diligent student, but nobody could know what he was. A Lifemaker *and* Deathmaker was unheard of. A violation of the balance of nature. I persuaded Headmaster Higgles to hire Mrs Crane as the school nurse and librarian to help keep an eye on Aeurdan, and she secretly used her own Lifemaker abilities to help him master his. Aeurdan's Deathmaker teaching, the power he was born with, fell to me. That was where I let everyone down. I should have spotted that he was growing too curious, too ambitious, for his own good. He always wanted to push the boundaries of magic to unnatural lengths. But alas, I did not.

"At sixteen, he left school early and began his quest to obtain the four remaining powers. He declared his intention for all to know. Of course, that became a necessity once the terror and kidnappings started. Someone had to claim responsibility for them. I'm not sure he ever showed remorse for a single act."

"But in the last twelve years, he hasn't found anything, has he?" pried Cas, turning around in his chair. "I mean to say, he still only has Lifemaker and Deathmaker powers, like me."

"*Only* Lifemaker and Deathmaker powers." Dr Bane laughed softly, a hollow sound. "Yes, Cas, that is all he has for now. But with every death, every kidnapping, as time went on and the Grand Council failed to find the Foretold, his followers grew. Fear and greed are powerful motivators. Even though you're here now, many still stand with him. They're enthralled by his vision. Amazed by his powers and how he's yet to be caught."

Is that why the Master of All broke into the school last night? Cas wondered. *Is he trying to find a way to get the other powers? Do the Abominable Archives hold a book, a device or something else that can help him take them?*

It was the only explanation that made sense.

If the Master of All was no longer seeking Cas – the one person who could stop him – it had to be because he didn't need to worry about being stopped if there was something which could help him succeed first.

Dr Bane shot Cas a piercing look.

"What do you know, Cas?"

"Nothing," Cas replied honestly. "That's why I came here to see you." He paused, then took a deep breath and finally dived in with the truth. "You heard what I told the Grand Council yesterday. I saw the Master of All trying to get into that secret room in the library – the Abominable Archives or whatever it's called. I want to know what's inside."

"Do you?" said Dr Bane thoughtfully.

Unlike the Grand Council, he wasn't denying that the Archives existed.

"You're a curious lad," Bane said. "I almost admire your brazen nature. Very well. As you may remember from your first visit here, Wayward School is home to some very unusual and potentially dangerous objects." He walked over to the locked, glowing cabinets in his office and tapped each of them in turn. "These are the shrivelled heads of five-hundred-year-old dead Oracles, perfectly preserved should the residues of power lingering inside them ever be needed." He moved away from the green glowing cabinet to the silver one. "This is the Orbialius, a one-of-a-kind object linked to the powers of life and death. Some say it can contact spirits on the other side. You may recognize it from the Oracle's ceremony."

"And that?" asked Cas, pointing to the bronze-tinged cabinet. The one housing the small glowing orb surrounded by spinning metal rings, which had always intrigued him.

"Oh, that," said Dr Bane, flicking the cabinet's glass and not deigning it worthy of a second glance. "That's the cupboard Mrs Crane decorates with odd clutter. I never keep anything important in there."

He strode back over to Cas. "The point I was trying to make is that Wayward School has been entrusted by the Grand Council to be home to many strange and powerful things. The Abominable Archives is a secret vault in the library where the ones that could wreak the most havoc in the wrong hands are contained."

Cas knitted his eyebrows together. "If it's secret, why are you telling me about it?"

Dr Bane gave him a one-sided smile and winked, before sweeping over to his desk and pulling something out of his drawer. "Because," he said, smothering his wrinkled, papery hands in lotion, "I know that if I didn't tell you, you would try to find out anyway."

Cas shrugged. He couldn't deny this was true.

"But I think that's enough for now," said Dr Bane, as he glided towards him in his dusky purple cloak, hand outstretched. "You're beginning to look quite peaky…"

Cas leant forward to squeeze in one more question, ready to insist he felt nothing of the sort, when a wave of wooziness washed over him. The edges of his vision grew faint and cloudy, as everything in the room became covered in a misty haze. The walls raced closer. His head felt light, lighter than air.

"Dr Bane…" Cas croaked. But it was pointless.

The last thing he saw was the Deathmaker tutor reaching out to steady him. Then just like that, no matter how hard he tried to fight it, he slipped into the growing abyss…

CHAPTER 18
PUGGLE
THE NUGGLE

WHEN CAS AWOKE, HE WAS SLUMPED, HEAD DOWN and drooling, on his desk in Madame Aster's classroom.

He groaned and peeled a wet, sticky piece of paper off his cheek, grimacing at the slimy gloops of saliva that dripped from it. Warrior was sitting next to him, bent over her own paper, scribbling ferociously so it looked like she was taking notes. In reality, she was drawing various doodles of Madame Aster being chased, burnt to a crisp and eaten alive by numerous imaginative creatures.

"Where am I?" Cas yawned, stretching out his arms under the desk so Aster couldn't see. Every inch of him felt leaden and achy, as if he had simultaneously woken from a deep slumber and hit the floor from a great height.

Warrior shot him a guarded, sidelong glance. "Second hour of double Order Studies," she said out of the corner of her mouth. "Dr Bane brought you in with some excuse that he found you wandering around the hallways in a daze." Then she went back to discreetly scribbling away on her paper without another word.

Yep, Cas thought. There was definitely still something off between them since the Scuffle.

Cas nudged her under the desk. Warrior jumped, banging her knee on the underside of the table, and raised her foot to give Cas a swift kick in the shins – but before she could, he whispered, "Don't you want to know how I got on with Dr Bane?"

His words did the trick. Despite how much she fought it, Warrior's features quivered into curiosity.

As quickly and quietly as he could, Cas told Warrior everything that he had learned. But whilst Cas couldn't deny that what he had found out about Bane's history with the Master of All was interesting, it wasn't the information he sought.

"Is that it?" Warrior snorted.

Cas let out a low grumble. "Sadly, yes. I didn't find out anything about what the Master is looking for in the Abominable Archives."

Truthfully, Cas's disappointment wasn't that deep. He was mainly glad of an excuse to talk to Warrior properly again. Her eyes had grown wider and her face friendlier with each passing word.

Turning away, Cas squinted at the blackboard. The

lesson topic – Myths and Theories of the Orders – was scrawled in smudged, chalky letters, beneath which was the word *Conduits*.

"What are *conduits*?" said Cas, making a half-hearted attempt to pay attention.

"Conduits," said Madame Aster loudly, overhearing Cas's question and jumping on the chance to make an example of him, "are magical objects through which the different powers from the threads are channelled." She frowned sternly. "Feeling better, Monsieur Darkbloom? Or would you like another snooze?"

Near the front of the class, Sam Du Villaine and the Snouts chortled. Surprisingly, Lucille elbowed her twin brother sharply, trying to get him to shut up.

Cas's neck and ears heated as he shook his head.

"Bon." Madame Aster spun on her heel, returning to the blackboard. *"As I was saying,"* she continued pointedly, "conduits are magical objects. Vessels through which the threads of power can be controlled. Would someone like to recap what we learnt at the start of the lesson for Monsieur Darkbloom, and tell us exactly what these objects are?"

Several students' hands shot into the air.

"Monsieur Embershade," said Madame Aster.

"No one knows exactly," said Fenix, shooting Cas a reassuring grin. He answered the question as if he were reciting the answer directly out of a textbook. "Each conduit is a highly coveted, ancient relic. Common belief is that there is one conduit that belongs to each Order. All of that Order's powers and abilities are channelled through it. People know the conduits exist, but not what they are. Only the Grand Council know, because it's rumoured that each Order has a conduit-keeper, whom they entrust with the object."

"*Magnifique.* And where do these conduits come from?"

This time, an eager Quinnberley Crestbourne beat Fenix to the punch.

"Nobody knows for certain. My dad's a threadologist, a sort of scientist who studies the threads of power, and he reckons they've likely been around as long as the threads themselves."

"*Bien aussi,*" praised Madame Aster. "Do you see, Darkbloom" – she narrowed her eyes into slits at Cas – "what you can learn if you bother to show up for the beginning of class?"

Cas sank lower in his seat.

"For many years, Others have wondered about the origins and purpose of the conduits. Threadologists believe they were created as a fail-safe. If an Order should abuse their power, or if a conduit should be misused or fall into the wrong hands – for instance, if the conduit-keeper used the conduit to turn an Order into an army – then the balance of nature could still be maintained by the conduit being taken away from the corrupt keeper, and all in the Order would lose their powers as a result."

At this, Cas perked up. *Lose their powers.* A thought unexpectedly and brilliantly bloomed in his head. His hand shot into the air.

"Yes, Darkbloom?" said Madame Aster.

"Does that mean these objects – the conduits – can give people powers as well as take them away?"

Madame Aster sighed. "Some believe so, yes. If the conduits have been around for many years, it is probable that at one point or another, a conduit-keeper may have been the last in their Order and needed to repopulate it. Of course, as Monseiur Embershade said, only the Grand Council and the conduit-keepers understand the exact workings of the conduits, so – yes, Darkbloom?"

"Are any of them kept at the school?"

Before Cas had even finished speaking, the classroom burst into hysterical laughter.

"Why would a conduit be kept here?" Madame Aster sniped, pretending to wipe an entertained tear from her coal-like eyes.

But the question wasn't stupid to Cas. He and the Abnormies shared a knowing look.

If the Master of All's aim was to acquire all six of the powers – life, death, earth, air, water and fire – and he hadn't come to Wayward School looking for Cas, he must have been looking for something that would help him achieve his goal instead.

The conduits sounded perfect.

Cas poked his hand in the air again.

Madame Aster wiped away another tear and her face fell. "What is it now?"

"You said that only the Grand Council know where the conduits are," said Cas, his mind buzzing, "but what if they get lost or stolen? Or something happens to the Grand Council? Is there a way to find them?"

Madame Aster's expression turned sour and thunderous.

"Oh no," moaned Warrior, her face and hair turning as white as a chalk. "Bad move."

"Why?" said Cas ignorantly.

"Madame Aster's husband is Ophelius Aster," hissed Warrior. "High Councillor of the Earthshapers."

Cas gulped. How hadn't he made the connection between the two?

I've just insulted one of the most senior members of the Grand Council, he realized, his heart sinking into his shoes.

"Monsieur Darkbloom," said Madame Aster coldly. Her murderous face was turning more outraged by the second. "You may be the Foretold, but I can assure you, the Grand Council know a lot more about how to look after the conduits than you. You are nothing more than a twelve-year-old boy. A nobody with a hero complex and shockingly bad grades in my class." Sam Du Villaine sniggered at that. "However," Madame Aster went on, much to everyone's bewilderment, "is anyone here familiar with the *seekerthing*?"

Almost every student in the room shook their head.

"I think my dad might have mentioned it once," Quinnberley muttered in a small voice. "But he said it was a rumour, a myth…"

"What's a *seekerthing*, miss?" prodded Neerja Gill.

They all waited for Madame Aster to explain or sketch something on the blackboard, but she pocketed the chalk in her hand instead.

"Nobody knows," Aster admitted, flopping down at her desk with a casual shrug of her shoulders. "Unlike the common belief in the conduits, *Mademoiselle Crestbourne* is right. The seekerthing is a legend. Even if it exists, nobody outside of the Grand Council has ever seen it. Hence its name, seeker*thing*. Those who believe it exists believe that only someone as strong and powerful as the threads of power themselves would be able to sense and find it. All the rest of us know is that the seekerthing would, in the wrong hands, be a very dangerous device. If you could only begin to imagine the damage it could cause if wielded by someone like—"

"The Master of All," finished Cas, the words slipping out before he could stop himself.

Madame Aster's expression turned furious again. *"I will not have that abhorrent monster mentioned in my class."*

The room fell utterly and fearfully silent.

Outside, the bells chimed, and everyone exhaled in relief as they began to pack up their things. But Cas sat there for a moment, thoughts and theories running through his brain at a million miles a minute.

The seekerthing.

He might've just discovered what the Master of All was looking for after all.

Over the next few weeks, Cas spent every waking moment trawling through every book in the library that might give him any indication what the seekerthing was.

The Abnormies were happy to help, and whilst Cas couldn't skip classes to do this, he could neglect his homework. As time went on, he found himself increasingly relying on the fact that he was the Foretold to give him a free pass for the upcoming end-of-year exams.

Unfortunately, there was no mention of the seekerthing anywhere.

Madame Aster was right. Mentions of the conduits were scattered here and there – in the same way one may know that nuclear codes or the secret service exists, but not what or where they are – but the seekerthing remained a phantom. There were no educated guesses about it in books by renowned threadologists. No hints in history books containing old Grand Council texts. Not even wild speculations by self-published crackpots.

When the dewy freshness of spring fully set in, even the Abnormies' interest in the seekerthing waned – and

Warrior had long since grown bored of tossing paper balls across the library for Hobdogglin to chase.

On the first day of April, the Abnormies had finally had enough.

Secretly, Cas had too.

He spent his lunch break dejectedly doing his second-favourite activity these days: sitting in the far corner of the library, peeking behind the re-hung tapestry and studying the Abominable Archives' lock.

It didn't seem to open using a normal key. Quite the opposite – it looked like you had to insert some sort of cog into a space in the door.

Cas was just about to call Fenix over for the umpteenth time, knowing he loved everything mechanical and tinkering, when Fenix, Paws and Warrior ambled over, swinging a picnic basket brimming with scrummy delights.

"That's enough," said Warrior, yanking Cas to his feet. "It's a beautiful day, the sun is finally shining and you're coming outside with us."

Cas supposed he should be grateful that Warrior seemed to have snapped out of her mood. At worst these days, she was occasionally off with him – a funny, distant feeling Cas couldn't quite put his finger on – but it had been so long since their Scuffle with the Du Villaines that he thought she must have got over their disagreement by now.

He sighed and started towards the shelves. "Fine. Let me just pick up—"

"No books," said Warrior firmly.

Paws and Fenix shot Cas an unsympathetic look.

"You're reading a lot, Cas, even for, erm, me," said Fenix.

Cas went to slump back down to the floor. "Well, I need to do something," he said, irritated. "I can't just sit here doing nothing. Not when the Master of All is out there and I still don't know what he wants."

Since security at the school had been tightened, the Master hadn't attempted another break-in – at least, not that anybody knew. Even so, Cas couldn't sit idly by. The answer about what the Master wanted felt so close, but also just out of reach.

"Today you can," ordered Warrior, heaving him up. "It's Paws's birthday. She's throwing a surprise picnic party by the lake."

"Surprise!" Paws sang from her wheelchair, razzle-dazzling her hands.

Cas glanced at her sceptically. "Aren't we supposed to be throwing you one of those?"

Warrior rolled her eyes. "Not in the Balance Lands. Here, the person whose birthday it is does the unexpected party-throwing."

Fenix nodded. "The birthday boy or girl can decide to throw their party at any time. Hours, days or months after their birthday."

"That's what makes it a surprise, you see," said Paws.

"Surely I can miss one—"

"No," Warrior interrupted him. "I'm throwing my party today too. *Surprise.*" The last word was as deadpan as a flat pancake.

"When was your birthday?"

"New Year's Day. Now, get a move on or else all the good spots by the lake will be taken."

When they wandered outside, it became clear that many other Wayward School students had also ventured out to enjoy the fresh air.

As Fenix and Paws tailed along behind them, Warrior frog-marched Cas down to the boating lake. But as they reached the water's edge, Lucille Du Villaine appeared from behind a tree and blocked their path.

She was alone.

"Hi, Cas," she said, smiling unsettlingly pleasantly. "Can I have a quick word?"

Warrior looked the silvery girl up and down. "I don't trust you to keep him in one piece."

Lucille's bright demeanour faded and she slipped back into her old, cold self. "Look, Riff-Raff," she barked. "I just want to talk to him. You can watch us from over there if you like."

Cas waved Warrior and the others on.

"It's fine," he said. "I'll catch up with you in a minute."

"But, Cas—"

"Look, I'll scream if I'm in trouble, OK?"

After making a gesture that told Lucille she would put

her foot somewhere extremely uncomfortable if anything happened to Cas, Warrior, Paws and Fenix walked over to another spot by the lake, worriedly looking back at him every other step.

"Where are your minions?" said Cas, glancing around.

Sam Du Villaine was nowhere to be seen.

Lucille twirled the hem of her grey Airscaper cloak uneasily around her finger. "Sam doesn't know that I'm here," she said quietly, as if she was afraid her brother might hear. "I just… I just wanted to…"

"What?" said Cas, already very bored. "Threaten me? Belittle me? Call me another stupid, horrible name?"

Lucille looked mortally offended. "*Thank* you," she murmured, the words sounding alien as they left her lips. "I wanted to thank you. You didn't tell anyone about me. About what you saw that night."

Cas groaned, exasperated. "I told you I wouldn't. There's nothing—"

Lucille held up her hand.

"There's nothing wrong with you," Cas concluded anyway.

She blushed. Cas couldn't believe what he was seeing. Lucille Du Villaine was *actually* flushing pink.

"Well, still, keep it to yourself," she said stiffly. Then realizing that might have sounded harsh, she added hastily, "Please. I'm not ready for people to know yet."

Cas gave Lucille the once-over. She was really quite

pretty when her personality wasn't so ugly. Cas wanted to say something else, to comfort her in some way, but in the end he merely nodded.

He knew what it was to feel like a freak. An outsider.

And whilst he couldn't help everyone knowing who and what he was, whilst he was trying to learn not to be afraid or ashamed of it, to take comfort in the knowledge that everyone had differences about them, he knew that some people weren't ready to share theirs yet.

This was Lucille's difference. Her secret. Her funny leg.

"I promise," said Cas.

Lucille offered him an incredibly shaky smile.

"Oh," she said, looking back at Cas as she strode away. "You can call me Lucie, by the way."

A warm, fuzzy feeling settled in Cas's gut. He carried the pleasant sensation all the way down to the lake, as he and the Abnormies hungrily dived into the basket full of treats and concoctions from Captain Caeli's Cakery.

Fenix told them that he had brought Steve, their Order Studies class's yellow-and-black-speckled salamander, outside for a change of scenery. It was his turn to look after the creature as part of their studies on Elementies, and he was keen to show off a new fireproof lock he had created. But when Fenix went to pull the salamander out of his bag, his face greyed and he dropped the creature's empty cage as if it had scorched him.

"Er, Fenix," said Cas slowly. "Did you accidentally leave Steve running riot in the Attic?"

Panicked, Fenix started riffling through his bag. But Steve the Salamander was gone.

Only a mangled metal lock, still dripping molten at the end, remained.

"It's all my fault," said Fenix despairingly, burying his head in his hands. "I shouldn't have tinkered with the padlock. How am I going to tell Madame Aster?"

"Don't worry," said Paws, patting Fenix's back. "We'll find Steve. He can't have gone far. I'll jump into Mogget and have a look around—"

The scabby cat around her neck yowled in disagreement.

"That's if the mangy mog didn't eat him," quipped Warrior unhelpfully.

Paws shot her an uncharacteristically sharp look. "That's not funny. How do you know it wasn't Hobdogglin?"

Hobdogglin appeared out of nowhere at Warrior's side. "Did you eat the stinky salamander?" Warrior asked him. Hobdogglin shook his abnormally small head. "See."

They all split up and started looking for Steve.

Just as the clock bells tolled to signal the end of break, Cas spied something near the shore.

"I've found him!" he cried out to the others, pointing to where a lizard-shaped yellow-and-black spot was perched atop Puggle the Nuggle. The Wavebreaker Elementie was wading in the shallows, munching on grass.

To Cas's surprise, the Abnormies' faces filled with dread.

"What?" said Cas. "I'll go and get him."

"You can't," said Paws.

"Why not?"

She furrowed her brow, clearly trying to read Puggle the Nuggle's mind. "Puggle is … *up to something*."

"Plus, there's rule 306 in the Wayward School handbook," said Warrior. *"Do not touch or ride on the Nuggle.* It comes after rule 305: *Don't feed the Nuggle* and before rule 307: *On pain of death, do not attempt to cuddle the Nuggle."*

Cas shot her a dubious look. "Wayward has more than three hundred rules?"

"Actually, more than five hundred," Fenix informed him. "They, er, have to with so many powerful Others around."

"I should know," grumbled Warrior. "Madame Aster made me copy them all out in detention once."

"It goes all the way from rule 1: *Don't run in the corridors* to rule 506: *Don't put salamanders down people's pants."*

Paws nodded enthusiastically. "Poor Mrs Crane was treating trouser burns daily before that one was introduced."

"Well, some people deserved it," huffed Warrior, suggesting she might have had something to do with the rule being drafted.

Cas waved dismissively. "I'm not going to ride Puggle," he said, ignoring their warnings and striding confidently up to the watery beast. "I'm just going to grab Steve off his withers – see, come here, little fella – WOAH!"

Unexpectedly, Cas felt a massive nip on his buttocks followed by a strong, rough bump. He was thrown into the air and grabbed hold of the only thing he could: the Nuggle's seaweedy mane. Steve the Salamander jumped off Puggle's back into Fenix's waiting hands as the Nuggle gave Cas another mighty shove with his muzzle, boosting him up onto his back.

Before Cas could say or do anything, Puggle reared and took off at a gallop.

"*CAS!*" the Abnormies hollered from the shore.

But their voices were drowned out by the sound of wind rushing past Cas's ears. Puggle the Nuggle bolted for several strides, before leaping into the air in a graceful arc and diving into the lake. Down and down he plunged into the icy depths, with Cas holding on for dear life. Water rushed past, plastering Cas's wet clothes to his body as they surged deeper still…

Panic rippled through Cas.

He couldn't breathe. His eyes stung and his lungs burned for air, until…

FLASH.

Puggle the Nuggle broke through the water's surface into a stinky, grimy pipe. Cas had just enough time to gulp in a mouthful of fresh air and realize that they had waygated into what appeared to be the sewers, before they were galloping again towards a bright light at the end of the tube. A thrilling wave of cold, familiar magic pulsed through him – they must be beneath the Deathmaker mausoleums. Then Puggle dived out of the end of the pipe and they plummeted towards another body of water below.

As soon as they crashed through the waves, Cas knew they hadn't returned to the lake. There was no flash of a waygate, and the watery landscape had changed. The waves tasted disgustingly salty. Schools of silvery fish swam by, twinkling like tin-foil-wrapped stars as they meandered through what looked like a gigantic underwater cityscape submerged by the sea. Gone were the algae-covered rocks of the lake; in their place were jutting obsidian boulders stacked so closely that they resembled towers and turrets. The fin of a great white shark loomed dangerously in the distance, and beyond that there was only vast, open ocean.

Cas's eyes stung as Puggle the Nuggle paddled on, oblivious to the fact Cas was drowning. His chest was on fire, his head was screaming and light spots were speckling the edges of his vision.

He had to do something…

Struggling to remain conscious, Cas slumped forward. He was only secured by being knotted in the Nuggle's seaweedy mane. All he could see was Puggle's dark bay body. But that was all he needed. With every ounce of effort left in him, Cas imagined taking control of the Nuggle's legs and commanding them to swim up. He imagined the creature's muscles moving to the whim of his magic ... paddling them to safety. The light in Cas's world began to grow dim...

FLASH.

Just in the nick of time, Cas and Puggle soared through the lake's surface, before the Nuggle unceremoniously bucked Cas off onto the bank.

He hit the ground with a *thud*, spluttering up water as his friends rallied around him.

"Casander!"

"Cas, can you breathe?"

"Are you all right? Where have you been?"

"Sea..." Cas coughed, drawing in enough air to get the words out before choking on the water he had swallowed again. "I didn't know ... Wayward had a sea..."

The Abnormies regarded him, puzzled.

"Well, it doesn't really," said Warrior. "Only a deserted sliver of one. But nobody goes there. We call it the Wide West of Wayward."

"It's on the edge of town," added Paws. "We use it to get rid of rubbish mostly because the tide draws it out. There's no beach, just cliffs. No one even goes swimming there; there's the risk you might swim out beyond the wards and not return before Wayward moves again."

"Or you could, um, go from swimming in deep water to a sudden, bone-shattering drop onto dry ground," said Fenix, "depending on where Wayward shows up. Hardly any wardsmen monitor there, because, you know, you'd have to somehow get past the wards, the sea and the sharks if you wanted to sneak in."

Cas blinked up at them through stinging eyes, incredulous. "And I'm only hearing about this *now*? You know we've been looking for how the Master—"

But a lilted voice cut him off.

"Monsieur Darkbloom," Madame Aster cawed, her shadow blocking out the sun as she suddenly loomed over Cas, hands on her hips and scowling. *"What do you think you're doing?!"*

"The Nuggle… I…" Cas tried to say, too faint and weak to properly explain.

Madame Aster didn't care. "Headmaster Higgles's office," she commanded, prodding her finger furiously towards the school. *"NOW!"*

CHAPTER 19
HIDERS AND SEEKERS

Soggy and sorry-looking, Cas sat glumly in the lobby leading to Headmaster Higgles's office, waiting for him to return.

Miss Grimbly and her parakeets kept looking daggers at him from behind her desk. "I told you hanging around with that horrible girl would bring you nothing but trouble," she scolded him, as the parakeets chirped in agreement.

But Cas didn't have the strength to tell her this had nothing to do with Warrior.

He felt simultaneously tired and wired. He was both buzzing to get back to the Abnormies to discuss how the Master was likely using the Wide West of Wayward to access the sewers, and busy thanking the threads that he hadn't drowned.

An hour later, Headmaster Higgles jollily strolled into

the lobby, belching and munching on his afternoon snack, a custard pastry crown.

"Oh, Cas, my boy!" the headmaster exclaimed, brushing crumbs from his cloak and hauling Cas into a hug. "What've you been up to? Did you get in the bath with your clothes still on? Happens to me all the time." Squished against Headmaster Higgles's long, spidery frame, Cas felt every one of the teacher's knobbly joints poking into his ribs.

He would've rather taken another round with Puggle the Nuggle.

Miss Grimbly got to her feet and glared disapprovingly. "Madame Aster caught him riding the Wavebreaker Elementie."

"Not intentionally!" Cas pointed out.

Headmaster Higgles shoved the rest of the pastry into his mouth, looking torn.

"Come in, Darkbloom," he said shortly, holding his door open. "Let's see if we can sort this out."

Cas followed the headmaster inside.

Hopeless Higgles's office was uninspiringly boring. The walls were painted a muted shade of blue and scattered with still-life paintings of food: a wicker basket full of vegetables, a half-eaten wheel of cheese, and a glorious cherry-topped ice cream sundae complete with sprinkles. The only interesting things in the room were Higgles's framed degree (Masters in Earthshaping, Fifteenth

Attempt, Laughable Standard) and a chaise longue on the other side of his desk instead of a chair.

Cas supposed it was better for napping.

"I'm sure we can let this little indiscretion slide," said Headmaster Higgles, plopping himself down on the seat and rummaging around in his desk. "I just need to fill out a form, a formality – let me see, where is it – oh yes."

The headmaster pulled a vast array of useless, hoarded stuff out of his drawer as he searched, bundling it onto his desk: a rubber eraser, a paper-clip ring, a ball made of elastic bands, a heap of multicoloured string, and a metal cog-shaped object.

Cas was just wondering how much it would all be worth at The Mint Exchange when his eyes lit up.

The cog.

His thoughts flew to the Abominable Archives' door.

"Headmaster," Cas drawled, feeling inspired, as Higgles dipped his pen in an ink pot and started to fill out the rule-break form. "I think I heard Cook Fiddlepot say that he was going to rustle up some chocolate eclairs for an early supper treat."

Headmaster Higgles instantly perked up. "Chocolate eclairs?" he said, licking his lips.

"I had one the other day," said Cas. "They're absolutely divine. Crisp, golden pastry. Fudgy chocolate. Oozy, gooey cream. I wouldn't want you to miss out."

For a brief moment, Headmaster Higgles seemed ready

to leap to his feet, but then he checked himself at the last opportunity. "Oh, well … no. No, perhaps later. I really ought to finish this first."

"Are you sure, sir?" said Cas, acting concerned. "You look a bit peaky."

The same trick Dr Bane had played on Cas sprang to mind as he focused his attention hard on Higgles, muttering *"Caput"* under his breath.

"What was that, dear boy?"

Cas's heart skipped a beat. "Oh, nothing," he said, and then gasped, feigning concern. "But the voices! Hearing words which aren't there is a sure sign you need to eat something, sir. *Right now.*"

Just then, Headmaster Higgles faltered, swaying slightly on his seat. "On second thoughts, perhaps you're right, Cas. I do feel a bit faint."

Cas could barely contain his smile. By some miracle, his powers were working.

"Stay here, Darkbloom," said Headmaster Higgles, pushing back from his desk so enthusiastically that the chaise longue toppled over. "I'll be back in a jiffy."

The moment Higgles lumbered out of view, Cas lunged forward and snatched up the metal cog. He shoved it inside his pocket and turned to go – but he couldn't resist the urge to quickly riffle through Higgles's open drawer. There were chocolate bar wrappers, used napkins, a photo of Higgles's mother who looked like a blobby pink slug in a wig … but also a recent newspaper clipping about the Master of All's attack on The Tyrannical Terrace and blueprints of the school – maps detailing every tiny passageway, secret tunnel and the routes of the sewers.

Shaking, Cas rummaged further in the drawer until his fingers grazed something curved and silver, wedged right at the back…

It instantly reminded him of the Master of All's silver mask.

Could Fenix be right? Was Higgles the informant?

"What on earth do you think you're doing?" shrieked Miss Grimbly.

Without hesitation, Cas pulled out his arm and slammed the drawer closed. The secretary lingered menacingly on the other side of the office, eyes slit-like and nostrils flaring. Cas raced towards the door, trying to streak past her towards the library. But Miss Grimbly was unnaturally limber and quick. She threw her brittle body into Cas's path, blocking his escape into the lobby.

Thinking fast, Cas clocked Miss Grimbly's parakeets behind her and focused on the crustiest-looking bird in the corner of the cage. This time, Cas didn't need words to direct his magic. His disbelief at what he had found and burning desire to finally break into the Abominable Archives was enough to spur his powers on.

He channelled all his energy into Polly the parakeet,

who suddenly stopped grooming her feathers and began to swell and grow like an inflatable balloon.

"My baby!" Miss Grimbly screeched shrilly.

Forgetting all about him, Miss Grimbly whirled around and dived across the room out of Cas's way. As she wrenched open the cage door, Cas let the parakeet deflate to its normal size. Then he took off, not stopping or looking back until he was outside the library's doors.

Slamming into them, Cas rattled the handles, but the doors were shut tight. Common sense told him it would be better to try and get into the Abominable Archives at night, when he was less likely to get caught. But after what he had just found in Higgles's office, there was no time to waste. Cas bounded up the secret passage to the Attic and flew down the trap-door slide into the room below.

As expected, the library was empty.

Even though she had left the Nurse's Quarters, Mrs Crane had been keeping an extremely low profile since the attack. Her cuts and bruises hadn't completely healed and Cas figured she didn't want to draw attention to herself. Ignoring the sound of books shuffling around on the shelves, Cas ripped the tapestry off the wall to reveal the door and jammed the cog into the slot. His breath caught in his throat when it worked. The wheels and mechanisms on the vault began to click, turning and whirring frantically as he heard heavy deadbolts and locks sliding open.

In a matter of seconds, the entrance to the Abominable Archives swung open.

A dark, cavernous room, illuminated only by the backlight flooding in from the library, greeted him like a gaping, open mouth. Obsidian rock walls stretched above Cas in a dome and the room was filled with countless rows of creaking shelves, holding more weird and wonderful objects than he had ever encountered. Some artefacts were locked inside cages or glass boxes, whilst others were inside ruby-encrusted vials or black, padlocked chests. The cavern sloped down to a caved-in dead end at the rear of the room, which looked like it had once led to somewhere deep below the school. A familiar, grimy stench rose from the cracked opening, but Cas didn't have time to dwell on where the archaic passage had once led.

Focusing on the shelves, he began picking through the relics and artefacts one by one, examining the dusty, scrawled labels tied to each of them. Despite the scribbled names on the labels, it was impossible to tell what many of the objects were. There were words and phrases Cas had never heard of, and some of the objects had labels written in a forgotten language Cas didn't understand.

Then he came to one that made his heart stop.

[ARTICLE NAME REDACTED]

Entrusted to Wayward School, Wayward, by permission of the Grand Council. Property of Curator Bane.

Something twinged in Cas's gut.

The label didn't say *seekerthing*, but it didn't need to. Madame Aster had said that nobody except the Grand Council knew what the device looked like or what it was really called, so they weren't very well going to scrawl it on a name tag.

This had to be what Cas was searching for. It *had* to be.

Just to be sure, he quickly scouted some other surrounding labels, but everything else was meticulously catalogued in a way the unknown object wasn't.

The withered, aged label was attached to a plain wooden box with a rusty hinge. Cas pried it open. A deep orange, gilded velvet cushion lined the inside, where a long, rectangular object sat snugly in a round divot in the fabric, sticking out awkwardly at one end. Cas couldn't see what the object was exactly; it was wrapped in copious layers of cloth. It looked like some sort of kaleidoscope or baton, maybe – but what was odd was that it didn't look like it fit properly in the box. And whilst the outer box itself was dusty, the dust around the object inside had been disturbed.

As he reached to peel the layers back, a voice rang out behind him.

"You won't find anything in there."

Startled, Cas snapped the box closed and spun round. Mrs Crane stood silhouetted in the doorway. She looked both stern and concerned, her arms crossed against her orange tweed dress and one of her pink-slippered feet tapping against the floor.

"I – I wasn't looking for anything," stammered Cas, shoving the box back onto its shelf with all the subtlety of a bull in a china shop.

Mrs Crane didn't look angry. She looked disappointed. Somehow this was worse.

"So, let me get this straight," she said, striding over to Cas and guiding him out of the vault. He cast one last, longing look behind him before the door whirred, buzzed and clicked shut, locking again behind them. "You just happened to stumble across the key to the Abominable Archives, which only the Headmaster has in his possession; and you just happened to find the library closed but accidentally found your way in anyway; and, let me guess, you tripped and fell, which made you put the key into the lock, opening the vault, and it was all a big misunderstanding that I found you nosily riffling through its contents."

Cas swallowed hard. "Um … oopsie?"

Mystified, Cas stared at Mrs Crane as she chuckled. "Look, I love stories, Casander. But that's a stretch to believe, even for me."

There was no point trying to hide it any more.

"I just wanted to find what the Master of All was looking for," Cas told her honestly. "The Grand Council don't believe that he's not after me. He's searching for something else now. I thought that if I could get to whatever it is first, I could keep it safe … stop the Master getting hold of it … at least until everyone took me seriously. Anything to prevent him coming back and hurting anyone else. It's my duty. I'm the Foretold."

In the blink of an eye, Mrs Crane looked very guilty. "No, Cas, it's not," she said considerately. "You're only a boy. A boy with an immense, unimaginable destiny, but it's still your job to learn and grow. Yes, you might be the Foretold. And one day you might defeat the Master. But you need to learn how to do it first and you don't need to do it alone." She paused, her slightly crooked front teeth clamped on her lip. "I know it's my fault that you feel this way, after what you saw him do the last time he broke in, but … sometimes bad things happen to good people, Cas. We can't stop them. We just have to be strong, pick ourselves back up and carry on.

"That's how we don't let the bad people win."

They stopped moving and Mrs Crane pivoted Cas to face her.

"The Master is not coming back, Cas," she said, holding fast to his shoulders and sounding more as if she was trying to convince herself than him.

"But he is—"

"He's *not*." Mrs Crane tightened her caring grip. "And even if he does, you, and anything else you think the Master of All might be after, are safe here. We'll protect you. It's not your place to protect me."

Mrs Crane released him and held her hand out for the key. Reluctantly, Cas turned and pried it out of the door.

323

"Just tell me one thing," he said, eyebrow quirked brazenly, before handing it back. "*Is* the seekerthing in there?"

Mrs Crane's mouth dropped open and her wild hair seemed to puff to twice its usual size. "The seekerthing?" she spluttered, taken aback. "No – I mean, it isn't – it's merely a rumour…"

Cas decided to take a leap of faith. "I know it's not," he lied. "Bane told me."

It was a huge gamble. A risk. But moments later, it paid off.

"Look, I couldn't tell you even if it was," concluded Mrs Crane. "Everything that belongs in that vault is classified information between the Grand Council and its keeper."

"Do you mean Dr Bane?"

Mrs Crane pursed her lips. She wasn't denying that the seekerthing was real, nor was she denying that it had been in the vault. This was a half win at least.

"Yes, Dr Bane holds on to all the most powerful artefacts at Wayward," she said warningly, as if this would somehow put Cas off. "They remain watched and guarded, either in the Archives or his office, which is *precisely* where this is going." Mrs Crane plucked the key from between Cas's fingers. "I knew Higgles should've never been trusted with it. I doubt you'll have the same luck sneaking it off my brother. But don't you dare think about going poking around his office for this or anything else either! Not only is it rude, but he couldn't tell you what or where half the stuff is in there anyway. I look after the decorating – my brother wouldn't know good taste if it bit him on the backside."

Cas knew Mrs Crane was trying to distract him by talking about sprucing up Bane's office.

But he was hardly listening.

His mind was still trapped inside the Abominable Archives. All he knew was that he had to protect the seekerthing – whatever it took.

By some miracle, Cas managed to make it to his last class of the day – Twisted Tongues and Languishing Languages – on time. He sat alone in class, still reeling from the afternoon's events. Once class had finished, Cas and the Abnormies trundled up to the Attic, fed-up and weary – but not too tired for Cas to tell them everything.

The Abnormies sat and listened with bated breath as Cas relayed all that had happened since leaving the lake.

"At least you didn't get in trouble for riding the Nuggle," said Paws, offering him a silver lining.

"Yeah," said Warrior, lying with her head hanging upside down off her bed. "If it was me, Aster would've made sure I got kicked out. Especially if Miss Grimbly nabbed me riffling through Hapless Higgles's belongings too."

Cas felt his heart deflate like Grimbly's gnarly old

parakeet. He hadn't even thought about the repercussions from running away from Higgles's office, let alone whatever punishment would surely be added on top when the headmaster found out Cas had stolen the key to the Abominable Archives.

What if being the Foretold didn't get him off this time?

"Now that we know the seekerthing is at Wayward School, we need to protect it from the Master of All," said Cas resolutely, concentrating on what was most important.

Whilst he was sure he wasn't strong enough to defeat the Master one-on-one yet, it was the best he could do until the Grand Council took him seriously and reinforced the protection around it themselves.

"We need to plan a brilliant new heist to rescue it," said Warrior, her voice dreamily excited. "Personally, I think your plan only failed because I wasn't involved."

The only trouble was, two gnawing suspicions were still niggling away at Cas.

The first was what he had discovered in the drawer.

"Of course Higgles would have maps of the school," said Paws rationally. "He's the headmaster. It's part of his job."

"Same with the, erm, newspaper," agreed Fenix. "He has to know what's going on near his school."

"As for the silver whatever-it-was you felt," said Warrior, "it could have been anything."

"But don't you think it's odd that such a bumbling

buffoon is in charge of Wayward School?" speculated Cas. "No, I know you said Dr Bane put Higgles up for the job so that he could do as he pleases," he interjected quickly, when Warrior shot him a look that implied they already knew the answer to this, "but if it wasn't only about Bane keeping the Grand Council sweet, it would be the perfect cover, wouldn't it? Nobody would suspect Higgledy-Piggledy Higgles of being the Master's informant."

"Then why would the seekerthing still be in the Abominable Archives? If Headmaster Higgles had the key, surely it would be long gone by now?"

That brought Cas on to his second suspicion.

"Except I don't think the seekerthing *is* in the Abominable Archives." He recalled the disturbed dust and how the long, rectangular device had looked like it didn't fit. "Or at least, it's not in the box it's supposed to be in."

The others merely gawked at him.

"So, what?" said Warrior, flipping the right way up on her bed. "Are you saying Bane switched the containers in case someone on the inside was working with the Master? Or the Master ever broke in himself?"

"Maybe. Either that or the seekerthing has been taken out of the Archives altogether."

"Then where is it?"

They all pondered long and hard but came up with nothing.

"Perhaps we're barking up the wrong tree?" suggested

Fenix. "Perhaps the Grand Council still have the seekerthing or it isn't what the Master is searching for at Wayward after all."

Cas hummed, unconvinced. "No, it makes sense that the Master wants the seekerthing – he needs the conduits to take the other Orders' powers. And I'm guessing that if he knew where the conduits were, he would've taken them already – which means he needs the seekerthing to find them. It *has* to be here. You should have seen the look on Mrs Crane's face when I fibbed and told her I knew it was. If the Grand Council still had it or it was stashed elsewhere, Mrs Crane wouldn't have been so alarmed. All she did was refuse to tell me where it was. She simply said that Dr Bane keeps everything valuable either in the Abominable Archives or in his office."

"Well, let's go and raid Bane's office then," said Warrior, leaping to her feet and pulling on her blazer.

"No, don't you see?" implored Cas, sitting down in the bay window. "Our next chance to get the seekerthing might be our last. We have to be sure of its whereabouts first. If Higgles is working with the Master then it won't be long before he figures out that I'm onto him, or he finds the seekerthing himself. Even a blind squirrel stumbles across a nut every once in a while. Besides, if we get caught again, we all risk being expelled."

Cas was so preoccupied and disappointed in his earlier efforts that he was unable to meet the grey, purple-flecked eyes of his own reflection. Instead, he gazed into the distance as too many thoughts to count raced through his head. He needed a new plan.

One that would succeed this time.

So, he had to decide: which was going to be his next point of attack?

The Abominable Archives again or Dr Bane's office?

Was the seekerthing under lock and key? Or hidden in plain sight for all to see?

At first thought, the idea of the seekerthing being on display in Bane's office was ludicrous. But maybe it was a plot that was brilliant in its simplicity. Neither the Master nor his informant would think that such a valuable artefact would be placed out in the open for anyone to gape at. Unless, of course, it was still in the Abominable Archives, stowed away under the wrong label to befuddle anyone who might try to steal it...

The problem was, now that it was in Bane's possession, there was only a slim chance of Cas getting his hands on the key again – and an even slimmer chance he would ever have enough time to sort through and decipher the other containers one by one.

The twinkling windows of the shops in Wayward Town were just visible over the horizon, glittering relentlessly, as if egging Cas on. They glimmered and sparkled like a constellation of fallen stars that had toppled down to the Balance Lands and never bothered to get back up. Cas refused to stop staring at them until he had made up his mind.

"Hey—"

Cas opened his mouth to tell the others his plan, but the words never left his lips. Something at the boundary of the school made the syllables die on his tongue.

Seconds later, he didn't need to explain.

The usually pearly wards had turned bright crystalline red as blaring sirens split the air.

CHAPTER 20
THE INFORMANT

As the piercing sound of sirens ricocheted through the school, Cas, Warrior and Fenix pelted down the spiral stairs, with Paws speeding along on the pulley system beside them. Despite the wardsmen unsuccessfully trying to usher everyone back into their dorms, the corridors were flooded by students in pyjamas and dressing-gowns. In a rushing stampede, they overpowered the orange-clad guards and hurtled down to the entrance hall, before erupting out of the grand front doors.

Cas couldn't explain the feeling in the air around them, the one which made everyone run towards danger instead of away from it. They should have all wanted to stay tucked up safely in their bedrooms.

But something felt different about this break-in.

Something was wrong.

The entire school spread out across the dew-drenched grass in front of the school. Shrieks and pointed fingers rang out from the onlookers, as Cas and the Abnormies pushed to the front of the crowd.

A single Heretic in the Master of All's signature garb stood silently glaring at them through the wrought-iron *WS* gates – *inside* the wards. He didn't move. He didn't speak. He didn't attack. Behind him, a horde of twenty similar figures stood waiting too.

"What's going on?" Paws asked, scooting forward in her wheelchair to get a better look.

Warrior shook her head, aghast. "I don't get it," she whispered, her breath blooming out in cold plumes in front of her. "The Master didn't set the wards off the last time he broke in, he just snuck in via the sewers…"

As she spoke, all of the wardsmen inside Wayward School piled out of the building to face the attackers. At least fifty, sixty, seventy more guards ran up the hill from Wayward Town, surrounding the Heretics on all sides. Flaming fireballs soared through the air towards the Heretics from the wardsmen, scorching and shaking the ground beneath them, which turned to quicksand at their feet. Yet still none of them fought or resisted.

A horrifying, terrifying thought occurred to Cas, as Mrs Crane flew up and down the line of students, waving her arms wildly. *"GET BACK INSIDE, ALL OF YOU!"*

Madame Aster, Professors Vulcan, Oxbow, Breezy and Everglade, and even Headmaster Higgles and Miss Grimbly were trying to contain the ruckus, but…

"Where's Dr Bane?" Cas scanned the raucous gathering hurriedly.

"I can't see him," Warrior replied.

Cas turned to the others, his eyes wild with panic. "The Master of All," he muttered urgently. Then more loudly: "It's a distraction. *This* isn't the real break-in; the real one's happening back in *there*." He pointed towards the school. "I bet you anything that after he failed to get the information out of Mrs Crane, the Master thought that Dr Bane must know where the seekerthing is."

Warrior glanced up at the window of Dr Bane's office, paralysed by fear.

This wasn't just about the seekerthing for her. Her father's life was on the line.

None of them needed to say another word.

"I'll scout ahead with Mogget," said Paws, giving the mangy feline a brisk stroke to wake her up. "Her cat senses are sharper than mine. Get Mrs Crane to take me back inside."

At the sound of her name, Mrs Crane skidded to a halt, her bright green, tweed dressing-gown practically luminous in the twilight. "Miss Grover-Rosales, what on earth are you doing – wait, no, don't you dare – BY THE THREADS!"

Paws's eyes rolled back in her head and her body slumped forward in her chair. At the same moment, the usually half-dead Mogget shivered to life, ears twitching and whiskers rustling.

"Just as Mogget thought. Disturbance on the first floor." Paws in Mogget's body loped off towards the school.

Warrior and Fenix followed suit, with Cas hobbling along as fast as his funny leg would carry him.

"COME BACK HERE!" Mrs Crane wailed, clinging on to the handles of Paws's wheelchair.

But the Abnormies were already too far away to hear.

They raced into the school and up to Dr Bane's office. The bolt-laden door was hanging off its hinges, severely mangled. Cautiously, Cas nudged it open and they crept inside, keeping their eyes peeled in case the culprit was still lurking.

But it was empty.

The study was a complete mess. Papers and torn, shredded paintings were scattered across the floor like snow. Dr Bane's mahogany desk and high-backed chair had been upturned, and the chains and animal skulls usually hanging on the walls were smashed to smithereens. The colourful cabinets that housed Dr Bane's eccentric collection broke through the gloom as their glows flickered unsteadily, dull and dying.

"Bane is gone," said Warrior, before she gasped, covering her mouth with her hands.

Four words were scrawled across one of the office's walls in what looked suspiciously like blood:

He failed to deliver

Cas picked his way over shattered glass and ceramics and bent to pick something up from the floor. He dusted off the cover of *The Book of Skulls and Skin* and placed it back on one of the remaining shelves, then wheeled around to the cabinets. They all seemed to have been roughed up but not ransacked. The jar of shrivelled heads teetered on the edge of its shelf, rocking precariously back and forth. The Orbialius from the Order Trials had been pulled out but was miraculously unharmed … and in the bronze-tinged cabinet, the hand-sized glowing orb with its spinning metal rings sat crooked amongst a hoard of other articles. Just then, Cas felt it again. The draw to the strange, spinning device. The rings whirled faster as he approached.

"The Master must've just been here," said Fenix, eagle-eyed, noticing the rocking heads jar too.

Paws in Mogget nodded. "I think I have his scent. We can still catch him."

Cas didn't know why, but he pocketed the spinning device. "Come on."

"This way," said Paws, pointing Mogget's paw towards the floor above.

335

They picked their way back through the carnage, trying not to stand on anything valuable, before rushing down the corridor, Cas taking the lead. As he hurtled around a corner, he ran slap-bang into someone.

Lucille Du Villaine.

She was dressed in a thick, fuzzy yellow dressing-gown and looking terrified.

"Have you seen Dr Bane?" Cas demanded, shaking her shoulders slightly when she didn't reply straight away.

Lucie was ghostly pale. "Two hooded men were dragging him into the library. But, Cas – you can't go in there. There was someone else with them … it was *him*."

Cas didn't need to ask who she meant.

Without another word, Cas changed direction and sprinted back down to the ground floor.

"Where are you going?" shouted Warrior as she, Fenix and Paws struggled to catch up. Surprisingly, Lucie Du Villaine scurried along behind them.

Cas didn't have time to ask what she was doing.

His mind whirred with panic, but it also felt sharper than it had in months. Memories and images, scents and smells were flashing through his brain.

"If the Master has taken Dr Bane to the library, we'll never catch him," Cas panted. "Mrs Crane gave Dr Bane the key to the Abominable Archives for safekeeping, so presumably the Master has it now. And I think the Archives lead to a way out."

He recalled the vile stench that had wafted from the caved-in tunnel at the back of the Abominable Archives. A distinctly repulsive smell that he had only smelt once before: when Puggle the Nuggle had taken him on his wild ride through the sewers. Paws had said the Elementie was up to something that day – what if Puggle had been trying to show him this?

"There's a blocked passage at the back of the Archives," Cas informed them. "I think it leads to the sewers. Since he destroyed the waygate mirror in the library, the Master is going to use the same way he broke in to escape. He'll clear the blockage in no time if he has an Earthshaper on his side."

"So, why are we running *away* from him?" puffed Warrior incredulously.

"Our best chance of stopping the Master is if we can cut him off. We need a different way into the sewers – and thanks to Puggle, I know where we can find one."

The five of them burst out of the back of the school, slipping and sliding across the slick lawn as it rolled down to the Wayward School graveyard. Cas noticed Warrior stumble at the sight of the mausoleums, but the thought of the Master escaping with Dr Bane seemed to urge her on.

They barrelled into the mausoleum where Cas had spent his first night at school. He quickly located a grate in the corner of the spectral tomb and together they tugged it loose. One after the other, they dropped down into the sewer below.

Cas grimaced as his feet splashed into the putrid, grimy water. He fought the urge to vomit as thick sewage curled around his ankles, grimly swirling green, dark brown and grey.

Lucie gave a sharp squeal as she plopped in.

Warrior shot her a daggered look. *"Shh."*

They paused for a moment, letting their eyes adjust to the darkness and listening. Voices, growing fainter. The Master of All was getting away, with or without the seekerthing in tow.

They had to find him and Dr Bane.

Fast.

Mogget's ears flicked. "This way," said Paws, once more using her incredible animal hearing to locate the direction of the noise. She slunk ahead along the edge of the sewer pipe, just outside the water's reach.

Fenix ignited in a *whoosh* of flames to light their way and Cas felt the characteristic bump against his leg that meant Hobdogglin had appeared. Warrior was preparing herself for a fight.

The sewer pipe sloped downwards, taking them somewhere far below the school. Cas felt the Deathmaker magic of the mausoleum fading, the threads of power which lingered there tugging on the threads inside him one last time in an attempt to call him back. Fenix's fire burned brighter as they travelled deeper into the earth. Soon, Cas felt the heat of the Firetamers' basement dorm, the Kiln, at his back. Yet the sewer pipe continued to slope further down still.

"Stay close," said Cas.

Eventually, the voices grew louder. The sound of fleeing footsteps grew nearer. Up ahead, the sewer pipe opened out into a cavernous hub, where six splashing pipes joined together in a circle of clearer shallows.

In the hollow, an uneven mound of obsidian rock protruded from the swirling grime, like an island in a nauseating sea. Flushed wrappers, screwed up homework sheets and clumps of toilet paper clung to the rocky island. But what churned Cas's stomach the most was the sight of who stood atop it.

Two hooded Heretics leered on either side of a cowed, bleeding Dr Bane, forcing him to his knees. Standing in front of them, disguised by his signature cloak and silver mask, was the person Cas had been born to defeat:

The Master of All.

Heart thrumming, Cas stepped forward, pushing the Abnormies protectively behind him.

The Master swept forward too.

"Foretold," he said smoothly. "I thought I heard you coming. We meet at last – or should I say, again."

He moved as if flying through air, soundless and deadly and graceful. When he reached the edge of the sewer island, he ripped off his mask and tossed back his hood, revealing soot-black hair, smokeless, flaming amber eyes and the face of a man much younger than Cas had expected.

The face of a man Cas knew.

"You," Cas croaked, recognizing the homeless stranger he had helped so long ago outside Captain Caeli's Cakery. The one who had caught the sand snoot.

"Yes." The Master of All chuckled. "I'm surprised the great and prophesied Foretold didn't catch on sooner."

"Aeurdan Darkbloom." Cas spoke the Master's real name through clenched teeth.

The Master of All pulled his lip back in a snarl. "Alas, I do not answer to that name."

"But it was your name, wasn't it," said Cas defiantly, "once."

To Cas's dismay, the Master threw his head back and laughed again, the hollow, blood-curdling noise echoing around the chamber. It was an empty sound, devoid of any true emotion and filled only with darkness.

"That was a false name," he said. "It was never my real one. It was the name I was forced to go by, because he" – he gestured towards Dr Bane – "didn't want anyone to know who I truly was."

Cas swallowed hard. "But I do," he said bravely. "I know who you are and what you've done. You killed your mother and took her Lifemaker abilities for yourself.

You've tormented and terrorised, kidnapped and killed in your quest for the other powers. But I won't let you take them. I *won't*."

The Master of All prowled closer.

"What an ignorant child you are," he said pitifully. "You believe the lies you've been fed because they're easier to swallow than the truth."

"No, *you're* the liar!" spat Cas, unsure what the Master was talking about. "Are you saying you aren't that person? That you haven't done all those terrible things?"

"You know nothing, boy," the Master snapped, a new note of fury alight in his voice. "Yes, I did those things and I used to go by that name – but it is not the one I go by now. Aeurdan Darkbloom was never my true identity."

"Then what is?"

The Master of All flung an accusing finger towards Dr Bane. "Aeurdan Bane," he declared. "Though my precious father would never want you to know that."

Behind Cas, Fenix and Lucie gasped. Even Paws gave a yowl of surprise.

But it was Warrior's reaction that scared Cas the most.

If what the Master of All was saying was true, and deep down she knew that Dr Bane was her real father, then that meant…

"You're no brother of mine!" Warrior cried, shoving past Cas and narrowing her eyes with unbridled hatred in the Master's direction.

Right on cue, Hobdogglin leapt to attention, *yip-yapping* and growling, before he took off at a run and launched himself, teeth bared, towards the Master's face. At the last moment, a shard of jet-black rock flew up from the island as one of the Master's Earthshaper Heretics moved to defend their leader. The shard pierced Hobdogglin's side and, with a terrible cry, the funny-looking creature disappeared in a plume of misty illusion smoke.

"NO!" howled Warrior, sounding as if her heart had been ripped from her chest. She fell to her knees, the dirty water of the cavern soaking into her jeans. She clawed desperately at thin air, trying to summon Hobdogglin back.

But the creature was gone.

Apparently for good.

"Silence!" the Master of All ordered, swinging a clenched fist in Warrior's direction. His powers sealed her throat, cutting off her tears.

Warrior opened her mouth to scream, but no sound came out.

"Now," said the Master, turning back to Cas, "it's just you and me."

Cas steeled himself. "Take me, but leave Dr Bane and my friends alone."

The Master of All swung round and yanked back Dr Bane's shaggy, silver-threaded head. *"This* Dr Bane? Your wonderful, perfect Deathmaker teacher? My, oh my, you really are naïve. Why would you want to save *him*? He's the one who's been helping me break in all year. He's the one who's *betrayed* you."

"W-what?" stuttered Cas.

His world felt like it had been unexpectedly and violently knocked off-kilter.

"Stop, Aeurdan," Dr Bane begged, bloodied and broken. A raw gash was oozing fresh crimson on his forehead. *"Please."*

Why isn't Bane doing something? Cas's mind rioted. *Why isn't he using his powers to save us?*

"I – I didn't have a choice," Dr Bane moaned.

The Master shot Bane a look of utmost disgust. "You had plenty of choices, Father," he retorted, his voice sounding more like a boy's than ever. He spun to face Cas. "Did he tell you what he did, Foretold?"

"Yes," said Cas, remembering his conversation with Dr Bane after Mrs Crane's attack. *The Master is baiting you,* a voice in Cas's head said. *Bane would never betray you. He's the one who sent Warrior to find you.* "Dr Bane told me that he brought you here from the Normie world, just like me. He told me that he knew what you were and what you had done, but he tried to help you anyway…"

"Help me?" The Master almost gagged on the words. "What a wondrously false tale my dear old dad weaves.

"Twenty-eight years ago, Dr Bane fell in love with my mother. He claims he had no choice now, but back then he *chose* to abandon us, including me, a baby, in the Normie world to rot. When I was eleven, I forced him to show his face again. After the unfortunate incident with my mother—"

"Her murder, you mean."

"Bane realized what I was: a Lifemaker and Deathmaker in one," the Master continued, as if Cas hadn't cut in. "He brought me back to Wayward, to train me, but didn't tell anyone what I was or what had happened. The Grand Council wouldn't have approved, you see. They would have locked me up in Nowhere Prison and deprived him."

"Of what?"

The Master of All's eyes glinted. "Of the same thing that he sees in you. An opportunity. A prodigy. A chance to manipulate somebody to become more extraordinary and brilliant than he could ever be himself.

"Dr Bane taught me how to control my Deathmaker powers and arranged secret lessons with Mrs Crane to teach me Lifemaker magic on the sly. Of course, the repercussions of my actions became clear when the fifth Order's powers began disappearing. But as their abilities dwindled, my ambitions grew. I was an Abnormie unlike any other. An exception to every rule. Not even the balance of nature could control me, so I wasn't about to let my cowardly father do so.

"After I left Wayward School, Dr Bane panicked. He scampered off to the Grand Council and tattled, but left out a few essential facts. Like how I was his son. Like how he knew what I'd done to acquire my powers and how he had been stoking my ambitions from the moment I arrived. Bane began working with the Grand Council to find me, tracking my whereabouts and hunting me down, in the hopes that they would get to me before I could get to them. Because he knew he would be punished or exiled for what he had done.

"But one day, a few years ago, I found him. People say I'm cruel, but I offered my father a deal. I had heard the Oracle's prophecy about you, Foretold. Bane could help me find you and end your life, or I would ruin his. Bane looked long and hard for the Foretold after that, sending his darling daughter here on secret missions to the Normie world to keep an eye out, just as I had my Heretics doing the same.

"Only, when he found you, something changed. His daughter didn't know about our deal and she managed to escape my Heretics with you unscathed, so Bane decided to play both sides. He protected you here at Wayward School, so that you stood a chance of stopping me, but he also continued to assist me – all to save his own skin. He created the distraction that allowed me to slip in through the town's wards at Christmas, after one of my Heretics heard that the Foretold was visiting from Wayward School. Shortly after, I met you, Cas. I would have done away with you then if your blithering friends hadn't blundered into view. But no matter. I waited. I bided my time. I planned to strike the school with my Heretics as soon as possible – then suddenly Bane fed me a new piece of information. I must've spooked him with the message I left with the Cricket boy.

"Bane informed me that there was something much more valuable than the Foretold at Wayward. He said I wouldn't need to worry about stopping the child who was destined to defeat me if I could succeed in taking all of the Orders' powers first. Bane said the Grand Council entrusted numerous valuable objects to Wayward School and among them, there was a device that could help me seek out the conduits – the very thing I sought."

"The seekerthing," Cas whispered.

The Master sneered. "You're smarter than I thought, Foretold. I broke into the school and tried to force its whereabouts out of Mrs Crane—"

"But she didn't give in," Cas interrupted, darting an accusatory look at Dr Bane.

The man who had trained Cas. The man Cas had trusted. The man who had secretly been working against them all and was partially responsible for everyone who had been hurt since Cas had arrived. Dewey Cricket. The Wayward wardsmen. Mrs Crane.

None of it was entirely Cas's fault.

"Unfortunately not."

"Well, don't get your hopes up," Cas told the Master crisply. "You don't have the seekerthing now and you'll never have it, because I'm not going to let you get it!"

Blood and rage thundering in his ears, Cas focused hard on the Master, ready to use his powers.

But the Master of All readied himself too.

Cas knew he couldn't really fight him. Knew he couldn't *win*. Still, he dug his hand into his pocket for the only weapon he had left: the glowing, spinning orb.

As Cas pulled the orb free, its spinning rings began to whirl faster. An ear-splitting screech tore through the chamber. It was as if the object was reacting to Cas and the Master's combined presence, to their immense power…

No, it couldn't be…

Madame Aster's words from Order Studies rang in Cas's ears: *Only someone as strong and powerful as the threads of power themselves would be able to sense and find it.*

It was.

The seekerthing.

The Master of All's eyes widened and his wicked smile grew. "You found it," he breathed. "I should have known that if I couldn't locate the seekerthing, you would, Foretold. You were prophesied, made directly by the same threads which this object senses." He held out his hand hungrily. "Give it to me."

Cas tried and failed to shove the device back in his pocket. *"Never."*

Snatching his powers away from Warrior, the Master of All turned them on Cas. Suddenly, Cas found his feet involuntarily moving towards him, sloshing through the sewage. Despite every effort he made to fight it, the Master had control of his muscles. Every ounce of control had been torn away from his limbs. It felt worse than any attack by his funny leg. More terrible than anything he had ever experienced in his life. He climbed like a stiff marionette up onto the island.

But at that moment, something extraordinary happened.

His funny leg broke through the spell.

It was as if the threads of power inside him could sense the threat before him and revolted. The sudden movement of walking had awoken the tingling feeling inside Cas's leg. The energy surged, greater than ever before, through his body and into his arm, too. He had never been more grateful for the fuzzy, prickling feeling. Never more thankful for the sparks as they fought back against the Master's control.

"*Obey.*" The Master's eyes protruded as he sensed his power slipping. "Hand it to me."

"Over my dead body," said Cas, gripping his fingers tighter around the seekerthing. The device shimmered and gleamed in the dim light. Then, in one swift motion, Cas smashed the object against the onyx rock of the island, shattering it into pieces.

"*NO!*"

The Master of All roared.

Cas's funny leg subsided and he honed his powers in on the Master. *"Ok—"*

But he had barely got one syllable out before he heard something whizzing towards him – and a sharp pain erupted in his gut. Cas looked down to see the same shard of rock that had snuffed out Hobdogglin sticking out of him as well.

Fenix and Lucie screamed. Paws in Mogget's body shrieked.

But Cas said nothing as he looked down, hands shaking, his eyes refusing to believe what they could see. Around the hole in his gut, where the shard protruded and there should have been a wound or blood, there was nothing.

Nothing but the misty, smoke-like tendrils of an illusion breaking free.

CHAPTER 21
WARRIOR BANE

EVERYTHING WAS A LIE.

Cas couldn't think of anything else as he stared at the shard sticking out of him. He reached down and tried to pull it free – but once, twice, thrice, his trembling hands passed straight through the obsidian rock, too panicked to solidify and take hold.

He was an illusion.

His entire life was false. His memories were nothing. He wasn't the Foretold. He was just a figment, an imaginary friend made real by…

His gaze shot over to Warrior, tears slipping down her cheeks as she stood to face him.

His best friend.

Warrior Bane.

The *real* Foretold. The One with a power greater and more unique than any the Master of All possessed.

But Cas didn't understand.

His life and death powers were real. The seekerthing had sensed them. He had still blinded Dr Bane, still frozen the Snout twins solidly in their tracks and manipulated the Nuggle's legs … unless those powers were Warrior's too. Unless she had imbued him with her Lifemaker and Deathmaker magic, in the same way she had created a hill with a face and Hobdogglin with his scaly legs and bright violet eyes.

Violet. Cas reached up and grazed his face. His fingers brushed against his own grey eyes flecked with purple.

Even his and Hobdogglin's features were the same. How had he not known?

Finally, Cas calmed himself enough to pull the rock shard free. The misty, smoke-like hole in his stomach closed. He patted his belly, but it had already healed, feeling whole and real again.

He could feel his heartbeat thrumming and hear quick, panicked breaths escaping his lungs.

But this was what Warrior did, didn't she?

She created illusions that were half real, half not. Illusions that were able to move and think and feel for themselves, to interact with the real world, but which were never actually born. Which never had a real body.

Now that I've found you, I can finally come home.

Cas remembered Warrior's words on the evening she had rescued him from Curious Mrs Crane's in the Normie world. For months, Dr Bane had been sending her there, against her wishes, to search for the Foretold. She hadn't wanted to do it any more. She had wanted to stay at Wayward.

I've never wanted to be the Foretold, Warrior had told Cas in the mausoleum.

So, she had created the one thing – the one person – that she knew could bring her home.

"Cas," Warrior sobbed in the present, her words muffled by tears. "I'm sorry."

Cas didn't know what to say. He thought of every inside joke they had shared. Every time it had seemed like they were the same person and she knew his thoughts … because she did.

Even the Oracle had sensed it in some way. *No aura, no existence. A nothing boy.*

"H-how long have you known?" Cas croaked out at last.

Warrior stifled a sniffle. "Not until now for sure," she answered softly, as if this was a reasonable excuse. "I thought maybe, on the night you ran after Lucille Du Villaine following the Scuffle, when—"

"You didn't want me to," Cas butted in. "When you said, 'I didn't say you could do that.'"

Snivelling, Warrior dragged a hand across her grubby cheeks. "Look, Casander. This doesn't change anything. You're still my friend. You're still you—"

"How touching," the Master of All sliced her off scathingly. Cas had almost forgotten that he was standing barely three metres away with the seekerthing in pieces at his feet. The Master strode forward and snatched Cas up by the chin. "Remarkable." A devilish glint twinkled in his eyes. "You feel so real. You can even touch me."

"He *is* real!" shouted Warrior.

"He's real to all of us!" Lucie Du Villaine added.

The Master glanced once at Cas, then at the shattered seekerthing. "You," he said, switching his gaze to Warrior and tossing Cas aside like a ragdoll. "You've lost me my seekerthing – but you may prove very useful yet."

"Don't touch her!" said Fenix, moving to guard Warrior.

In the same instant, the Master's Earthshaper Heretic sent another fragment of rock soaring towards the Firetamer. It stopped barely centimetres away, scratching the tip of Fenix's nose.

Paws hissed angrily, hackles raised and hair standing on end.

"Come to me." With a lazy curl of the Master's finger, Warrior started moving towards him in the same rigid way that Cas had done.

"Aeurdan," Dr Bane begged, his eyes popping at the sight of Warrior. "Don't—"

But the Master of All slapped Dr Bane's silver, shaggy head back. Dr Bane toppled, motionless, into the sewer water.

"Sister of mine," said the Master, examining Warrior like precious treasure. "You and I are going to do incredible things together. You're better than any seekerthing, Warrior. Much better. You're the real Foretold. The one who can bring illusions to life and imbue them with powers. If you join my side, no one will be able to stand against us in my quest for the Orders' powers."

"*STOP!*" Cas bellowed, as the Master of All and the Heretics closed ranks around her. They swallowed Warrior in an undulating mass of purple and white, moving as one towards a clear patch of water, looking ready to jump.

They were going to use it as a waygate.

"*Okuli,*" said Cas, focusing on the unsuspecting henchmen.

The Heretics staggered back, clawing at their eyes, momentarily blind.

"Warrior, *run*!" Cas bawled. "*Muskuli.*" He clenched his fist to create a searing cramp in the Master of All's leg.

The Master cringed in pain and let Warrior go. She rushed forward, her face hopeful – but at the very last second, the Master snatched at her wrist and hauled her back.

"You're not going anywhere, little sister," he grunted, as the Heretics stumbled out of their dark trance.

The chance to escape had gone.

Before Cas could act again, the Earthshaper Heretic sent separate fragments of rock flying towards Cas and his friends.

"Two choices," the Master snapped, offering Warrior an ultimatum. "Join me and I'll let your friends live. Or try to escape and watch them suffer."

"Don't do it, Warrior!" Cas yelled, summoning all of his courage as the daggered point of the rock edged closer.

Warrior tugged fiercely against the Master's grip, straining to see her friends' faces, trying to figure out another escape route. But there was no way out.

She had no choice.

"I'll come with you. Please, just let them go," pleaded Warrior quietly.

"NO!" Cas shouted as the Master and the Heretics gathered around Warrior once again, sucking her into their shadows.

As one, they leapt through the waygate and disappeared from view.

"No, no, no," stammered Cas, dread and fear and all things terrible brewing inside him. The rock shards dropped away, and he waded over to where they had vanished, staggering through the sewage as fast as he could.

With a frustrated scream, Cas smashed his fist into the clear pool of water. Even if he knew how to use a waygate, there was no way of following the Master and Warrior without knowing where they had gone.

A clattering sound echoed from the large pipe they had originally come from. Mrs Crane appeared in the gaping black hole, wheezing and dishevelled. Orange-clad wardsmen spilled out of the tunnel behind her.

"Cas – Paws – Fenix – *Lucille Du Villaine*?" Mrs Crane panted, her tweed dressing-gown splattered with filth. "What's going on – where's Dr Bane? *Where's Warrior?*"

Cas couldn't even bear to look at her as he sank down onto the island, clutching the broken pieces of the seekerthing in his hands.

"She's gone," he whispered, looking at the glimmering remnants. "She joined the Master."

And I don't know how to get her back.

CHAPTER 22
HEROES

BY THE TIME MORNING BROKE OVER WAYWARD, there was no sign of Warrior, the Master of All or Dr Bane. The wardsmen searched every nook and cranny of the sewers for hours, refusing to believe that they had been so close to catching the Master, yet once again he had slipped away.

But Warrior and the Master had disappeared into the unfathomable depths of a waygate, undoubtedly to some unknown and terrible place. Meanwhile, it didn't take a genius to figure out that Dr Bane must have scarpered. There was no trace of him to be found.

As the sun crawled into the sky, Mrs Crane and the Abnormies clambered out of the sewers into the honey-hued dawn, only to find themselves surrounded by Wayward School in chaos. The small band of Heretics who had created the distraction had been arrested, but wardsmen were still crawling everywhere. Blind to their thunderstruck faces and shivering skin, those above ground immediately swarmed them and bombarded the Abnormies with questions.

Cas couldn't bring himself to speak.

Thankfully, he didn't need to. Smoothing her untameable salt-and-pepper hair down into less of a frizz, Mrs Crane took charge, ushering Cas and the others towards Headmaster Higgles's office.

A soft touch on Cas's arm made him turn around as they departed. Lucie gave him a comforting, secretive smile and then slipped away before either Sam or the Snouts could notice she was missing. It was as if she had never been with the Abnormies at all.

It wasn't any calmer when they reached the foyer of Higgles's office. Paws's body was waiting with Artemis Grover and Diana Rosales, who smothered her in a cacophony of cooing and fussing once she was safely back in her own form. A girl with shockingly blue hair, who introduced herself as Fenix's sister, made him chug reviving hot chocolate as if his life depended on it. Feeling lonelier than ever, Cas numbly let Mrs Crane guide him into the headmaster's study, before promptly closing the door.

The Grand Council were ready and waiting.

High Councillors Hephaestus, Aster, Du Villaine and Brooks stood like silent sentinels, regarding him with a mixture of concern and despair.

"By the threads, what's happened here?" seethed High Councillor Du Villaine, her mouth taut as she raked her fingers through her silver-grey hair. Purple shadows hung below the wrinkles next to her eyes.

"Let them explain," High Councillor Hephaestus said sharply, visibly shaken but gesturing for Cas to take a seat with a kind smile.

Both Cas and Mrs Crane sat down on Higgles's chaise longue. Cas opened his mouth to speak, but words failed him once more.

Mrs Crane placed a soothing hand on his shoulder. "Tell them."

And so, with a deep breath, Cas did.

He told the Grand Council everything – or at least, everything that he could bear to say aloud. He told them about how he had deduced that the Master was after the seekerthing. About breaking into the Abominable Archives and discovering the device was in Dr Bane's office instead. About the Heretics and the diversion, and how the Master had tried to escape out of the school with Dr Bane via the sewers, before—

"Captured," Mrs Crane chipped in, gripping Cas's hand tightly. "Dr Bane, my brother, was captured. So was one of our students, Warrior."

"Warrior Bane?" said High Councillor Aster curiously. "Dr Bane's ward?"

Cas didn't doubt that, as Madame Aster's husband,

359

High Councillor Aster was very familiar with Warrior's name.

"His daughter, yes," said Mrs Crane. She didn't clarify to the Grand Council if she meant adopted or real, but she and Cas shared a knowing look. "We don't know where the Master of All has taken them both. He likely wants my brother for information and Warrior as a hostage."

Out of the corner of his eye, Cas saw an anxious bead of sweat drip down Mrs Crane's brow. On their way up from the sewers, Cas and the Abnormies had confessed everything to Mrs Crane – right down to Warrior's choice and Cas being ... what he was. *So, why is she lying?* Cas wondered. *Why doesn't she want the Grand Council to know the truth?*

"I see," said High Councillor Hephaestus, panic spiking her voice. "What about the seekerthing? Did – did *he* take it?"

Cas shook his head stiffly. "No, I destroyed it."

He brought out the shattered pieces of the seekerthing and braced himself for the torrent of disapproval that was sure to come.

It never did.

For a brief moment, the look of concern on the High Councillors' faces deepened. Cas knew that feeling. The one of coming so close to having the thing you sought most, and then, *poof,* in the blink of an eye it was gone.

For the High Council, it was catching the Master and protecting the seekerthing.

For Cas, it was Warrior. His friends. A chance at a real life in the Balance Lands.

Any hope of either had been obliterated.

Unexpectedly, Hephaestus let out the breath snagged in her throat. "Good," she said, her shoulders relaxing in relief. "Thank you, Cas. I think I speak for all of us when I say you did the right thing. You're exactly the Foretold we were promised."

The Foretold.

The words made Cas feel sick. Bile clawed its way up his throat as the syllables churned in his stomach like something rotten he had eaten.

"I'm not," he began, summoning what little courage he had to admit what he knew he must.

But Mrs Crane squeezed his hand tighter, cutting him off.

"Foretold?" High Councillor Du Villaine choked out bitterly. "Don't make me laugh. This brat of a boy has been absolutely useless!"

"He tried to warn us about the seekerthing," argued High Councillor Hephaestus. "As I recall, *you* were the one who was most dead set against revealing to the boy that it was at Wayward."

"Yes, for this exact reason. He only went and smashed it up! The Master of All was here. He was within our grasp. This wet lettuce of a Foretold let him get away!"

"He's a twelve-year-old boy, Tyrannia!" rebutted

361

Hephaestus protectively. "He may be the Foretold, but how on earth could he be expected to stop the Master by himself when we've been trying and *failing* for the last twelve years!"

"The main thing is that the Master's plan was thwarted," said High Councillor Aster, his voice as calm and serene as ever. "Without the seekerthing, he's no closer to finding the conduits and getting the other powers than he was before."

"So, in essence, Casander *did* stop the Master of All," added Brooks, shooting Cas a proud grin. "We can't thank you enough."

A wind whistled around their feet, growing more blustery by the second, as High Councillor Du Villaine clenched her jaw so hard that Cas was afraid her teeth might fall out. The other Grand Council members refused to back down, though, instead heaping praise on Cas, thanking and congratulating him.

Eventually, Du Villaine had no choice but to accept Cas's victory.

After a great deal of back patting and hand shaking, the Grand Council members finally departed, until only High Councillor Hephaestus remained.

Cas tried to hand back the broken remains of the seekerthing.

"Keep it," Hephaestus said. "As a reminder of what you achieved last night. The Balance Lands owes you a great debt. Stay strong, Casander Darkbloom, and before long we'll truly defeat the Master of All, together."

Cas couldn't stay in Headmaster Higgles's office a second longer.

As soon as the Grand Council had left, he took off like a bullet towards the lake, somewhere that had become one of his and Warrior's favourite spots. He dropped cross-legged to the ground, watching Puggle the Nuggle terrorising Wayones walking by, and pulled blades of grass from the soil furiously.

A few minutes later, someone joined him.

It was Mrs Crane.

"Why didn't you let me tell them?" The words burst out of Cas with all the bottled-up emotions of the last few hours.

The old Lifemaker librarian calmly sat down next to him and drew out a pair of knitting needles from her pocket. She shrugged, clicking the needles together casually as she observed the Nuggle too.

"Tell them about what?"

"All of it," said Cas, shell-shocked. "About Dr Bane betraying us and running away. About Warrior joining the Master of All's side, not being taken. About me being … being…"

Cas's voice cracked too much to get the words out.

It cracked like the big, empty hole inside him now. Except it wasn't a hole. It was a chasm. An endless, bottomless pit, which he was tumbling helplessly into, with nobody to break his fall.

"Firstly," said Mrs Crane, still knitting, "I didn't tell them about Dr Bane because – well, he's my brother. He did something wrong, very wrong. We all know that – but he does too. That's why he's likely gone into hiding."

"But you suspected him, didn't you?" deduced Cas. "Even before we told you that he had been helping the Master. I heard your conversation in the Nurse's Quarters and … it was you, wasn't it? You were the one who removed the seekerthing from its original box and placed it in Dr Bane's office. That's why, even when the Master got hold of Dr Bane, he didn't know that it was there – because neither did Dr Bane. You couldn't have trusted him if you did that."

Mrs Crane sighed, letting her needles rest. "I did, yes. I knew the Grand Council trusted my brother with everything valuable at Wayward – and whilst I love him dearly, that doesn't mean I think he always makes the wisest decisions. In my younger days, I used to courier equally valuable objects for the Grand Council myself, remember."

"And Warrior? Why didn't you tell the Grand Council about her?"

"What good would it have done," Mrs Crane asked

364

him, "to tell the Grand Council that the real Foretold, their one and only chance of defeating the Master, had joined his side? If I had told them the truth about Warrior and Dr Bane, both would be hunted like the Master. They would be seen as just as guilty."

But Warrior isn't, thought Cas.

Yes, Warrior might've lied to him for a while. She might have hidden the truth about who and what Cas really was – but she had said that she hadn't known herself for certain. At least not at first. And even if she had, what did it matter really?

Warrior was his friend. She had sacrificed herself to save the Abnormies.

They owed her their lives.

"You don't seem surprised," said Cas gloomily, staring at his knees. "About me being an … *illusion*."

There. He had said it.

Mrs Crane shrugged again, as if Cas had told her something perfectly plain and ordinary. "You seem pretty real to me."

"But am I?"

She reached out and pinched his arm. "You *feel* real."

Cas wriggled out of her grasp. He knew he wasn't. His head still didn't want to accept it, but he couldn't forget what he had seen in the sewer. How the shard of rock had passed straight through him and left only misty illusion smoke in its wake.

He might be able to physically interact with the real world, to see and think and feel for himself, but there was also something about him that wasn't entirely *there*.

"You're not an illusion, Cas," said Mrs Crane, shaking her head. "You're a creation, same as the rest of us. One of Warrior's creations, sure, but aren't we all created from someone? As his daughter, Warrior was created by Dr Bane. Dr Bane and I were created by our mother and father.

"But we are not those people. We are not our makers. We are the makers of our own destiny. The threads that created you exist within me, and Paws, and Fenix, and everyone else too. We're all made of the same stardust at the end of the day."

He hadn't thought about it like that.

"To answer your earlier question," Mrs Crane continued, "I suppose I'm not surprised, in a way. No, I don't mean I knew that you were what you are – but I always suspected Warrior was capable of magic as powerful and impossible as this."

Cas's heart sank as he remembered. "It's because Dr Bane Gleaned her when she was younger, isn't it? The night he locked her in the mausoleum."

"Yes," said Mrs Crane, looking mildly surprised that Cas knew. "I think that's why she's always been so good at her illusions – the Gleaning forced that part of her powers out of her – but also, I suspect, why her life and death powers were suppressed until she placed them into you as well."

Mrs Crane hooked her finger under Cas's chin and forced him to look up.

"Promise me something, Cas," she said.

Cas swallowed nervously. "Um, what?"

Mrs Crane smiled. "If I tell you a secret, you have to promise to remember it and tell as many people as you can."

Cas wasn't sure he had heard her correctly until the librarian winked.

"Whatever people tell you about who and what you are, always remember this: normal doesn't exist. Everyone is different, from the points of our fingers to the tips of our toes. Being *different* is what's normal. It's what makes each one of us magic, each one of us strong."

Her words tugged on the threads of power inside him. Illusion – no, *creation* – or not, he felt more alive than ever.

They both climbed to their feet, the energy from the threads causing his funny leg to start twitching.

"So, what am I supposed to do now?" Cas asked.

"For now, I think it's best if you remain the Foretold," said Mrs Crane thoughtfully. "For your sake as well as Warrior's."

"But I'm not—" Cas protested as Mrs Crane sauntered away.

"It doesn't matter." She tapped her nose over her shoulder. "You don't have to be the Chosen One to be a hero."

The final weeks of term passed very quickly and very slowly all at once.

Every day, Cas spent each second that he wasn't in class helping in the search for Warrior. The Grand Council assured him they were sending highly trained Others to scour every place the Master might be hiding, but unfortunately their search turned up nothing.

Warrior and Dr Bane's portraits were printed on the back of every issue of *The Threadly Times,* which meant that other people were looking for her too. Cas even recounted his showdown with the Master to Wilibert Waffle, the reporter from the Mini Questial, in order to drum up publicity – something which didn't produce any leads but only encouraged the crackpot news predictors over at *The Oracle's Eye* to write wild tabloid stories about the Banes being found safely one week, then chopped up in cans of cat food the next.

The only saving grace was that Cas knew that wherever Warrior was, she couldn't have come to any harm. If there was one thing he was certain about when it came to Warrior's powers, it was that her illusions couldn't remain alive if she wasn't.

He was gradually coming to terms with being one of her creations, though a few questions still dogged him day to day.

Like now that Warrior was gone, would Cas be forgotten? Would he fade away to nothing?

Or would his memories disappear?

But for now, he was still existing, still thriving. He could only be grateful for each day and take them one by one.

When term came to a close, Cas discovered that one of the perks of still pretending to be the Foretold was that he had been excused from all of his exams.

A generous act that turned out to be one of Headmaster Higgles's last.

The idea that Higgles could ever have been the Master's informant seemed ridiculous now. In their end of year assembly, Higgles announced that he was going to take an early retirement.

The school was too busy applauding loudly to hear whatever he mentioned about going on a much-anticipated cheese tour of Balance Europe or becoming a professional napper. But Cas suspected that, without Bane pulling the strings, Higgles was having to do his job properly for the first time and he had realized just how hopeless he truly was.

The only lingering question was who would take over in his place.

Their deputy headmaster, Dr Bane, obviously wasn't an option.

"Why, you're related to him, Mrs Crane," said Headmaster Higgles, dragging the blushing librarian up onto the Atrium's dais. "I believe you'd do a splendid job."

The whole room grew critically silent, but Cas couldn't think of a better person.

"Headmistress Crane!" He stood up and started chanting. *"Headmistress Crane!"*

On either side of him, Fenix and Dewey Cricket rose to their feet and joined in. So too did Paws, Quinnberley Crestbourne, Bracken Moonstrike, Ellie Green, Neerja Gill and almost everyone else – including the Snouts, until Sam Du Villaine roughly tugged them back down into their seats. Lucie didn't stand, but Cas saw her muttering the chant under her breath.

Upon their release from the Atrium, the students piled outside into the grounds to soak up the last rays of the hazy, marmalade sunshine.

The Abnormies strolled down to the docks by the Wavebreakers' boathouse so they could bid goodbye freely, and Cas and Fenix rolled up their trousers to dangle their legs in the lake's cool water.

"What are you doing this summer, Cas?" asked Paws.

Mrs Crane was going back to the Normie world over the holidays to check up on Curious Mrs Crane's and Cas was going to join her. He was determined to spend every waking moment searching for Warrior, and he supposed the Normie world would be a good place to look too. On the off chance that Warrior managed to escape, Mrs Crane thought she might hide out in one of her favourite places there. Obviously, there was the curiosity shop, but also an animal sanctuary that Mrs Crane had taken Warrior to multiple times on holiday, where she liked to feed a group of stubby-legged Shetland ponies who were all named after famous gangsters.

Cas thought they must have reminded her of Puggle the Nuggle. Of Wayward School and home.

"I thought the Grand Council didn't allow Others to have any real ties to the Normie world," said Fenix, alarmed, when Cas told them.

"Well, Mrs Crane says that some rules are made to be bent, even if they can't be broken," Cas replied. "And I think after getting away with all we have this year, I agree."

"I'm going to help my parents at the Elementie Emporium," said Paws happily.

Meanwhile, Fenix told them he was going travelling.

"Keep your eyes peeled for Warrior," Cas instructed them. "Send me an Airscaper letter the moment you see or hear anything."

"Promise you'll write to us as well," said Paws, stroking Mogget, who was lounging on her lap, belly-side up, tail curling contentedly.

Cas glanced at them uncertainly. "Are you sure you want to hear from me?"

371

"Why, erm, wouldn't we?" said Fenix.

"Because I'm – I'm—"

"A creation," Paws and Fenix chimed together. They laughed. "We know. You keep saying."

"But you're more than that to us," emphasised Paws.

"You're our friend," said Fenix.

Despite every worry and doubt still niggling away at him, Cas smiled. He had to keep reminding himself that being a creation was just another difference about him. Like his violet-flecked grey eyes and long, gangly arms. Like his funny leg.

Without his differences, Cas wouldn't be Cas. Just like Paws wouldn't be Paws and Fenix wouldn't be Fenix.

Being different was good. It was normal.

"I'll write," Cas promised, his heart feeling fuller than it had in weeks.

"Promise you'll write to me, too?" said another voice.

They spun around to see Lucie walking towards them. She plopped down onto the deck beside Cas, as if she was part of their gang, sticking her feet in the water.

He supposed she was one of the Abnormies now.

"Where are Sam and the Snouts?" said Fenix fretfully, glancing rapidly from side to side.

"Back up at the school," said Lucie. "I left them trying to stuff some poor Wayone into his own suitcase. But you still haven't answered my question." She stared straight at Cas. "Do you promise you'll write to me, too?"

"Of course."

She scrawled her home address, a place called Sallowfen Mansion, on a screwed-up bit of paper. "So, what now?"

Cas sighed. "I don't know," he responded honestly. "I guess we wait and see what the summer brings. All I know is that we can't stop trying to find Warrior. We can't stop trying to defeat the Master. It isn't going to be easy, and it probably isn't going to be soon, but we'll do it."

"Together," said Paws, offering them her hands.

Cas, Fenix and Lucie joined theirs together.

"Together."

"How can you be sure?" said Lucie, watching Cas with a smidge of apprehension. She hadn't spilled his secret about being a creation, just as he still hadn't revealed that she was an Abnormie.

"Someone once told me that you don't have to be the Chosen One to be a hero," said Cas reassuringly.

And as Cas sat on the dock with Paws, Fenix and Lucie beside him, the setting sun igniting the sky in a blazing fury of gold, he knew that it was true.

He was going to save Warrior and stop the Master of All.

He was going to be the hero of his own story.

AUTHOR'S NOTE

Personally, I believe that very few of us grew up "normal".

Now, I know what you're thinking: it's easy to look at the grown-ups in your life and assume they've always fitted in. In contrast, maybe you feel like there's something different about you. Something nobody else can understand or that you can't explain.

For me, my difference was a rare neurological movement disorder called Paroxysmal Kinesigenic Choreoathetosis, a condition that causes jerking movements in my right arm and leg which I can't always fully control. Or, as I always called it, my funny leg. One of my earliest memories is speaking to my parents about how to hide my disorder on the first day of school. I could pretend to stumble or hang back from my friends to "tie my shoelaces", because there was no way I could explain something that I didn't understand. Even the doctors were left scratching their heads. Scans and tests drew a blank regarding what caused it. Medications and special diets didn't work. And if nobody else could make sense of it, then kids at school couldn't possibly either. And sometimes people can be cruel about things they can't comprehend.

Maybe if individuals with unique traits like mine had been shown more in the media growing up, life would have been different. But I never saw myself represented in books or on TV or in films. It was always "normal" people living "normal" lives. Characters didn't have to worry about their arm lurching into a spasm when they whipped out their wand to fight Voldemort. Or risk hobbling along so slowly that they would be caught by the White Witch in Narnia. Hence, it's no wonder I was worried about my peers' reactions, when being different was seen as "abnormal" or "weird".

Yet as I grew up, I quickly realized that everyone has their unique bits, their quirks. Whether you're scared of heights, have diabetes, use a walking stick, or even have a funny leg, we all have our differences – in the same way we can have brown hair or blonde, differently coloured eyes, or some people are tall or short. Our differences are what make us special. What make us, well, us. Without your differences, you wouldn't be you; I wouldn't be me. And can you imagine how boring the world would be if we were all cookie-cutter versions of the same?

So, the next time you feel like you don't fit in, just remember that your difference is your greatest strength. *Casander Darkbloom and the Threads of Power* was written precisely for this reason, as an ode to my twelve-year-old self – not because it was the type of story I would've wanted to read when I felt out of place, but because it was the one that I *needed* to. Therefore, I hope that you find something of yourself within these pages. Or at the very least, that Wayward and the characters who live there are a collection of places and people that you can call home.

ACKNOWLEDGEMENTS

Buckle up, kids, because here comes the soppy bit.

First of all, I would like to thank YOU. Yes, YOU, sitting and reading this right now. And pancakes, for fuelling the majority of writing this book into the wee hours of the night.

Mostly the pancakes.

No, seriously, thank you, dear reader – for picking up this book and giving Casander, Warrior, Paws, Fenix and all at Wayward School a chance. This book was never intended to be written ("I'll never write a children's fantasy!" she infamously exclaimed into the void), but it was for a very special reason close to my heart, and so I hope that you've enjoyed coming along on this crazy journey and the many more adventures to come.

Next, I would like to thank Josephine Hayes and Jordan Lees at The Blair Partnership. My agents, my superstars, my knights in shining armour. Jo was the first person to ever read *Casander Darkbloom and the Threads of Power* and Jordan is the one who has championed it the whole way through. You made sharing my – and by extension, Casander's – story less scary. Never judging, always encouraging. For ever on hand. Neither Cas nor I would be here today without you. Thank you to everyone else at TBP involved as well, including the hard-working legal and foreign rights teams. Many thanks to my incredible editors, Denise Johnstone-Burt, Emily McDonnell and Megan Middleton at Walker Books, for being considerate and respectful, insightful and passionate, but most of all for giving Casander the best home. A big shout out too to Maia Fjord, my designer at Walker, and Nathan Collins, my illustrator, for your incredible artistic talent and somehow managing to pull images of characters and places directly out of my head. There's a good reason I could never find any nit-picks or faults.

To M, my best friend, my soulmate, for always being there even when you're not. To my parents, for supporting me through everything. To Mum, for even in the darkest of times, telling me to "write, write, write!". To Dad, for the rare "well done" and always telling me that I couldn't do something, making me want to prove you wrong. To Isobel, for being the perpetually annoying pain in my backside who kept me going. To Ellie CG, Ellie R and Lauren, for being the ultimate cheerleaders, and the WymCol Gang for the same – even when we're scattered and apart. To my grandparents, for the never-ending support. To Holly, for all the late-night doggy cuddles whilst drafting. To Becki Ali, for being my first editor aged 7 (I promised I would one day credit you). And to every English teacher who put up with my fifty-page-long short stories and let me doodle fiction at the back of the classroom, instead of cracking on with the actual work.

Hailing from Norwich, the City of Stories, **P.A. Staff** is a science communicator and vet by day, writer by night. Growing up with a rare and unexplainable neurological condition called Paroxysmal Kinesigenic Choreoathetosis, she now writes stories featuring heroes with similar differences for the next generation, as an ode to her twelve-year-old self. *Casander Darkbloom and the Threads of Power* was created to tackle the universal themes of embracing your differences, conquering people's perceptions of them, and learning to be your own hero who is neither held back nor defined by them.